CINDERELLA'S
∽SHOES∾

*

ALSO BY SHONNA SLAYTON

Cinderella's Dress

CINDERELLA'S
~SHOES~

SHONNA SLAYTON

Entangled Publishing, LLC
2614 South Timberline Road Suite 109
Fort Collins, CO 80525
Visit our website at www.entangledpublishing.com.

Entangled Teen is an imprint of Entangled Publishing, LLC

Edited by Stacy Abrams and Lydia Sharp
Cover design by Alexandra Shostak
Glass slipper (c) cosma/Shutterstock
Background (c) BMJ/Shutterstock
Woman (c) coka/Shutterstock
Legs (c) Petar Paunchev/Shutterstock
Interior design by Sabrina Plomitallo-González,
Neuwirth & Associates

Print ISBN: 978-1-63375-123-1
Ebook ISBN: 978-1-63375-124-8

Manufactured in the United States of America

First Edition October 2015

10 9 8 7 6 5 4 3 2 1

For Rebekah

The air chilled Nadzia to her core as she ran down a dark passageway into the deepest part of the castle. A single torch on each wall cast a pale, flickering light on the uneven damp stones. She was crushing the muslin-wrapped bundle in her arms, but she daren't let go her grip. Tears threatened to spill out of her tired eyes. Was it only last night they had held the annual ball? Today the world was upside-down.

The queen should have allowed her to stay for the baby to be born. The child would have been like a little brother or sister she never had. All these months helping the queen prepare—knitting the soft blankets and sewing the tiny clothes and the little nappies. Now someone else would help Kopciuszek care for the wee one.

She choked back her emotions. There would be time for self-pity once she made it to the mountains. Back to Esmerelda. At least if the queen had to send her away, she was sending her back to the only mother she had ever known. Hopefully the old woman was well. Nadzia felt a quick pang of guilt that she hadn't been back to check since moving into the palace. She didn't mean to be so ungrateful. Life had just gotten busy. *And comfortable.*

She paused at a junction where the passage split in two. It was to confuse and divide any attacking army that made it this far into the castle. After a slight hesitation, she chose left.

"Nadzia!" Her name echoed against the walls.

She stopped. Hope rose. "My queen?" Nadzia retraced her steps. Had Kopciuszek changed her mind?

Several corners later, she found the young queen braced against the wall breathing heavily and holding her rounded stomach.

"Is it time?" Nadzia rushed forward and knelt, hands reaching up to feel the baby elbowing its cramped space.

"No. I'm just out of breath. I forgot to give you something."

Nadzia squinted in the dim light. Dangling from the queen's other hand were her shoes. *The* shoes.

Clear as a mountain stream. Delicate as a crystal goblet. Legendary as the queen herself.

"Those, too?" she squeaked.

"One. You must, so you can find me again."

Nodding, Nadzia took one of the delicate slippers. "What if I should fall and break it?"

The corners of the queen's lips curved up, pushing dimples into her cheeks. A movement in contrast to the urgency of the day. "You won't. The shoes are made of diamonds."

∽ ONE ∾

New York City, 1947

The Memorial Hospital looked like a small castle plucked out of a fairy tale and dropped smack in the middle of New York City. Originally built for cancer patients as a kind of wonder-building, it had been a disappointment, not a cure for cancer at all, and had since opened up to patients with other ailments.

Kate Allen thought it was the prettiest building in the city with its classic red brick turrets and arched windows, but that was only on the outside. Inside, there was no hiding the sickness of the patients, despite all the flowers Princess Kolodenko had ordered up for the special day.

The visiting princess had purchased every last arrangement from the neighborhood florists, from white carnations and pink roses to the more exotic calla lilies and purple orchids. Caught up in the excitement, the nurses buzzed about the circular room, setting out vases stuffed with bouquets amid the patients in the tower. The flowers' heady scent covered up the sterile smell, making the room as close to a mountain meadow as Princess Kolodenko could transform it.

Kate sat with her aunt, Elsie, watching the fuss being made for them. Elsie's mind was clear at the moment, for which Kate was grateful. Over the years, dementia had been taking over her aunt's memories, and no one was ever sure who Elsie would be when they visited her. But today was an important day, one that they hoped Elsie could enjoy with them.

"Are you nervous?" Aunt Elsie focused her attention on Kate.

Nestled in the hospital bed, Aunt Elsie looked so frail, though her white hair was beautifully done up in a bun with a white orchid pinned to the side. "Not about the ceremony. It's what comes after that I'm worried about."

Kate's gaze followed Princess Kolodenko making rounds to the patients, like they were her subjects and she was comforting them. The circular rooms were specially built to help the nurses see to each patient, and the center ventilation tube was supposed to help keep the air fresh, but the layout didn't leave much room for privacy. The princess looked like an old-time movie star, so elegant and full of life, even though she was as old as Elsie.

Kate nervously chewed her lip. *Just how does one serve a royal family?*

Elsie reached out to hold Kate's hand. "You will lack for nothing. The Kolodenkos are generous. And most of the time, the job is quiet. No fuss. Every so often the stepsisters' family tries to take what is not theirs, and that makes for excitement."

Even though the descendants of the stepsisters, the Burgosovs, were in jail, Kate felt a tingle run down her spine. The brothers, acting on a mission from their mother, had tried to trick her into giving them Cinderella's ball gown in exchange for information that might lead to finding her father, who was missing in action. They'd planted the idea that the glass slippers could help Kate find her dad just like they had helped the prince find Kopciuszek, the Polish Cinderella.

The Burgosovs had been lying, though. They didn't have the magical glass slippers at all. But now Kate couldn't let the idea go. Could it be possible? Could the glass slippers be used to find a loved one? Could they be used to find her dad?

Aunt Elsie continued, unaware of Kate's musings. "It will be different now, a Keeper living in America. Perhaps one day you will go to Poland? You look like a Polish girl. Tall and pretty and your hair is a lovely shade of brown. Or in future, one of your daughters will go?"

Unwillingly, Kate blushed. Her thoughts immediately flew to her boyfriend, Johnny, as they so often did. Her aunt and uncle both assumed she and Johnny would marry soon, despite her protests that she was too young to be seriously considering such a thing. During the war all kinds of girls got married right out of school, but now that the war was over, they didn't have to rush. Besides, the Kopciuszek dresses had so overshadowed everything in her life these past few months, she was still waiting for the new normal to feel normal. In light of the war's ending, and then Kate becoming Keeper, even graduation had come and gone with her hardly realizing it.

"Perhaps Poland one day," she answered. A safe answer.

The ceremony today would help. It would make Kate the official Keeper of the Wardrobe for the Kolodenko royal family, taking over from Aunt Elsie. The role had evolved from the medieval tradition of a servant overseeing care of the royal clothing and accessories, to the preservation of three particularly important dresses. The Kopciuszek dresses.

"If we were in Poland, we could have ceremony in a beautiful garden." Elsie gave an apologetic smile.

Kate shook her head. "If you had stayed in Poland, who knows what would have become of the dresses? And the Keeper role would have gone to someone else."

Princess Kolodenko made one last visit, speaking with an elderly woman sunk deep into a hospital bed, before returning to Kate and Elsie. She looked around, frustration etched on her face. "Where is that granddaughter of mine? Nessa must be here so she will know what to do when it is her turn."

Kate followed the princess's gaze to the door, wondering what kind of girl Nessa was. Did she like knowing she was a direct descendant of Cinderella, or was she mad that no one had told her until recently? Ever since the Kolodenkos had arrived in New York, they hadn't spent enough time with Kate for her to know what to expect from them. First impressions suggested Nessa would be easy to be Keeper for. She was sweet and generous, though seemed prone to losing track of time.

As Keeper and Princess, Aunt Elsie and Princess Kolodenko had an almost sisterly relationship, but they had grown up together knowing the secret. Kate and Nessa had only recently learned about their families' linked history. No one had told Kate what they expected her to do when Nessa finished her schooling in America. If the princess went back to Europe—either to their current residence in Italy or their family home in Poland, would Kate have to go with her?

Nessa burst into the room just then, carrying a large bowl filled with oranges, lemons, and apples. Princess Kolodenko frowned disapprovingly at her granddaughter's lateness, but Nessa only shrugged in response. Her soft black hair and rosy cheeks made her look more like a descendant of Snow White than Cinderella. "I thought I should add my part. Since the war ended I can't get enough of this fruit. Would you be a dear?" She handed the heavy bowl to Kate before pulling a small box out of her pocket. "I also brought a special token for Kate." Since Kate was holding the fruit, Nessa opened the box for her. Inside was a silver brooch. A royal carriage. "May our friendship exceed your service to my family. Thank you for giving of your time and talents." She tilted her head regally while glancing up at her *babcia*.

Princess Kolodenko nodded approvingly.

"Josie helped me pick it out that day you were busy outside watching the display window." Nessa winked, the formalness gone and a secret shared.

While Nessa and Josie, Kate's best friend, had been shopping, Kate had been outside Harmon-Craig department store in front of the famous Cinderella window display talking with Johnny. *Kissing* Johnny, if truth be told.

"Another symbol of Kopciuszek's story," Nessa said as she pinned it to Kate's collar.

"It's beautiful," Kate said. She leaned over to show Elsie, whose expression was starting to fade. *Oh no, Elsie. Hang in there a little longer.*

Princess Kolodenko motioned for Nessa to wheel over the curtained dividers to give them some privacy. Then she reached out and they all held hands.

"Elsie, Kate," Princess Kolodenko began in a quiet yet commanding voice. "You represent generations of faithful servants. You seek no personal glory. No fame for yourself. Your loyalty is as solid as the Tatra Mountains in Poland. These values may seem old-fashioned in this changing world, but they are virtues you should be proud to posses."

She focused on Elsie, and the two old friends looked kindly at each other. "Thank you for your service, my friend. You have been faithful to the end. I pray the rest of your days be lived out in satisfaction that you made your family proud."

Kate swallowed down the sudden lump that formed in her throat. Poor Elsie. After years of guilt for betraying her sister, to hear these words of forgiveness—what a gift from the princess. Princess Kolodenko let go of Elsie's hand and took up Kate's, cutting Elsie out of the circle. She peered fixedly into Kate's eyes.

"Do not think of your task as trivial. By keeping these valuable items for us—" She glanced at the three bundles, lined up touching one another along the edge of Elsie's bed:

The ragged and patched servant's work dress.

The magical satin ball gown.

The glorious white and flower-accented wedding dress.

"You help us keep incessant greed out of our family. You help protect our family from destroying ourselves from within."

"What about the glass slippers?" Kate asked, hoping for a hint to their whereabouts. "Am I to keep those, too?"

The princess shook her head. "Those have been lost to our family. All the more reason we need your help in keeping these dresses safe."

"Were they lost in the war?"

"Let me finish the ceremony, dear," Princess Kolodenko said. She turned to Elsie and took the amber necklace from her thin hand. This was the necklace Kate's *babcia* had brought with her to America and given to Kate as a family heirloom. Until recently, Kate had no idea of the significance of the amber necklace, or that Babcia had taken it from her sister. As Fyodora clasped the necklace around Kate's neck, she whispered, "I understand you have already worn this necklace."

Kate hesitated before nodding slightly. Princess Kolodenko's kind words about loyalty and not seeking glory hadn't always been followed in this servant family.

"We've never expected perfection, Kate," Princess Kolodenko said, as if sensing Kate's thoughts. She turned Kate around and spoke directly to her. "Our family is well acquainted with greed, and the effect of the dresses on us is strong." She glanced at Nessa. "We only ask that you try to keep your heart's intention toward servanthood. Your actions will follow." She smiled widely. "Do you, Kate Allen of the line of Keepers of the Wardrobe, solemnly agree to uphold the traditions of your family in protecting the Kopciuszek dresses?"

"I agree." Her voice came out quiet, timid. As she spoke, she noticed sparkles begin to fall around her. She lifted a hand to catch one and it melted like a snowflake in her palm.

Nessa giggled, trying to catch her own sparkles. "What is this, Babcia?"

"Magic." Princess Kolodenko smiled, then continued. "And do you solemnly agree to remain loyal to Kopciuszek's descendants, to uphold their rights and privileges with the dresses?"

Kate hesitated. Her answer would truly link her to this royal family and their wishes. She glanced at Nessa, who gave her an encouraging nod. "I agree."

Behind Princess Kolodenko, Nessa clapped excitedly.

The princess raised a delicate eyebrow before continuing.

"I bestow on you the title of Keeper of the Wardrobe for the Kolodenko family. Guard our treasures well."

While Kate shared hugs all around, the churning in her stomach that she'd been pushing down all day forced its way back.

All the smiles. All the congratulations. All the confidence everyone had in her was overwhelming. She had seen the quiet times and she had seen the "every so often. . ." as Elsie had put it. The stepsisters' descendants could be formidable. And they wanted the dresses more than she did.

✎ TWO ✎

The prop closet at Harmon-Craig department store was a mess. Kate and Johnny were tasked with going through all the boxes and inventorying every lightbulb, wire, bauble, and pillar. Their boss, Mr. G, had suddenly decided that it was past time for a master list. Although he knew exactly what he had and could generally find it within seconds, it was the other window dressers who needed a list.

"How is your aunt Elsie?" Johnny asked. His muscles flexed as he pulled down a dusty box from the top shelf. He started sorting while Kate observed his square jaw, set in concentration. That one strong feature stood for everything she loved about him. He was dependable, focused, and somewhat unreadable. Okay, maybe she didn't love that last part. She wished she could always tell what he was thinking. It would make her life so much easier.

He set aside silver balls, white garland, and plastic snowflakes. Watching his hands, she wanted to reach out and hold them. Stare into his eyes behind those new glasses of his. Brush his dark brown hair across his forehead. "Is she adjusting to living in the hospital?" he asked.

Kate blinked, embarrassed her mind had been wandering. Johnny had no idea how cute he looked in his characteristic white T-shirt and jeans. The time they had spent apart writing letters during wartime had been fun—she had a nice collection of missives showing their progression from friends to more-than-friends, but being together was way better. The butterflies in her stomach could attest to that. To think, they could have a complete conversation in one sitting instead of taking weeks to talk over something.

"She was with us through most of it, and she loved the spectacle Princess Kolodenko made for her."

Kate sat beside the Christmas box and wrote down the items Johnny was pulling out. If she kept busy with him like this, she wouldn't get caught daydreaming. He was all she wanted to think about lately.

Neil, one of the older window dressers, came in and grabbed a bolt of shimmery fabric. "Oh, hello, Kate. I-Is your mother working today?" He nervously patted the top of the bolt, shaking loose the material.

"Yes, she's here until seven o'clock. Did you need something from Women's Wear? I'll run and get it for you." She made for the door.

"No, no. I don't need anything from Women's Wear. Just wanted to talk to your mom is all." He cleared his throat. "I'll be going now." He backed out of the room and took off.

Was he blushing? Kate felt a pit in her stomach. "You don't think he's going to ask my mom on a date, do you?"

Johnny shrugged, letting out a burst of air. "He might. Do you think she'll say yes?"

"No. My dad. She wouldn't." The pit in her stomach shifted. "I don't *think* she would." It had never occurred to her that Mom might start dating again. "We haven't had any real confirmation about what happened to Dad. She can't start seeing anyone. Can she?" *Oh, this is bad.* "What if Mom starts dating and then they find Dad?"

"There comes a time when you have to move on—" Johnny started, but Kate stopped him.

"No. I don't want to talk about it. My brother is tracking down some leads. He'll find something."

"I don't mean to be disrespectful, Kate, but short of finding Cinderella's missing slippers, I don't know how your brother will find anything new. It's been—"

Kate held up her hand. "It's been too long. That's what everyone keeps saying. But Mom and I can't quite believe it. She still won't look through Dad's things that the army returned. She's still hoping . . . Wait. Why would you mention the slippers?"

Johnny looked sheepish. "That's what those Burgosov men said. I know they were trying to trick you, but why would they come up with that particular lie? They didn't seem like the brightest fellows, so maybe they let the truth slip out."

Kate leaned back and stared at the ceiling. That was

exactly what she had been thinking. "Did I make a mistake?"

"You followed your intuition, and it paid off. They didn't have the slippers, and they didn't know about your dad. Doesn't mean the shoes aren't real."

"I wish I could talk to them again."

"The guys in jail? You're kidding, right? Why don't you just ask Princess Kolodenko?"

"I did, but she told me the shoes were lost to the family. The Burgosovs are the only ones who can help."

Johnny gaped at her. "Do you hear what you're saying? You want to risk talking to those criminal brothers to get information on a pair of fairy-tale shoes that don't belong to you, and whose owner seems to be satisfied that they're gone. She's not even looking for them, is she?"

Princess Kolodenko didn't have the need that Kate did. One of her granddaughters had died in the war, but they knew what happened to her. There was no mystery for them to solve. No need to risk anything. Kate raised her eyebrows in a look that she hoped said, *Yes, it sounds foolish, but I'm going to do it anyway.*

Johnny laughed. "Anyone hearing us outside this room would think we were loony."

Kate smiled, and soon began laughing herself.

Johnny sobered. He leaned forward and searched Kate's eyes. "How do you think the shoes will help you find your dad? Didn't the prince have to go door to door until he found Cinderella?"

The last of the laughter floated out of Kate. "I don't know. I thought maybe if I wore them, they would guide me to him." She cringed. "Silly, right? But the dress is unusual. What if the shoes are, too? What if they *do* find people? I have this crazy connection to a fairy-tale family; I should be able to use it when I need help."

"Okay," he said. "I'm in. Whatever you need me to do."

Kate relaxed. He didn't think she was crazy, and he wanted to help. "Swell. First, I need to talk to the Burgosovs." She shuddered when she said their name. She never thought she'd have to see them again, and she couldn't believe she was initiating a meeting. "Do you think they're still here?"

"I know how to find out." Johnny pulled a card from his wallet. Agent Gillespie's business card.

"You keep that with you?" Kate asked.

He grinned. "It's not every day you get an FBI card. Makes me feel like a spy." He tucked the card back in his wallet. "I'll call him after work." He handed her the notebook and pen. "Ready for another box?"

Kate flipped to a new page, ready to start recording inventory again. After they zipped through a few boxes, Johnny sat down beside Kate. "Dad and I aren't taking the ship with the rest of the film crew. We're flying out ahead of them this week. We'll be at the Kolodenkos' estate the same day we leave. Sure was nice of them to offer their place to us. Flying beats almost a week on the ocean, don't you think?"

What is it with boys and airplanes?

"Floyd says there's nothing like flying." Kate refrained from voicing her thoughts about Johnny leaving early to work on his dad's movie in Italy. And about the Italian girls so interested in the foreign American soldiers who helped liberate their country. Her brother, Floyd, had written several of his "sugar reports" about the girls he had met while serving over there. "And it will give you lots of time to tell your dad about school."

"Hmm. Right."

"You've got to talk to him soon. Our semester will be starting when you get back."

"I know, I know. I've tried bringing it up, but then the conversation goes another direction. He's got big plans for me and my brother, and I don't want to spoil it for him."

"He's going to find out eventually. Like in September."

Johnny pulled out another box. "You know what should happen? You and Josie should audition for the movie in Italy. It'd be a snap for you."

He said it with a straight face, but the longer she studied his expression, the harder it was for him to contain his laughter. Finally he caved with a loud guffaw.

Kate looked around for something to throw at him, settling on a mound of beanbags. She pelted him with one after another. "Nice, Johnny Day."

He protected his face with his arm, laughing.

They had first met at an audition for one of his dad's

movies, and she had ended up sprawled on the floor, almost taking him down with her. She'd tried very hard to forget that day. Well, at least the embarrassing parts of that day. She met his gaze and it reminded her of looking into his eyes that first time. The connection was so striking she had felt like she was staring into Frank Sinatra's baby blues. At first she hadn't known he was the son of Wallace Day, owner of both the film production company and Harmon-Craig department store where she and her mother worked.

"But Josie found out this week she is interning with a costume designer for the summer. Not even Miss I-Want-to-be-a-Star herself would give that up for a bit role in your dad's latest film."

Johnny stopped laughing. "I'm serious. Then you could come with me." He grinned. "You're kind of growing on me." He started repacking the box. "At least see me off at the airstrip? Then when no one is looking, I'll sneak you aboard."

A summer in Italy? Kate was glad Johnny wasn't looking at her as she struggled to keep a happy face for him. She didn't know if she could visit the place where her father had gone missing in the war.

"Besides, that way you won't get too far ahead of me in your window design training," Johnny added.

"Ah!" Kate flung more beanbags at him. "You're never serious."

He lunged for her, capturing both her hands in his strong grip while he pummeled her with beanbags.

The door opened and in walked a pretty blonde, Fran Marshall, one of the store models. She quickly took in the scene of Kate and Johnny fighting over the beanbags. Her eyes narrowed at Kate before fixing on Johnny. "There you are. Your dad wants you in the meeting about our trip to Italy." She smiled at him like he was the only one in the room.

Fran Marshall was going? Kate raised her eyebrows, silently asking Johnny. He let go of her hands.

"We're in the conference room upstairs." Fran crossed her arms and waited.

"Don't finish without me, Sparky," Johnny said to Kate as he walked out the door with Fran.

Despite Johnny's using his nickname for her, which he only did when he was flirting, the insecure, jealous corner of her brain woke. Kate let the last beanbag fall. Why hadn't he told her Fran was going? She must have a role in the movie. The last big thing Fran had done was the baking soda commercial. Out of sympathy, Kate's mother had kept her in the store's fashion shows. Not that Kate was jealous. Or worried. It was just Fran. She had bigger issues to worry about.

But if she did go to Italy, she could spend her summer with Johnny and do her own research into Dad's disappearance. It was unlikely she'd find anything the others hadn't turned up, but at least she could say she tried everything to find him. And if she were able to find the glass slippers, she could do what no one else could.

∽ THREE ∾

Johnny never did come back to the prop closet after his meeting. Kate waited past her scheduled work hours, but eventually gave up and went upstairs to let her mom, assistant manager in Women's Wear, know that she was going home.

"Did Neil find you?" she asked, studying her mom's face for her reaction. She was wearing more makeup today than usual. A new shade of red lipstick.

"Yes, he did. I'll see you at home," Mom answered, not giving anything away. She was holding several empty hangers and started for the back.

"What did he want?" Kate followed her. *And is that a new perfume, too?*

Mom waved her hand flippantly and kept walking. "To talk to me, not you. Quit being so nosy. I'll see you at home."

Honestly. I only wanted to know for her own good.

Back at home, she called Josie, who immediately came down from her own apartment upstairs.

"Tell me again. Exactly what did Fran say, and how did Johnny look?" Josie tucked her feet under her on the sofa, balancing her plate of sliced peaches and toast on her lap. Her dark eyes focused on Kate.

"She came in and snatched him up like she was his boss. He barely looked at me before toddling after her."

"And she said 'our' trip to Italy? As in, Fran Marshall is going with the movie crew?"

"She must be one of the actresses."

"I don't believe it." Josie jutted her arm in the air. "For one, I'm Italian and I've never been to Italy. Two, I should be in the movie. After all, now I've got connections, right? With you and Johnny. Could he get me on the movie?"

Kate gave Josie a horrified look. "He teased me about auditioning, but I can't ask him that. Remember when I found out he worked for his dad? He accused me of trying to use him to get into that movie I auditioned for."

Josie slumped back into the cushions. "It's not like my parents would let me anyway. I'm lucky Mom convinced Dad I could switch schools to study fashion design. Interning with Bonnie Cashin this fall is good enough for me. I don't need to be in a movie—I'm going to help design costumes. Though I'd do a better acting job than that Fran. Aargh. I can't believe it."

Kate smiled. Good ol' Josie. Voicing the exact thoughts Kate was thinking but too proper to say.

"You're not worried Fran is going to try to break up you and Johnny, are you?"

"No." Kate answered a little too quickly. Sitting alone in the prop room, that had been exactly what she was thinking. Fran had a way of claiming things that didn't belong to her.

Josie took her plate into the kitchen. "I'd better go. Mom wants me to help with dinner tonight."

As Kate stood in the doorway waving good-bye, a telegram boy was looking at the numbers on each door as he walked down the hallway. Goose bumps flecked her skin as she remembered the telegram they got during the war telling them that her father had gone missing while working with the Monuments Men in Italy.

Her father, an art professor, had joined the army so he could help them avoid bombing any historically or artistically important sites. If he hadn't gone missing, he might be part of the group her brother was with now, finding the proper homes for all the stolen artwork uncovered in salt mines and castles and ordinary people's homes.

Josie raised her eyebrows as the boy passed her and stopped in front of Kate.

For a brief moment, Kate's breath caught. *Not Floyd.* The war was over. He wasn't involved in any fighting. He'd flown planes at the end of the war, but now he was mostly grounded, as there was a glut of pilots.

"Kate Allen?" the boy said.

"Uh, that's me." Kate took the telegram.

Josie followed her back into the apartment. "What is it?" she asked.

Before Kate had closed the door, she had torn into the envelope:

```
ROME, ITALY
KATE ALLEN
NEW YORK CITY, NY

DADS BOX. DIAMOND.
-F
```

Kate read the telegram twice. The first time in relief. *Floyd is okay*. The second time in confusion. She shook her head. "I don't know what he's talking about." She showed it to Josie. "Sometimes Floyd can be so irritating."

"Do you think it's code?"

"Maybe. But the war's over; their letters aren't getting censored like they used to."

"Well, it's got to be important. Your brother is too cheap to waste money on a telegram just to bug you."

"You'd be surprised what a brother would do. But okay. Let's say it's for real." Kate marched into her mother's room and dug through the hope chest. "Maybe the box my mom's engagement ring came in? If she still has it, it would be in here, but that's still not *Dad's* box. Look, she did keep it." Kate showed the small ring box to Josie. Empty.

Josie pored over the telegram. "The initials spell DBD. Read it backward, it would say . . . nothing. If we took every second letter: DDBX, okay, not that. I give up," Josie said. "I'd have made a terrible spy in the war."

"And if it's for real, why send it to me instead of Mom?"

"Maybe it's a gift for your mom. He might have bought it ahead of time and told your brother to give it to her on their anniversary, not knowing when he'd be back from the war. How romantic," Josie said, passing back the note. "Check his toolbox."

"Hmm. Maybe. It would be like Floyd to forget something like that." Kate sighed. "You know I think Neil at the store asked my mom out?"

"He's one of the nice ones, isn't he? Didn't give you a hard time about helping in Windows like some of the other guys did." Josie frowned. "I bet that feels weird for her. Did she say yes?"

That wasn't the reaction Kate was expecting from Josie. Her best friend was supposed to share her hope of Dad returning. Kate shrugged, masking her frustration. "She told me I was nosy." *"Concerned," "worried," or "angry" are better words.*

A lump formed in Kate's throat as she dragged the rusted green toolbox out from behind the piles of shoes and forgotten mittens in the closet. Dad was the last person to have touched the box. Many of his other belongings had been packed up and taken down to storage. Mom must have thought they'd need the tools even though the super took care of the minor repairs in the apartment.

She snapped the silver latch open and when she lifted the lid, the sliders on the corners squeaked in protest.

Looking at the contents, Kate laughed. Nestled in with the hammer, various screwdrivers, and wrenches were artist's brushes and tubes of paint. Anything could be in there.

She poked around but didn't see a jewelry case. At the bottom of the box were screws and bits of wire and various mechanical pieces whose function Kate could only guess at. "No diamonds." She reread the telegram, as if new words could have formed.

"Let me know what you find," Josie said, retracing her earlier steps out the door. "My mom'll be calling soon if I don't get up there fast-*veloce*."

"Bye." Kate dumped everything out of the toolbox. She took a cloth and wiped the inside clean, even stopping to examine the cloth to see if anything sparkly got swept up. Nothing.

She carefully returned all the contents, organizing as she went. The tube of burnt umber had at one time spilled over the top, and her dad's fingerprint was forever imprinted on the side. How strange to think he could be dead—going by what the army said—when here was his fingerprint. His identity. She slowly sucked in a breath, and then let it out. It was the little things that caught her heart by surprise.

After removing the paint tube, Kate shoved the toolbox back into the closet. She padded softly to her room and went immediately to her hope chest, the one Aunt Elsie and Uncle Adalbert had given her.

She placed the paint tube onto one of the top trays, wondering again what her brother's message meant. The mere hint of a new mystery made her want to check on the Kopciuszek dresses. She wished she could shrink them down and carry them with her wherever she went so she would always know where they were and that they were safe.

Perhaps all the Keepers of the Wardrobe had felt this heavy weight. Her grandmother certainly had. In fact, she had at first refused the role before changing her mind. But by then Aunt Elsie had already taken over.

The hidden panels of the chest slid easily, evidence they were made by a master craftsman. Kate removed the blankets and tablecloths and sheets she had started collecting for her future home. Then she pressed firmly on the bottom until it gave way and the wood pressed back against her fingertips. She removed the panel and confirmed the packages were still neatly lined up together like three best friends at a sleepover.

Her hand hovered over the middle package. The ball gown. The most important dress of the three and the one that the Burgosov family would do anything to get. Though the two Burgosov men who tried to steal it were in jail, their mother, Ludmilla, was still out there plotting. Kate could almost feel it, that sense when someone is watching you. Knowing she was alone in the apartment, she resisted the urge to look over her shoulder.

The amber necklace around her neck began to warm.

It always did when the ball gown was near. The pine scent floated up, making her room smell like the forest where the amber originated. She wondered what Poland was like, especially now, after the devastation of war. Was anything left from the days of Kopciuszek? How many other treasures of theirs had been lost?

Floyd had been amazed at all the stolen artwork the Monuments Men uncovered. He said it was proving difficult to find the proper owners for so many of the pieces. It was especially hard when an owner had been killed, and they had to track down the next of kin. Too many families were receiving boxes of trinkets instead of seeing their precious loved ones walk through the door.

Like the box the army had sent Mom, which lay untouched on her dresser.

Kate had asked her once, "Why don't you open it?"

"Lots of reasons," Mom had said. "If I look at the mementos he took from home, along with the items he collected on his travels, it would be like I know all there is to know about your dad. And that would be the end. No more mystery. At least, not that we could ever learn. I would be holding the last items he had touched, maybe learn the last bit of fun he had. See the last words he had written. I can't handle that. It would be overwhelmingly sad."

"It might also be healing," Kate had countered. Yet the box still sat, sealed and unopened. *Dad's box . . . that's it! Dad's box.*

Kate dashed into the bedroom. The box was at its usual place on her parents' dresser between Mom's jewelry stand and Dad's catchall tray. It wasn't very large. About the same size as a shoebox. Mom had told them to give away Dad's clothing, just save whatever he had in his duffel bag. It had to be the box Floyd meant, and why he'd sent Kate the telegram, not their mother.

Kate wrestled with her conscience. She felt like she needed permission to cut through the tape, but the one person she ought to get permission from would say no.

Without stopping to talk herself out of it, Kate went straight to the kitchen, grabbed a knife, and sliced through the four sides.

With shaking hands, she opened the box. *Sorry, Mom.*

At first glance, the items inside could have belonged to any soldier. Shaving kit. A postcard of some city in Italy. A few Italian coins. But upon closer inspection, she found items specific to her dad. Three small books of art prints. A leather-bound sketch journal. A small stack of V-mail with Mom's handwriting.

Kate sat down hard on a kitchen chair. There was no jewelry. No diamond. If this was the box Floyd was talking about in the telegram, he was wrong. And Kate had opened it for nothing.

Curious to see what she had written her dad, she flipped through the V-mail sheets to see if he had kept any of her letters. To save space on transport, letters were first censored, then transferred to microfilm before being sent overseas. There, they were printed out before going to the soldier, but at only 60 percent of the original size.

She found one of her letters:

Hi Dad,

Hope everything is all right where you are. We are doing fine here. Floyd is being a little overprotective but Josie has figured out a way to get past him. Don't worry. It's not like we are trying to do anything wrong, we just don't want him along. Mom gets to organize the Spring Fashion show next year. I bet she's already told you. Holy Toledo, but it's all she talks about. School is good. We're going to a movie tonight—Above Suspicion. Wish you could go with us.

Kate

She couldn't read any more. The tightness forming in her throat threatened to choke her if she did. To think — the everyday things she'd written to him when in a few short months he would go missing. She should have said more. Told him she loved him and was proud of him for what he was doing for the world.

As she was putting the letters back, her hand nudged the journal and she noticed a piece of paper sticking out. It was the drawing she had sent him of the amber necklace so he could have a copy made for Mom. Names and numbers were scrawled in the corner. She turned the page over and read the words: *diamond* and *Elsie*. A shiver traveled up her arms. Whenever Elsie was involved, the trail inevitably led to Kopciuszek. It was possible Dad stumbled upon a connection when he was looking for a matching amber necklace.

She flipped through the journal, sketch after sketch of the Italian countryside, some houses, some people. No drawings or other mention of a diamond. She closed the book and stroked her hand over the leather. It was Dad's favorite brand of journal, but expensive. He liked to go outside, find a comfortable place to sit, and sketch with the 2B pencil that he always carried tucked into his shirt pocket. Her fingers traced over a bump sticking out of the spine near the binding. A rock must have gotten in. She needed to dig it out so it wouldn't leave a dent in his sketches.

It was slow going, as she didn't want to puncture the leather. But there was a small hole in the seam, and she worked and worked the small rock down until she could pick it out.

She gasped as she held it up to the window. It sparked with blue light like ice crystals on snow. That was some rock, all right.

It was the diamond.

❧ FOUR ❧

"Y ou girls need anything?" Kate's mom asked as she breezed through the apartment. "Josie? Anything you want me to tell your mom?"

"No, Mrs. Allen. Just that I'll see her later."

"All right. And Nessa, thanks for taking Kate to the airport later today. Josie's mom had me committed to this fund-raiser weeks ago. You girls enjoy."

The door shut, and Josie jumped up to turn on the radio. She danced a little jitterbug back to the sofa where the girls were working. Nessa had come over to help teach Josie how to tat lace. Apparently tatting was also a skill passed down in the Kolodenko family.

Aunt Elsie had taught Kate the art of lace-making as part of her education to be the Keeper. The ball gown was trimmed in lace, as was the matching shawl. Kate needed to know how to fix any holes that might develop and teach the next Keeper how to make the compli-cated pattern. Despite being all thumbs at first, Kate had developed quite a talent for it. The rhythm of the shuttle and the thread felt comforting. But Josie was having as much trouble getting started as she had.

"It won't flip," Josie complained. She was firmly planted between the two of them, which was appropriate, since she liked being in the middle of the action.

Kate held back her giggle. She knew exactly how frustrating it was to try to get the thread from the shuttle hand to flip onto the ball thread as you gently pulled. "Loosen your left hand. You're holding it too tight."

"Honestly. If I loosen it, it falls off my fingers."

Nessa held out her hands to demonstrate. "You'll get the hang of it with practice. Are you nervous, Kate? I know I'd be, meeting my boyfriend's mother for the first time as he flies off in a plane, leaving you there, having to, what is the word?" She leaned over and asked Josie.

"Chitchat."

"Yes, chitchat."

"I wasn't very nervous until you brought it up."

"Nah, it works out perfectly, since we're coming along," Josie piped up. "You get to say good-bye, and meet the mom, with the support of your good friends to back you up. Then later we all get to help Nessa do more shopping."

Nessa and her grandmother were returning to Italy via ship later in the week so Nessa could finish getting ready to move to America for college. Their current trip to New York had been unexpected, as they left straight from a vacation in France when they'd seen a photo of the famous Cinderella Window in the fashion papers. They had thought they'd lost the dress forever until that photo appeared. Nessa wasn't prepared to stay in New York. She wanted to go home for the summer and finish her packing.

And before they left, they wanted to get in a few more purchases. Apparently certain goods were still hard to come by in Europe.

"Girls, that reminds me," Nessa said. "Did you hear the news? Princess Elizabeth is engaged. There have been rumors about it for ages, but now it is official. I must find something to wear to the wedding."

Josie's mouth gaped. "You got an invitation to the wedding of the future queen of England?"

"Not yet, but we go to all the royal weddings. I'm sure we'll get one." Nessa said it without any guile as she continued to study her tatting pattern. Being used to such events, she couldn't relate to how that would sound to two average girls living average lives in an average apartment building in New York.

Looking bug-eyed at Kate, Josie grinned. "I hate when I don't have the right dress to wear. You don't want to overshadow the bride, but with all the royals, you can't be demure either."

Nessa looked up and smiled at Josie. "Exactly. You understand my problem."

Josie winked at Kate. "Why don't you wear the ball gown from the Cinderella windows?" she suggested.

Kate pulled too tightly on her thread and made a knot. The Cinderella dress wasn't a dress to be worn willy-nilly. She picked out the knot, listening for Nessa's response.

"I hadn't thought of that," Nessa said. "What a great idea. I'll have to ask Babcia what she thinks."

No, not a great idea. Nessa didn't know enough about the dress to wear it in public yet. What if something happened to it? The princess would have to take it to England all by herself and get it back to Kate in one piece.

"Isn't a ball gown too fancy for a wedding?" Kate asked.

"A *royal* wedding," corrected Josie.

"I'll see what the other girls are planning to wear before I decide."

The knot in the lace Kate had been working on fell out, and with it the little bit of tension she had been feeling. She was being overly protective. Nessa always dressed immaculately and was driven around by a chauffeur. Surely the girl could manage a ball gown. Or Kate could travel with her. She would hobnob with the other servants in the back halls of Buckingham Palace while they waited for the dancing to be over. Kate hadn't realized how much she still didn't know about the Kolodenkos' expectations of her until now. Since she hadn't grown up knowing the secret, she had a lot to learn. It seemed everyone assumed she knew what she was doing. They forget that Elsie's explanations were spotty at best.

"That's one problem solved," Josie said. "Kate, did you

ever figure out what Floyd's strange message was about?" Josie returned her focus to her tatting, but Nessa looked up sharply.

"What strange message?"

Kate kept her eyes on her shuttle and thread. She hadn't planned on telling anyone about the diamond until she had worked out its purpose, and why her dad had hidden it inside his sketchbook. It was such an unusual gem. A blue diamond. She wouldn't have known it was a diamond if Floyd hadn't said so. She wanted to take it to Tiffany to see what the jewelers there thought of it. They had the famous canary-yellow diamond in the store, but she didn't want them asking any questions. She'd learned her lesson with the dresses—unusual things should be kept secret until you knew all the facts.

Having to keep secrets about killed Josie, so Kate was reluctant to say anything to her. If the diamond were an anniversary gift for Mom, no big deal. But if the diamond were linked to something else, like the reason Dad went missing in action, that would be a detail she should keep quiet until Floyd could give her more information.

"Kate? What message?"

"Oh, uh . . ." she started. She pretended to be side-tracked by a particularly difficult stitch in her tatting. Could Nessa be trusted? Her own mother and grandmother hadn't told her about the Cinderella dresses until a few weeks ago. It was Nessa's older sister who'd known about them and was to inherit them. Kate looked up to see both girls staring at her. *If only Josie hadn't said anything.* But how was her friend to know the underlying currents in her family?

"Her brother sent her a cryptic telegram mentioning the words 'Dad's box' and 'diamond.'" Josie put down her tatting and opened her eyes wide at Nessa. "What do you make of that?"

"Who's he in cahoots with?" Nessa said, looking to Josie for slang approval. "Diamonds are one of my favorite topics."

"The message didn't make much sense," Kate said. "Hopefully he'll send a follow-up letter explaining it better."

"But if he sent a telegram, timing is important," Nessa persisted.

Kate avoided looking at Josie. "We searched in his toolbox but didn't find anything."

"Where else could we look?" Nessa asked, pulling her thread taut to close off a ring. She stood, hands on hips, to survey the apartment. "We'll help."

"No, it's okay. Floyd'll send a follow-up letter. With him, the message could mean anything."

"Does your brother often play tricks?" Nessa asked. "I've only a sister to compare, and she wasn't much for tricks. She was always so serious." She blinked rapidly, her brown eyes swimming with tears. "I am sorry, it still hits me every so often."

"Do you want to talk about it?" Josie asked.

Nessa shook her head so slightly, Kate knew it was a sensitive subject. It was the same way she felt when well-meaning friends wanted her to talk about what happened to her dad.

Lots of people refused to discuss what happened during the war. It was as if they needed time to process, and if they spoke about it too soon, they'd be releasing the memories too quickly.

"We should probably get ready," Kate said. She put her tatting supplies into a bag.

Josie grabbed Kate by the shoulders and shoved her in the direction of the bathroom. "Hair and makeup first," she said. "This is the last time you'll be seeing your honey for a while and you want to leave the right lasting impression."

"Honestly, Josie." Kate rolled her eyes.

"May I remind you about Italian girls? Starving for some fun after a brutal war?" She put her hands on her hips. "Trust me on this. I've seen how flirty my sister can get."

Kate caught Nessa's eye, and the two burst out laughing.

"What? What did I say?" Josie asked.

Giggling, Kate answered. "How flirty your *sister* can get? How about you?"

Josie gave an exaggerated bow. "Fine. I stand accused. But you know I'm right. Let me just tidy you up a little."

As Josie set to work, Kate tried not to let Josie's words get to her. Johnny never seemed to pay too much attention to the girls who were trying to be noticed, but some girls were awfully persistent. Like Fran. How long could he hold out before he noticed them? Her?

Either Kate and Johnny's letters would sustain them over the summer, or things would fizzle. She'd never perfumed her letters, but this summer she might need to.

∽ FIVE ∾

Nessa had a hired car that she had been using during her visit to New York. A smooth Cadillac with a divider window separating them from the chauffeur just like in the movies. Kate and Josie were surely seeing a side of life they had only dreamed of before. Kate glanced at Josie's rapturous expression as she burrowed into the tan leather seats, and she stifled a giggle. Josie might never recover.

"Sorry about this, Kate," Nessa said for the hundredth time on the way to the Memorial Hospital. "I tried to explain we were in a hurry, but my *babcia* wouldn't listen. She wants to see where the planes leave America."

"We'll still make it," Kate said, hoping her voice sounded more optimistic than she felt. They were driving so slowly she could watch the car's reflection in the buildings they passed. When the turrets of the castle-like hospital came into view, she volunteered to run up and get Princess Kolodenko.

The atmosphere in the tower room was subdued, with nurses walking whisper-quietly between beds. Elsie's eyes were closed, her white hair fanned out over her pillow. Princess Kolodenko was rubbing hand cream into her friend's gnarled fingers while Uncle Adalbert sat opposite like a sentinel, reading his paper. He nodded at Kate as she approached.

"Hi," Kate whispered as she pulled up a chair. "Is she asleep?"

"No, just relaxed," Princess Kolodenko said. In silence, she continued to massage Elsie's hands. She pressed her thumb into her friend's palm, stroke after stroke.

Kate tried not to tap her foot to show it was time to go.

Elsie cracked open her eyes. When she saw Kate, she smiled and closed her eyes again. "That girl, you are," she said in Polish, her voice quiet like she was waking from a dream, or falling into one.

"Here, take over for me," Princess Kolodenko said. "I'll go freshen up and then we can leave."

Kate reached for Elsie's hand and tried to copy the princess's movements. Elsie's hands were delicate, with soft skin stretched across knuckles.

Once the princess had gone, Kate spoke. "My brother had me look into my dad's belongings that were sent back from Italy." She lowered her voice to a whisper. "He told me to look for a diamond."

Adalbert folded down half his newspaper and looked at Kate with one eye. "Did you find one?"

She nodded in the direction of her purse, where she had tucked the loose gem securely into an inside pocket. "I found it hidden in the spine of his sketchbook."

"Have you told anyone?" His voice rose and he put the paper in his lap.

"Not sure who to tell. Especially since Dad had also written the word 'diamond,' along with Elsie's name, on the sketch I drew of the amber necklace." She looked around to see if Princess Kolodenko was returning. "I feel like I should keep it a secret for now."

Nodding, Adalbert reached over to brush Elsie's hair away from her forehead. "I think that is wise. In her distressed moments, Elsie has said the word 'diamond.' I thought nothing of it until now. What do you think the connection is?"

"I don't know."

Elsie shook her head, eyes still closed. "I don't cry teacups like I used to. Show me."

Kate glanced at Adalbert before focusing back on Elsie. Her aunt said random words when she couldn't think of the correct one.

He shrugged, as he often did when he didn't know how to respond to Elsie. "Let me see it, Kate. Quickly, before Fyodora returns. Maybe I'll know something about the setting."

"There is no setting; just the diamond." Kate dug it out and passed it to him. "A blue diamond."

"Esmerelda. Dresses. Shoes." Elsie opened her eyes,

squinting them so her forehead wrinkled. It was as if pulling out these nouns took great effort. She turned her head to Kate. Her look was so intense it made Kate's heart skip a beat. Her expression reminded Kate how agitated Elsie became the day Kate showed her the servant dress in the Harmon-Craig window. Kate had asked her where the shoes were and Elsie went hysterical. It took Johnny coming by to calm her. Back then, Kate assumed Elsie was just shocked at seeing the dress on display in the Cinderella window. But what if there was more? What was trapped inside her mind?

Adalbert examined the square diamond. "I'm sorry. Without a setting, I can't tell anything about it. I thought maybe it would remind me of something. I have several jeweler friends who enjoy teaching me about their craft, but I've never seen a diamond cut in this way before. Square with beveled edges, and the right size for a large ring. Nor have I seen one this color. Are you sure it's a diamond?"

Kate sighed as she reached for the gem. "I'll just have to wait until I hear from Floyd, then."

"*Nie!*" Elsie said. She grabbed the diamond out of Adalbert's hand, all the while letting loose a string of words that Kate couldn't understand.

Adalbert interpreted. "She is saying much nonsense words. Nothing makes sense."

At that moment, Princess Kolodenko returned. She took in Elsie's agitated state and met Kate's eyes. "What happened?"

The heat rose up Kate's face. The princess had left Elsie so peaceful she was almost asleep. Two minutes with Kate and Elsie was in the midst of hysterics.

She turned to Princess Kolodenko. "Can you make sense of what she says?"

Frustrated, Princess Kolodenko tried to translate. "Her words are mixed. I think she is saying things about the dresses, things that happened in the past. And the necklace being lost, but you know about that. Your *babcia* had it. It was never lost. And the . . ." She studied Adalbert's face.

"The shoes," he said. His face took on a questioning look. "Did she say diamond shoes?"

Kate's mouth dropped as she stared at the two. "You mean the glass slippers?" Her voice rose at the end. "The glass slippers are made out of diamonds?" She focused on Adalbert. "Did you know about diamond shoes?"

He shook his head, looking as genuinely shocked as Kate was.

Princess Kolodenko chewed her lip as if considering what to say. For the first time, Kate noticed a resemblance to the more free-spirited Nessa. "Yes, the Kopciuszek slippers. They have been missing from our family for as long as anyone can remember. I've been told they were made of diamonds, though I have never seen them myself."

Kate needed a minute to take this in. She thought the dresses were valuable, mostly because of whom they once belonged to. But diamond slippers? Holy Toledo. The diamond Elsie was clutching couldn't be a coincidence. The way she was holding on to it so tightly. If only she could tell them how it related to Kate's dad.

"Were they blue diamonds?" Kate asked.

"*Nie*," the princess said sharply. "They were clear, like glass."

The princess's eyes darted back to Elsie, as if looking for confirmation. But Elsie was still talking, her fingers making motions like she was picking something up and burying it. Adalbert leaned in, closely listening. "Elsie says her mother told her the diamonds in the shoes were once plucked out."

Princess Kolodenko shook her head. Speaking over Elsie, she said, "Impossible. The shoes cannot be broken. People have tried, but the diamonds hold together no matter the force."

Elsie's mouth set in a firm line. She looked at Adalbert with pleading eyes. She spoke again in Polish.

Princess Kolodenko crossed her arms, still shaking her head.

Kate looked to Adalbert for translation. If there was ever a time when she needed Elsie to communicate, it was now. The princess was hiding something. Talking about the shoes was making her visibly uncomfortable.

"Her words are jumbled," Adalbert said. "I couldn't even understand as much as Fyodora did." He sounded resigned, like he was ready to give up.

Kate had to make them understand. "It's just that I'm wondering if the slippers could be found . . ."

"Then you could use them to find information about your father," Adalbert finished. "Like the Burgosovs told you."

Kate nodded, studying the princess. Would the royal family be willing to let her use the shoes *if* they could even find them? There was still so much about the family that she didn't know.

"You are the Keeper of the dresses. Do not concern yourself with the shoes. No one in recent memory has even seen the Kopciuszek shoes." She gently touched Kate's shoulder. "I know you want Elsie to communicate some hidden secret. But her mind . . . It is not as it was." She glanced at Adalbert and frowned in sympathy. "We should go," Princess Kolodenko said, her voice tight. "We don't want you to miss saying good-bye."

"Right," Kate said, reluctant to leave while Elsie still gripped the diamond. She couldn't wrestle it out of her hands in front of Princess Kolodenko.

Adalbert leaned in, straining to understand Elsie, who continued to speak slowly, deliberately, but in nonsense words as far as Kate's understanding of Polish could allow. "I will stay with her until she falls asleep," he said. "Will I see you later, Kate?" He looked at her meaningfully.

She nodded. Oh yes, and hopefully he'd have the diamond back. She followed the princess out the door, with one last glance back. *What are you trying to tell us, Elsie? What are you remembering?*

SIX

Their chauffeur drove up the circular drive at LaGuardia Field and dropped them off in front of the Marine Air Terminal. According to the official airport-time clock outside, they had twenty minutes until Johnny's flight was scheduled to leave. He was probably already on board. Maybe he would see her wave from the observation deck.

She had been to the airport once before, when Floyd had brought her and Mom out on one of his plane-spotting trips. He wanted so badly to share his passion for flying with them, he even paid their ten-cent fee at the turnstiles to the observation deck. He explained the differences in the Boeing and the Douglas DC and the other planes, but to Kate, they all looked the same.

"Well? Where to?" Josie asked.

There was a loud roar and they all looked up, squinting against the sun to see a plane rising into the blue sky.

"We're supposed to meet in the passenger waiting area

near the globe. I think it's this way." Kate led them toward the rotunda with more confidence than she had, but there was no time to waste. While scanning the crowd for Johnny's dark brown hair, she dodged passengers lugging suitcases that looked like oversize briefcases.

They found the globe but no sign of Johnny or his family. The waiting area was filled with nicely dressed folks waiting to fly out or waiting to meet someone coming in. She exhaled a little too loudly, and Princess Kolodenko patted her shoulder. "Keep looking, dear."

While Josie and Nessa talked about the Art Deco mural, Kate dug through her purse for the piece of paper that had the Days' flight information on it. She found a grocery list, the sketch of the stone cottage Johnny had drawn for Elsie, but no airline information. It was probably sitting on the counter in the kitchen.

Suddenly, hands clasped over her eyes and she froze, trying not to spill everything out of her handbag. Her heart leaped. "Those better be the hands of Johnny Day," she said, faking an irritated voice. She peeled off the fingers as she spun around.

"Sparky. What took you so long?" He grinned, obviously pleased he'd surprised her.

"Sorry, we got held up at the hospital."

"Elsie?"

Kate bit her lip as she thought of her aunt, wild eyes and clutching the diamond with a death grip. "She's had a little spell. I'll tell you about it later, if we have time." She hoped Johnny would get the message and lead her off to be alone. There were several things she wanted to talk to him about. The sketch in her purse had just given her a new idea.

"We've got plenty of time now."

She frowned. "I'm not going to make you miss your flight."

"Oh, you're not. There's been a delay because of mechanical reasons. That means my mom is trying to talk my dad out of flying because the plane is broken, and therefore going to crash just like that Baltimore flight back in May."

"Oh, don't say that. Fifty-three people died in that crash."

He waved someone over. "And speaking of Mom, here she is."

With such little warning, Kate's stomach barely had time to somersault before a petite woman, all smiles, came and gave Kate a welcoming hug. Mrs. Day had to tilt her head to not hit Kate with the wide brim of her straw hat, and her dangling earrings tickled Kate's cheek.

"It is so nice to finally meet you," she said. "Johnny's never introduced me to a special girl before."

"Aw, Ma." Johnny put his hands over Kate's ears. "Don't tell her things like that."

She cast a loving look at her son. "Well, it's true."

Kate grinned. She'd never seen Johnny so embarrassed before. It was a nice change from her being the one with the glowing face. "I'm happy to meet you, too," Kate said.

"Take her to the Sky Bar outside and buy her a little snack," Mrs. Day said while reaching for her purse. "Birdy and your father are still out there watching the planes."

Johnny stopped her. "I got it, Ma. You girls want to come, too?" he asked Josie and Nessa as they rushed up from the direction of the shops.

"You bet," Josie said.

Nessa handed Kate her shopping bags. "Be a dear and hold these for me? Thanks."

Without thinking, Kate accepted the bags and followed the group outside. The Sky Bar was a small snack shack on the observation deck. Johnny bought them all Cokes and they spread out along the crowded area. Nessa and Josie headed straight to one of the binocular stands while Kate and Johnny held back and found their own place at the railing. Johnny's sister, Birdy, spotted them and waved at Kate.

Kate dropped Nessa's bags and waved back.

"Why'd Nessa give you her bags?" Johnny asked.

"I think she's used to having people do things for her." Come to think of it, Nessa often began her sentences with "Be a dear," followed by a demand.

"Are you sure I can't convince you to go with me?" Johnny bumped his side against hers and stayed there so they were still touching. They watched a small truck pulling a cart loaded with luggage up to a plane.

"All the way to Italy?"

"You should have auditioned for the movie."

"I'm sure the other actors would love it if the producer's son's . . . friend . . . ended up with a role."

He laughed. "My *friend* would be great as an extra."

"Don't you use locals for extras?"

Johnny shrugged.

Kate pulled the pencil sketch out of her purse. She started opening it when Mr. Day called out to them.

"Hey kids, it's time. Come on, Johnny."

"I'm not expecting you to find it, but here, take it with you." She raised her voice as another plane took off. "I just want to know the significance of the place. Elsie had you draw it for her, and my dad obviously saw it, too, since he sent me a watercolor of it. It might be a clue, one the army doesn't have."

He pointed to the roof. "That gingerbread trim is pretty distinguishable. Like many things in your life, it's a cottage from a fairy tale."

"Why do you have a picture of our gardener's cottage?" Nessa came up from behind, and was looking at the drawing with a curious expression.

"This is on your estate? My dad made a painting of it." Kate couldn't believe a clue to her dad's whereabouts had been right in front of her all this time. "Why didn't you tell me he'd been to your house?"

Johnny grabbed Kate's hand and pulled her toward the building. "Let's walk and talk," he said.

"I don't know about your dad," Nessa said a bit

defensively. "The estate is quite large and spread out over several valleys. We've got more than twenty farms, and we had all kinds of military men pass through from every country you could think of. We hid a lot of them in our forests and abandoned buildings. You said your dad was in Italy for the artwork? It's possible he came through. Imagine if he did. That was before you and I knew . . ." She glanced at Johnny. "About each other."

They walked the length of the observation deck and back into the building. Johnny held the door open for the girls. Nessa went in first, still talking. "You could ask my *babcia*. I spent most of my time keeping the children occupied. And I try to avoid the *babuszka*, our gardener. She's, well, quite mad, to be honest. My mother made us bring her fresh bread and jams, but we would wait for her to go inside, leave it on her doorstep, knock, and then run." Nessa laughed. "She must have a cottage full of baskets for all we left her." Nessa put her hand on Kate's arm. "I'm sorry I don't know any more. I will ask around when I get home, though."

Kate refused to let go of the new hope growing. If Dad had been to the Kolodenko estate, there was a chance someone there could give them more information. This was the best news she'd heard in a long time. The diamond was another unanswered question, something else just out of her reach. But a known place could be revisited. Surely someone would remember her dad.

"I'll even bring the *babuszka* some pastries and see what she knows." Nessa held up her hand. "Don't get your hopes up. Your Elsie has problems with her memory, but at least she is sane. This woman, though . . . I've never known her to make sense my entire life. She's always lived in her own strange world."

"You forget, I'll be there, too. I can help." Johnny squeezed Kate's hand. "We'll ask around and see if we can piece together who he knew and where he went."

They caught up with Mr. Day and the others. Mrs. Day's arms were crossed, her head shaking. When she saw Johnny, she broke from the group and strode toward them. "It's decided. You are not getting on that airplane today. I don't trust it and I don't want the two of you on there. Your father, stubborn man," she said, shooting her husband a look, "will go on ahead and you can meet him there with the rest of the crew." She turned to Princess Kolodenko. "Better yet, Johnny can escort you and your granddaughter." Mrs. Day held her hands up to her chin like she was praying. "A perfect solution."

Johnny's gaze lifted to his father, who shrugged in defeat.

"But it's perfectly safe, Mom," he pleaded. "The pilot wouldn't fly if he didn't think it was."

Kate could sense his frustration, but was impressed he kept his tone respectful.

Mr. Day came over and gave Johnny a hug. He whispered in his ear, loud enough for Kate to hear. "You can fly home with me. Don't worry, I'll get you on a plane yet." He clapped his son on the back. "Time to fly."

He waved a general good-bye to the group. To the Kolodenkos, he said, "I am looking forward to seeing your estate. Any message you want delivered?"

Princess Kolodenko held out an envelope. "For my husband. Thank you."

Lastly, he kissed his wife. "I'll send you a telegram when I arrive."

After Mr. Day left, they all went onto the observation deck to watch the plane take off.

"I'm sorry you don't get to fly," Kate said, resting her hand on Johnny's arm.

"It's not all bad, staying behind. It means I get an extra few days with you." He smiled, but his eyes didn't light up.

Kate slipped a little closer to him. She was happy he wasn't leaving yet, though she didn't have the fear of flying that Mrs. Day did. "I'm not as fun as a first airplane ride. But I think I can help you take your mind off it."

He tickled her side. "I'm counting on it."

She pushed him playfully away. "It won't all be fun and games. We've got a criminal to interrogate."

SEVEN

Kate sat in a hard plastic chair at the Criminal
Courts building, waiting for Agents Gillespie
and Bristow to come for her. She rubbed her
sweaty hands on her skirt, crossed and uncrossed her
legs. Johnny wanted her to wait for him, but he got pulled
into another planning meeting for the movie and couldn't
make it. She wasn't about to call him away just to hold
her hand when talking to the detectives or the Burgosov
brothers. With all the guards around, she couldn't be safer.

To avoid eye contact with anyone else in the waiting
room, she'd been watching a tiny beetle crawling along
the baseboards. *Where is Gillespie?* The man across from
her stared at her with a blank expression. From the looks
of him, she couldn't tell if he was here to help someone or
hurt someone. Averting her eyes, she dug into her purse
for a stick of Wrigley's gum. The gum had been hard to
come by during the war, but gratefully, she could buy it at
any corner store again.

"Miss Allen," Gillespie said as he strode into the room, hand outstretched. "You wanted to see me? Is there something you'd like to add to your statement?"

"Didn't Johnny tell you?"

"He talked with Bristow. Did you want to wait to talk to him, too? He should be here in an hour or so."

Kate looked nervously at the rough-looking guy across from her and felt like a snitch. She whispered to the detective, "No, I don't want to wait. Is there somewhere we can talk privately? I have something to show you."

He nodded and motioned for her to follow him. He led her into another room, to a paper-cluttered desk in a long line of desks. It looked more like what she'd imagined a newspaper room to look like than a police station. "A little more private here," he said, motioning for Kate to sit down in a chair. "They're letting me borrow this desk while I wrap things up with the Burgosovs. I'll be taking them back with me to Europe as soon as possible. They're going to help us trace back some of the art they took." He sat down, folding his hands on the desk, and waited.

"So, does that mean they are being cooperative?" Kate's hopes rose. This might be easier than she'd thought.

The detective grimaced. "I wouldn't say that exactly. But we'll take what we can get." He pulled out a pen and notepad and looked at her expectantly.

She checked to make sure her pendant was safely hidden under her blouse before pulling out her drawing of the necklace. "I—" She started to speak, then realized she couldn't tell him the significance of the heirloom. He didn't know anything about the Kopciuszek story. She bit her fingernail as he took the paper from her to examine it. "Have you seen any jewelry like this?" She pointed to the notations her dad had made. "Or do you recognize the street or the name written here?"

Gillespie held the paper up to the light while he took a slow drink of some very black coffee.

"Yes, this street in Warsaw, I know." He dropped the paper to the desk and tapped his finger on the name. "Not much left now. Heavy bombing."

"But you are familiar with it?"

"Sure. It used to be a hotbed of underground crime before it got blown to bits."

Kate cringed.

"Sorry. Poor choice of words. But this name." Gillespie tapped the paper again. "Punia. It sounds familiar." He riffled through his desk until he found a particular manila envelope. He opened it and searched through the papers inside. He flicked a page with his fingers before turning it around to show Kate. "Aha. Here it is."

There was a short typed report and a grainy black-and-white photo of a side profile of a figure with a hat pulled low over the face. Not much to go on.

"A petty thief. That is how he came to be on my list, mostly harmless. But more importantly, we've long suspected him of being a go-between. He gets items for other people. Legally or not. By day, we think he is a jeweler.

This could be one of his designs, but I can't tell. He leans toward the flashy." He pointed to Kate's drawing. "Where did you get it?"

"I drew it for my dad. He was going to get a necklace made up for my mom. But he added all the rest—the name and the street. I, um, was curious and I know you know a lot about European art so I thought I'd ask." Holy Toledo. Her palms were sweating and she hadn't even gotten to the hard part yet.

The detective rose but Kate remained seated. There was one more thing she wanted.

"Yes?"

"Are the Burgosovs still here?"

The detective pointed with this thumb. "Cooling off in the cells at the Tombs next door."

"Could I ask them something?"

"Oh, honey. Bristow told me you wanted to see them. But that's a bad idea. You don't want them figuring out you're the one who ended their life of crime, do ya? We've got it all squared away. No need to mess with it."

Kate shook her head. Of course not. But she needed to know about the shoes. What did their side of this legendary feud know?

"That's a girl. Off you go now. Let me know if there's any other mystery I can help you solve."

Disappointed, Kate stood to leave. She bit her lower lip as she watched the detective put away his pen and paper and drink the last of his coffee.

He noticed she was still there. Sighed. "What do you want to know? I'll get it out of them."

Maybe there was hope after all. "Are you sure I couldn't talk to them? It wouldn't take long and I won't let anything spill about how they were caught. They know things about my family." She sat back down. "And I need to see their eyes when they answer."

He tried to hide a smile, but Kate knew she'd hit a chord. He must have agreed there was something about looking a person in the eyes.

"Please?" she added.

"You will talk through a telephone, separated by glass, but you'll be able to see their beady eyes. I will sit with you. Do you need to talk to both of them?"

"Can I start with the big one? He seems to know the most."

"You're a good judge of character." He groaned as he stood and stretched. "Come with me."

Kate followed the detective into the inner rooms of the Department of Corrections. "You're lucky they're still here," the detective continued. "We'd have processed most guys out of here by now, but since we're taking them soon, we've kept 'em close."

When a door of bars clanged shut behind them, Kate's heart nearly stopped. Then it kicked into high gear, flooding her system with adrenaline. Cinderella herself would be amazed at all the trouble her dress and shoes were causing in the modern era.

Gillespie led her into a small room with two chairs and a telephone hanging on the wall. He motioned for her to sit in the chair and they waited, staring through the glass into a matching room.

"You sure?" he asked.

Kate nodded, her mouth dry as sandpaper.

After an eternity of the detective trying to make small talk, the door opened and in walked the leader of the Burgosov boys. Tall and with thick shoulder muscles hiding his neck, he was dressed in the solid gray uniform of a prisoner, but ambled in with an air of aloofness, like he disdained the very air in the place. A recent cut on his cheek looked like it would turn to scar as it healed. He stopped short when he saw Kate, his eyes widening in surprise, then he grabbed the phone and grinned, revealing the gap between his two front teeth.

Kate slowly reached for the receiver. As soon as she held it to her ear, she heard, "Little American girl. Did you forget something?"

Her mind went blank. All she could remember was the feeling of fear when she found this man waiting for her in her apartment. Gillespie was right. The Burgosovs could have forgotten her, moved on. She shouldn't be giving them reason to dwell on her. But she was here now. She'd already poked the giant. "The shoes," she whispered. When he didn't comment, she said it louder. "The shoes. Tell me what you know about them."

He smirked.

"Please," she added.

The man tilted back in his chair, looking relaxed and in control of the situation. "I already told you we no have the shoes." He shrugged. "I have a heart. No needless suffering, I say."

"But what do you know about them?" Dare she mention the diamonds? "Do you know when they were lost? How they were lost?"

"Lost?" He chuckled. "Is that what they tell you?"

Kate squeezed the phone hard. "Do the Kolodenkos have them?" She tried to keep her voice light, like she didn't care they might be lying to her.

The man leaned forward, bringing his chair down with a *bang*. Detective Gillespie put a hand on the table. Kate could feel him tense.

"They can only wish for them. Is the other family who is keeping the shoes. The other stepsister."

Kate's breath caught in her throat. Then they were real. The shoes had survived just like the dresses had.

He smiled, but nothing about the smile was friendly. "You want to find shoes? Go to Poland. Tell the people you are looking for Malwinka." He winked. "That is all you need to do. Then wait. She will find you. Even if you have changed your mind, it will being too late for you." He slammed the phone down on his end and, without a further look, he and his guard started to leave the room.

Kate stood and slapped her palm against the glass. "What people? What people!" He turned around, but she could tell he wasn't going to say any more. She quickly pulled out the sketch of the cottage. "What about this place? Is it important?"

He squinted to see the sketch, then laughed and turned back, this time walking out and letting the door close behind him.

Kate hung up her end of the phone line, feeling Gillespie's stare. "Okay. Well, thanks," she said.

"Was that helpful?"

"No. Yes." Kate hoped he wouldn't ask more. As a detective, he must be dying to know what the big deal was about a pair of shoes.

He pointed back with his thumb. "That wasn't about Cinderella's glass slippers, eh?" He snorted. "'Cause, remember, we caught them with the Cinderella dress from the display window." He noticed Kate's expression. "Sorry, bad joke. We try to lighten things up around here."

He led her back out the way they came and even walked her to the front door. "You said your dad was one of the Monuments Men, yes?" All joking was now out of his voice.

She nodded.

"I'll ask around. See what I can find out for you." He held the door open for her.

"That means a lot to me. Thank you." Kate wandered out of the precinct, thoughts all a jumble but hopes rising. If the Burgosov man was telling the truth, then she would find the shoes. All she had to do was track down this

Malwinka person and somehow convince her to let Kate have the shoes. Not completely impossible.

"Johnny!" He was running down the sidewalk, darting around pedestrians.

"I got here as fast as I could," he said, out of breath. "How did it go?"

"Better than I thought. I have a new lead." She grabbed his arm. "But I need to go to Poland. The other line of stepsisters has them."

"I don't like the sound of that. What about Princess Kolodenko? Can't she get them back?"

"I'll talk to her, but she'll brush me off. She's acting funny about those shoes. Apparently, they're made of diamonds."

"Holy Toledo. Now I'm interested." He rubbed his hands together in an imitation of Scrooge. "Never could understand what was so great about a glass slipper."

Kate raised her eyebrows. "Yes, well, it gets better. I wanted to tell you at the airport, but there were too many people around. Floyd sent me a telegram to look for a diamond in Dad's things. I found one. It was a blue diamond, and it's what set off Elsie's last episode. She recognized it."

"So the shoes are blue?"

"I don't know. Princess Kolodenko says the shoes are clear, but she's not interested in them. If anything is going to happen, I'll have to make it happen." She ran the amber pendant along its chain. She was the Keeper, after all, and it was her job to watch over the royal wardrobe. Aunt Elsie had taught her that the commitment extended not only to a single princess, but to the family line.

Johnny draped his arm around her and steered her down the sidewalk. "You mean I won't have to smuggle you to Europe in my suitcase after all?"

Kate laughed. "I don't know. You might have to. I don't think my mom will let me go." To pay for the trip she'd have to tap into her college savings.

"Do you trust me?" Johnny asked.

"Of course."

"I have an idea."

EIGHT

Kate was about to slip through the front door when Mom called her back in.

"Would you set the table, please? They'll be here any minute."

Arggh. Kate closed the door in frustration. It was because the Kolodenkos were on their way over that Kate was trying to sneak out. She had to intercept them in the hallway so she could tell them what she'd learned.

Her initial excitement about tracking down the shoes had worn off, and her practical side had risen up to tell her all the reasons why it was too hard to do and how she would fail. She decided to get all the facts before bringing up the trip with her mom.

"Regular plates?" she asked.

"I don't think the Kolodenkos eat off of regular plates. Get out my good china."

Mom had been busy in the kitchen all day, which was

so unlike her. Apparently, she wanted to make sure the Kolodenkos felt welcome, and to thank them for all the time they had been spending with Aunt Elsie. Kate set the table in record time and dashed out the door to find Uncle Adalbert coming down the hall.

"Good. Close the door, child. I must speak with you alone," he said. He dug in his pocket and pulled out a little cloth bag. "Here is your diamond. Elsie would only give it back to me after I promised her you would go to—"

"Poland?"

He nodded, his face grim. "And you are willing?"

It was inevitable. "I'm nervous, but yes. Did Johnny tell you?"

"There is more. I sense the princess is being cautious with us. She knows more than she is saying. Johnny told me what you found out from one of the Burgosovs. This Malwinka cannot be trusted."

Kate's arms erupted in goose bumps. "You know her?"

"I know *of* her. She is quietly dangerous. Don't let her kindness fool you. Be careful what you share with her. And with Princess Kolodenko."

"Do you think this particular diamond could have come from the shoes, but Princess Kolodenko doesn't want us to know?"

"I do not know the significance of the diamond, but it has meaning."

The door opened behind them, and Kate's mom looked

out, exasperated, at Kate. "Come on in." She tugged Kate inside. "Good evening," she said to Adalbert. "I've got the paper ready for you while we wait for the others."

He shrugged, indicating he had more to say, but followed Mom inside.

When the others arrived, Kate hovered in the kitchen, hoping Princess Kolodenko would step in and they could speak semiprivately about Malwinka.

"Join us, Kate," Nessa called out.

"Oh, I'm just tidying up in here. I'll be out in a bit," Kate said. She puttered around, waiting long past a respectable time for keeping guests waiting.

Mom eventually came in. "It's time to serve the food. Why are you hiding out in here? Take in the veggies for me, please."

Kate was fidgety all during the meal. She tried to catch Princess Kolodenko's attention, but she was busy talking to Adalbert. It seemed like the Kolodenkos had something on their minds, too. Nessa kept smiling at Kate. A big, bright smile that she couldn't keep down. And Kate was positive she saw Fyodora wink back at Nessa's big grin.

"What are your summer plans?" Mom asked Nessa. "Are you going to stay here and get settled for school?"

"No. Our trip out here was so unexpected, I didn't have time to take care of things back home, so I need to go back. I don't mind the Atlantic crossing. The waves don't seem to bother me."

"I mind," Princess Kolodenko said. "This is my one and only trip to America. I will be happy to settle back home."

Mother kept the conversation rolling, oblivious to the looks being passed around with the mashed potatoes. "We got a letter from Floyd today," she said.

"Did you read it?" Kate asked. She could feel Adalbert and Nessa both lean in.

Her mother gave her a sideways glance. "Of course I read it."

"And? What did he say?"

"Just the usual. Hints about the girls he's met. Places he's seen. He's been transferred to the collection facility in Wiesbaden. He says he was warned that the job can be tedious, cataloging all the artwork, photographing it, and researching the owners. But there can be lots of excitement still for uncovering a great work or finally tracking down who it belongs to."

"Did he say anything about me?" *Or about a diamond?*

"You can read it later. I've told you the important parts."

"I've a few art pieces missing from our home in Poland," Princess Kolodenko said. "I should send him a list. Once they were taken, I never expected to get them back. People have a way of holding on to things and believing they are the rightful owner."

The conversation continued on about art until Nessa, clearly unable to hold back, burst out. "Can I tell them?" she asked.

Princess Kolodenko waved her hand in a queenly gesture, giving permission.

Nessa practically leaped from her chair with excitement. "When Johnny was booking his cabin, he found out if we wait a few days longer, we can take the trip to Europe on the *Queen Mary*. Babcia won't mind the travel so much if she can go on such a luxurious ship. They have restored it to the way it was before the war, before they used it for transporting troops. Plus it is the fastest."

"How exciting," Mom said. "All the celebrities go on the *Queen Mary*."

"That's not the best part. Babcia says Kate can come home with us for the summer." Nessa turned to Kate with a wide grin.

Kate drew in a quick breath. She looked at Fyodora, who was nodding, confirming the news. Then Kate looked at her mother, whose face reflected her own shock.

"Forgive my granddaughter's excitement," the princess said. "She meant to ask if Kate would like to go, and to tell you that we will take care of everything. You will have none of the worries. And then Nessa will have someone to help her prepare for her move to New York."

"Our treat," Nessa added. "And maybe we could squeeze in a trip to Poland?" She looked to Princess Kolodenko for approval, but the princess only shook her head slightly.

"We will have to apply for Kate's visa immediately," Princess Kolodenko continued. "I know someone who can take care of that. Tickets are available for the ship; Johnny already found that out."

Nessa flashed her Cheshire grin. "I made him keep quiet about it so I could tell you first."

Do you trust me? He had asked her. He figured out a way to get her to Europe. They wouldn't have to rely on letters all summer.

Mother interjected, "I have some money put away. My factory job paid well and—"

Princess Kolodenko put up her hand. "Kate will be our guest. It is our pleasure. Our villa is much too big for just my husband and me. With Nessa's mother in France and Nessa coming here in the fall, it would be lovely to have the rooms filled up for the summer."

Kate could hardly believe what she was hearing. Could it be that easy? She mouthed the word "Johnny?" to Adalbert. He briefly met her eyes and nodded before looking away.

Nessa clasped her hands together, begging. "Can she go?"

"Well, I—I—" Mom wiped the corners of her mouth with her napkin before excusing herself from the table and locking the bathroom door behind her.

"Oh, dear," Fyodora said. "That was probably not the way to bring it up. I'm afraid we have scared her. I should have thought."

"What do you mean, Babcia?" Nessa asked.

"Kate is all she has left. Europe has taken her husband

and her son, and now her daughter." She sighed. "I need to make this right. Excuse me." She folded her napkin and placed it carefully beside her plate.

Kate checked herself. She hadn't thought about her mom in all this mystery. Maybe it was time to let her in on the secret, too. Originally Aunt Elsie didn't want Mom to know, but Mom had changed during the war years. She wasn't focused on impressing the elite women she served at the department store anymore. She was settled now. Content. The news about their family history would have a different effect than before. *Or she might think I'm crazy and not let me go anywhere with the Kolodenkos.*

Princess Kolodenko knocked softly on the bathroom door. "Deborah? I am terribly sorry. I did not ask you to travel with us because I thought you would not want to go because of your work. But we would like you to go, too. In fact, I insist. We cannot take Kate from you. You must come and see our beautiful country. Even after the war it is still beautiful, and you must see it."

The lock clicked open, and her mother came out. Her eyes were rimmed in red, and she looked away like she didn't want anyone to notice. "I'm sorry," she said. "Of course Kate can go. What a thrilling summer it will be for her."

"And you, too."

Mother shook her head. "You are generous, but I'm not ready." She met Kate's eyes and gave a slight smile. "Maybe soon, but not now. I'm working on it."

Kate smiled back. *Mom is okay.* It didn't feel like the right time to tell her about the family legacy. And if Kate read between the lines properly, she wasn't going out with Neil, either. At least, not yet. But Neil would have ample opportunity while Kate was gone, and Mom could get lonely in the apartment by herself. The thought churned Kate's stomach.

Nessa grabbed Kate's arm. "Let me help you pack." She went straight to the bedroom and knelt by the trunk on the floor. "They're in here, aren't they?" She stroked the wood. "Mind if I have a fast look?"

Kate closed the door and shrugged like it was no big deal. The dresses did belong to the Kolodenkos, after all. There was no reason at all that Kate should feel so possessive about them. She'd known about the dresses longer than Nessa, she'd had them in her possession longer, and she always would have them as long as she kept them for Nessa. As she sat on the bed, she pushed the creeping tendrils of jealousy down deep. Elsie never told her about these kinds of feelings. She thought the Keeper was supposed to be immune from the pull of the dresses. From the greed they created.

But when Nessa started poking and probing the wooden chest, Kate jumped up to intervene. Now, the dresses may not be hers, but the chest was. "I'll do it." Deftly, Kate triggered the release, pulled out the three packages, and laid them on her quilt.

Nessa bounded over to the bed, clearly unaware that

Kate was a bit miffed at her. She ripped open the middle package and shook out the ball gown. Holding it up to her shoulders, she danced around the room, letting the fabric drag on the ground. Kate rushed over and lifted the skirt, following Nessa as she danced.

"Be careful," Kate said, trying to use a playful voice.

"Oh, it'll be fine. Your room isn't even the least dusty. The first Cinderella probably walked through the mud in this thing." Nessa thumped down on the bed. "The first Cinderella." She looked up at Kate with wide eyes. "Can you imagine being her?"

Kate shook her head. She had already tried. And she'd tried walking in the shoes of her own great-grandmothers. Touching the physical objects they had touched helped, but it was still mind-blowing to think of the fairy-tale legacy.

"What do you think I can do with this dress?" Nessa asked slyly.

"Excuse me?" Kate said. *Wear it carefully* was what she was thinking, but likely not what Nessa was getting at.

"You know. *Magic?*"

"What did your grandmother tell you?" Kate didn't know what the dress was truly capable of, either. Elsie said it magnified people's emotions, and Kate had witnessed that already.

Nessa frowned. "Not much. She talks like it is just a pretty dress, but we all know about what happened the night the Burgosovs tried to steal it."

Did she ever. Kate wasn't supposed to let the dresses be so publicly displayed, and then to have the Burgosovs come along and seemingly set the dress on fire . . . Her career as a Keeper had almost ended before it had started.

"About that night." Kate wrestled with how much to tell Nessa. She didn't like how the older girl was sounding about the dress. "I have a theory."

Nessa pushed the bundles away, clearing a spot for Kate to sit with her. Kate shook her head. She needed to pace for this one, just like Elsie used to do when she talked of the dresses.

"Elsie warned me the dress has personality. It didn't make much sense to me at first, but now that I've had time to think about it, it does."

"What do you mean?" Nessa prettily lifted her right eyebrow. Her delicate features made her look a bit like a fairy herself.

"It's hard to explain. It's almost as if the dress can take care of itself."

Nessa stretched out on her side, resting her head on her hand. "Interesting. What else?"

Happy to have Nessa's attention, Kate continued. "And I feel something, too, when I'm near the dress." She held out her necklace. "For instance, hold this."

"It's warm," Nessa said in wonderment.

"Even when Adalbert and Elsie first arrived, it happened, but I didn't understand why. The necklace and the gown are connected." Kate took a shaky breath, even now thinking about the dress catching fire. "And then, when we were setting up the window displays, the dress gave out a shock when one of the men touched it. It protects itself."

Nessa picked up the ball gown and examined it.

Kate was trying to instill a sense of awe and reverence in the young princess in the hopes that she would help make Kate's job as easy as possible.

The princess got up on her knees. "That's what I mean. What else can this dress do? Can it make someone fall in love with me like it did for Cinderella?"

"Oh, I think the prince was already in lo—"

"And will it bring me fortune like the Burgosovs think it will?" She shot a furtive look at the door. "My grandmother won't admit it, but the war not only devastated our family, it has also taken its toll on our finances. We could use a little magic there."

Kate bit back what she was about to say regarding the glass slippers. She didn't like the direction Nessa was headed. Kate had a feeling she would have to keep a sharp eye on this particular Kolodenko. Kate was Keeper of the Wardrobe to Kopciuszek's legacy, to the whole family, not Nessa. She was to protect them from the greed.

She gave Nessa a tentative smile as she watched the princess tear into the package with the wedding dress and examine the jewels on the bodice. This wasn't going to be as easy as she thought.

NINE

The next few days were a whirlwind with getting all the paperwork in order and trying to contact Floyd to let him know she was on her way. And then she had to tell Josie she was leaving for the summer.

"My treat," Kate said, waving at the bank of tiny windows at the Automat. "Whatever you want." She jangled her nickels as she waited.

"I wish you would just tell me already," Josie said. "I haven't got much time for lunch. We're working on a rush order, and I want to make a good impression. A recommendation from Bonnie would mean a lot for my future career."

"Do you want me to pick for you?" Kate asked, still waiting for Josie to finish her rambling.

"No, I can choose my own food, thank you very much." She hastily dropped in the nickels and put macaroni and cheese, green beans, and apple pie on her tray. "There. Now tell me why you are being so nice to me today."

"I'm always nice to you," Kate said as she made her own selections. She led them to a table, all the while feeling Josie's eyes burning a hole in her back.

"Spill it."

"Fine. I'm going on a trip this summer."

Josie made a face. "Oh, is that all? Going to the beach again?"

"Well, I will get a good look at the ocean." Kate dragged out the suspense, either trying to make it a little fun for Josie or merely putting off the inevitable.

"Tell me already." She looked at her wristwatch. "I gotta go in five."

"Italy." Kate squinted her eyes closed and hunched up her shoulders, waiting for the outburst. Her confession was met with silence. She peeked. Josie was pushing the macaroni around her plate with her fork.

"Did you hear me?"

"Yeah, yeah. Italy."

"And?"

Josie set the fork down. "What? Do you want me to say it? All right. Your life is charmed, Kate Allen. Charmed. I think you and I were switched at birth. You are living the life that I should be living. You're not even Italian."

Kate threw her hands in the air, mimicking Josie's gestures. "And that's the passion I was waiting for!"

Josie frowned and lowered her eyes. "Don't make fun of me, Kate. You know it's true."

An outburst would have been less guilt-inducing.

"I wish I could take you with me. But your life isn't so shabby, either. Who is the one who got to go to the Central High School of Needle Trades when my mother said no way? And who is interning with the famous Bonnie Cashin, youngest designer to make it on Broadway? And who is it I saw standing at the corner talking to that tall blond?"

Josie's face turned bright red in a blush Kate hadn't seen on her in years. "You saw that? What do you think? He's a dreamboat, isn't he?"

Kate smiled her agreement, but kept them on topic. "Besides, we're practically sisters, so I'm practically Italian."

"We *are* practically sisters, so you should find a way to hide me in your suitcase."

Kate sighed. "You know I would."

Josie was quiet, and the metallic clinking of forks and china around them grew louder. "I'm happy for you. You've been through a lot, and it's nice to see something good happening to you. I'll visit Aunt Elsie while you're gone."

"She doesn't scare you anymore?"

Josie shrugged. "She hasn't screamed 'Ludmilla!' at me lately, if that's what you mean. Nah, she's swell. She kind of grows on you."

"Thank you." Josie was everything a girl could want in a best friend. "Think about what you'd like me to bring back for you."

"Could you swing an Italian boy?"

"Ha-ha. You'll have to go get one yourself."

"A girl can dream."

After lunch, the two went back to Harmon-Craig. Before parting at the entrance to go their separate ways, Kate gave her a tight hug. "You know I'd take you if I could," she said. "We would have so much fun." She let go and sighed wistfully. Sure, she'd have Nessa to show her around, but it wouldn't be the same without Josie.

"No way I'm going in there to talk to Mr. G for you," Josie joked as she waved good-bye.

Kate frowned. Mr. G was the next hurdle. She had to find a way to get time off for the summer while still having a job when she came back. She never knew with the temperamental Mr. G, and she hoped he was in a good mood.

Kate knocked on the open door. "Mr. G?"

He looked up, talking on the phone, and waved her in and motioned for her to take a chair.

She edged past a giant stuffed bear standing near the door, and had to move a box filled with silk butterflies before she could sit.

He hung up the receiver. "That was Cecilia Staples. She was updating me on my Christmas order."

"If you need me to go over there, I'll do it. Anytime. Well, anytime after this summer." Cecilia Staples had a wonderful warehouse filled with display props. She built specialty displays for most of the stores on Fifth Avenue. She was amazing.

His eyes narrowed. "Is there something special going on this summer?"

"Fyodora Kolodenko has invited me to go back with her to Italy." She hoped that by invoking the name of Fyodora, Mr. G would be more inclined. He had been in awe of the princess ever since she had practically walked out of his window, his art come to life. The manikin he used for the Cinderella dresses had been modeled after a chance photograph he had taken in Europe, a photograph of Princess Kolodenko in her younger days.

"You're not asking my permission, are you?"

Kate tensed. Even after working with Mr. G for years, he still made her nervous. "I-I . . ." she stammered. "I thought I should talk to you about it. I would like to continue working for you when I get home."

He leaned back in his chair, hooking his hands behind his head. "On one condition."

She waited. He seemed to enjoy making her sweat.

"You get me photos while you're there, and I'll consider you still working for me."

"That's a generous offer, sir," Kate said, wishing she could take him up on it. "But I don't own a camera."

Mr. G popped out of his chair.

Kate blinked in surprise. Ever since he and Miss Lassiter started dating again, he seemed to have boundless energy.

"You are in luck. I recently bought myself a new model. You may borrow my six-twenty flash."

"Oh, no, sir. I couldn't take your camera." *What if something happens to it?*

He reached into a bottom drawer and pulled out a black box camera. "Nonsense. It's a Brownie. Easy to use." From the file cabinet he pulled out several rolls of film, which he lined up on his desk with the camera.

Kate was tempted. "Do you mean it?"

Mr. G nodded. "It was a trip such as yours that I went on as a young man." He closed his eyes like he was imagining his early days. "You can't put a price on inspiration. You never know what you will find when you set out on an adventure."

He pointed to a bulletin board filled with black-and-white photographs of the Eiffel Tower, the Leaning Tower of Pisa, and another landmark Kate didn't recognize.

"Do you know how to operate the Brownie?"

Kate shook her head.

Mr. G pointed to the lights. "Turn those off, bobby-soxer. You'll want to do this in a darkened room so you don't expose the film." He popped open the camera, pulling out a square frame. He handed her a film canister. "Open that. It's 620 film. That's what you need to buy. Attach the film to the spool here."

On the second try, she got the film to stay.

"Now, you wind it around the frame, then put the box back together." He demonstrated turning the dial until the window showed the number one. "It's ready. Now, to take my picture we need to attach the flash. I don't want to waste a bulb, so we'll go outside for that. But here is how you attach the flasholder. It's a little awkward, but you'll need it for indoor shots."

After Mr. G showed her the finer points of operating the camera, they went out into the street. "Take my picture by the display window," he said. He posed, arms crossed, facing the window, looking like he was examining his work.

Kate chose the focus at five to ten feet. She lined up her shot in the viewfinder, and pushed the exposure button. *Click.*

"Excellent," Mr. G said. "Now wind it to the next frame." He pointed to the tiny window on the camera, which revealed a number two after several twists of the winding knob.

"You got that?" he asked.

"I think so. Can't wait to see how your picture turns out."

They returned to Mr. G's office where he loaded her up with the flashgun, spare bulbs, and more film. "I'll start you off with these rolls, but you might want to buy more. I've got my own equipment, so I'll develop the film for you when you get back. My only fee is that you allow me a copy of whatever catches my eye."

"Swell. I'll do my best, Mr. G. Thank you." Kate refrained from jumping and clicking her heels. He was being so generous, she barely knew what to say.

"And Kate?"

"Yes, sir?"

"Have fun."

Next up for good-byes was at the Memorial Hospital. Mother was the only one going to see them off at the pier the next day. Adalbert intercepted Kate at the entrance. "It is not a good day today," he warned. "She does not recognize any of us. She is sitting, staring at the curtains. I am sorry for you to see her like this before you leave."

"I understand. But we take Elsie any way we can get her."

While they walked up to Elsie's room, Adalbert reviewed Kate's plans for finding the shoes. "I am second-guessing," he said. "Maybe you should tell the Kolodenkos your plans. You have so little information."

"I've toyed with telling them, but the timing has never been right," Kate answered. Although her gut warned her not to tell Nessa. And every time she'd planned to speak with Princess Kolodenko, they'd been interrupted. Surely on the ship they'd find a quiet moment where Kate could tell her the good news about the shoes.

"I have been asking around for the location of Malwinka. My friends, some say the name is familiar, like a legend, but no one knows how to find her. You will have to try yourself. She has not been like Ludmilla, which I always thought surprising. I wonder why she does not come after the dress like the others do."

By now they had reached the top of the stairs. Adalbert paused with his hand on the door handle. "I wish we could go with you, then continue home to Poland." He shrugged. "But with Elsie the way she is, we stay here. Besides, even now, Poland is not the place for me, a Jew, nor someone like Elsie, who married one. You would think after the war, people would be kind, but no. If my home survived the bombings, someone else is living there now. Someone else is wearing my clothes. Someone else is using Elsie's dishes. They would not welcome us home." He opened the door.

"I'm sorry, Uncle." It was the same story for many of his friends. They were not going back to their homeland.

Elsie was just as Adalbert had described. She was propped up against her pillows and staring, unblinking, at the curtains. Kate took a deep breath. Elsie may never know she stopped to say good-bye, but she, herself, would know.

"It's good to see you, Aunt Elsie." She spoke in Polish. "I'm leaving in the morning."

A slow blink was the only movement Elsie gave. Kate took that to mean she had at least heard Kate's voice. Thinking a hug was out of the question, Kate reached over to squeeze Elsic's hand. At first, the older woman resisted and tried to pull away, but then her fingers relaxed.

After a moment, Kate let go. "I will try to find what's been lost."

✑ TEN ✑

Day two on the ship and Kate still hadn't gotten used to the constant motion. Her stomach lurched with each crest and dip of the waves. Now she understood how Aunt Elsie could have been sick her entire trip from India to North America when she and Adalbert escaped the war. Elsie had spent all her time down below with the dresses, and Kate was beginning to see the wisdom in that.

Nessa had called her up to the Sun Deck for some fresh air, but really, Kate was realizing, Nessa wanted her there because she was bored and needed someone to play cards with. The movie people were not on vacation, but working as much as they could before reaching Italy, including Johnny. Most of the crew had gone over already, but there were several who stayed behind to finish up props and whatever other materials they couldn't readily get in Italy and were making the crossing now.

A cold ocean breeze constantly blew across deck. The

wind should have been refreshing, but the nauseating smell of brine was doing nothing to help her stomach. Everywhere Kate looked there was water. Perhaps she should go back to her room so she wouldn't have to see the cause of her suffering.

"I win," Nessa said. "Again." She frowned. "You know, you're not giving me much of a challenge here. Next round, how about you look at your cards instead of staring off into the sea." She waved her hands in front of Kate's face.

Kate blinked and focused back on Nessa. "Sorry. I was just thinking."

"Care to share?"

Do I? Kate fingered her necklace. She'd been thinking about what Adalbert had said. She needed the Kolodenkos' help. But even though Kate and Nessa shared a suite next to Princess Kolodenko's on the Main Deck, they hadn't seen the princess since they boarded. Nessa said her *babcia* would probably remain in her rooms the entire trip. And since Nessa had a friend, the princess wouldn't need to make a special effort to leave her cabin.

Kate had never seen anything so nice as their suite. Their bedroom had two twin beds and a vanity, and there was a separate dayroom and an adjoining bathroom, all styled in Art Deco. If only she were well enough to enjoy it.

"It's about the dresses, isn't it? You're nervous that we brought them with us instead of leaving them hidden or with Adalbert. Babcia says as long as they are kept somewhere safe, you don't have to walk around with them everywhere you go."

"I know I can't have them with me all the time," she said quickly. But, yes, she was nervous about bringing the dresses back to Europe. Europe was where all the Burgosovs lived. At least in America she knew exactly where the two Burgosovs in New York were, and they weren't going anywhere near the dresses. Although if her plans worked out, she'd be tracking down the family line of the other stepsister. She hoped they were less intense about the dresses and more willing to help her find her dad.

Nessa continued talking as she shuffled the cards. "You would have been more nervous to leave them behind. Besides, we'll have more fun with the dresses here. We can test them out."

Kate looked at her sharply. "What do you mean, 'Test them out'?" Her senses were not so dulled as to not be alarmed.

Nessa's face took on a sly look. "Aren't you even a little curious to see what they can do? Ever since your friend suggested I wear the ball gown to Princess Elizabeth's wedding, I've thought of nothing else. We'll have to plan a ball, of course, so I have an excuse to wear it." She frowned. "Grandmother has never hosted a ball before. What reason can we come up with to have one? It's too late to celebrate the war being over." A smile overtook her face. "What about in the movie your boyfriend's dad is making? Do you think he might have a ball scene?"

"I don't know. It's a movie about the end of the war. There might be some kind of dance."

Nessa dealt the cards, looking smug. "Once he sees our ballroom he'll have the writers put in a scene, I just know it. The room is irresistible. And then I can wear the dress." She punctuated each word with the snap of her cards. "Your turn. *Ora tocca a ti.*"

Kate squeezed her forehead. She wasn't in the mood for Nessa's cheerful Italian lessons. And the more Nessa talked, the more Kate feared her whole time in Italy would be spent coming up with excuses to prevent Nessa from wearing the ball gown. This trip was her only chance to solve the mystery of her father's disappearance. She couldn't waste it.

"Do you think I'll meet your brother?" Nessa asked.

"We didn't hear back from him. I hope he hasn't already left for Germany." Kate had sent Floyd a letter to tell him she was on her way to Italy and where she was staying. Princess Kolodenko had offered to arrange a meeting if he was still in the country. "If we miss him, do you think we can go to Germany?" Kate really wanted to hear more about Poland, but was anxious about coming right out and asking. She didn't want Nessa to know how badly she wanted to go, and Princess Kolodenko changed the subject any time Poland came up.

The ship rocked and Kate clung to the table, her stomach rising in her throat.

Nessa leaned back comfortably in her chair and waited for Kate to get hold of herself and lay down her card.

Kate swallowed with difficulty. Sweat broke out across her forehead. She dropped all her cards on the table. "Gotta go." She hoped she could make it to the privacy of the nearest bathroom before her stomach overwhelmed her.

After she'd regained control, Kate returned to the deck. Nessa had found a new card player, Johnny, and when he saw Kate, he leaped up to help her back to the table.

"You're not looking so good," he said.

"Thanks for the compliment," Kate joked. She put her head on the table.

"Do you want to go lie down?"

She shook her head. "In a minute. I need to gather some energy first. You can finish the game."

"I don't mind quitting," he said. "She's beating me."

"No quitting," Nessa demanded, waggling her finger. "I don't like to lose, but I also don't like to win because someone is letting me."

Kate took a steadying breath. "When do you think we'll go to Poland?" she blurted out.

"Oh, darling." Nessa felt Kate's forehead. "You're worse off than I thought."

Kate closed her eyes as another wave rocked the ship. "What do you mean?"

"They're rebuilding, to be sure, but our villa in Italy is much more luxurious than anything we might get in Poland. Trust me, you'll want to stay in Italy."

"But you're the one who said—"

"I know. I was only trying to talk you into coming back

with us. And besides, the place where Adalbert and Elsie lived is no longer Poland, but Ukraine. Do not tell her the borders changed; she will only be upset. Besides, her neighbors are gone, too. Those who survived the war have been expelled." Nessa played her hand, and the wind picked up and blew the card away. "Oh! Be a dear and get that for me, Kate? You are closer." She took a sip of her Shirley Temple that she must have ordered while Kate was in the ladies' room.

Johnny shot a look at Kate before retrieving the rogue card.

He'd complained to Kate more than once that she was letting Nessa walk all over her. But he didn't understand Kate's position. Everything was so new, and she didn't want to jeopardize her role as Keeper. Nessa was used to being waited on; it was no big thing. It was becoming more of a deal that he wouldn't let it go. He kept pushing her to stand up for herself.

"They can treat people like that?" he asked, again looking pointedly at Kate. "But this is peacetime."

"War. Peace. Sometimes it's hard to tell the difference," Nessa said. "It happened to my family, too, a long time ago. We should own a string of castles."

"What castles?" Johnny asked.

"Poland is dotted with castles. Millions of them—well, hundreds. They're everywhere. Had my family not been ousted, we could have had our pick to stay in any one of them."

"If Poland had remained a monarchy, you mean," Johnny said, an annoyed edge in his voice. "And if you could have held on to it for hundreds of years. When was it your family had to leave?" He put down a card.

Nessa made a small squeaking noise, but Kate couldn't tell if it was in protest to what Johnny said or the card he played.

"We'd like to go to Warsaw," Johnny said. He started rubbing Kate's back. Slow circles.

Her stomach still rolled with the waves, but now her skin tingled. His comforting touch reminded her of when she was sick and Babcia would stay up with her, soothing her the same way. Except this was better. She smiled. She could even forgive him for being such a pain about Nessa.

"No reason to go to Warsaw," Nessa said. "When we say there is nothing left—there is literally nothing left. You'll see when we land and start driving through Europe." She played her hand. "It would be a waste of time."

Kate's smile fell into a tight line. She couldn't look at Johnny. She already knew what he was thinking.

When Nessa spoke again, her voice had softened. "But it would have been worse if not for people like your dad, Kate. I'll show you the ancient buildings he and the others protected from the bombing. You can't easily move a fresco painted on a wall."

Kate sighed. Nessa sometimes came off curt, but she did understand. Kate gave Johnny one of his pointed looks back. He quirked his eyebrow at her, and then it hit her. Nessa had yet again managed to turn the topic away from finding her dad. She buried her head back in her arms on the table. She needed Nessa's blessing. She needed Nessa to be focused and helpful. Since Kate didn't know any Italian and limited Polish, she needed Nessa for everything.

Kate lifted her head, sensing a break in her nausea. How was she going to get Nessa on her side? The girl seemed interested only in shopping and the dresses. Oh yes. That was one topic Nessa was very interested in — Kopciuszek.

"Can I get you some water?" Johnny asked.

She nodded. "That'd be great." She waited until he was far enough away to not hear them. For the moment, she thought it important that Nessa not know how much Johnny knew. The secret was supposed to be kept in the family, and the only reason Johnny knew was because Adalbert had a feeling that Johnny would one day be joining the family, and so he'd told him.

At the risk of revealing too much, Kate decided to dive in. "What do you think happened to the glass slippers?" Even though she didn't say Kopciuszek or Cinderella, she still glanced over her shoulder at the couple sitting closest to them. They were both reading, seemingly not interested in the young people playing cards.

Nessa leaned forward conspiratorially. "I don't know, but I'd be interested in finding them. I've been thinking about this. There is a series of frescoes at our residences. All fairy-tale-type scenes, now that I think about it." She smacked her forehead. "I should have known something was different about my family. I still can't believe I was the last to know."

"What about the frescoes?" Kate prompted. She knew how Nessa felt, being the last to know. The secret was even more well-kept in her family.

"There is only one at our place in Italy. It is a dancing scene. And I bet Kopciuszek is in it."

A flicker of hope tickled Kate's insides. "Do you think it could hold a clue for us? How old is it?"

"Oh, ancient. Although I doubt it goes all the way back to the original Kopciuszek, but certainly hundreds of years ago. You're not used to seeing old things, living in New York. Everything in Italy is old. Well, used to be before the war. Now new buildings are going up all over to replace the old."

"What about the other frescoes?"

"At our residences in Poland, but Babcia hasn't the heart to go see what survived yet."

"What if we went and looked for her?"

"We'll see," Nessa answered vaguely. She lay down the last of her cards. "Oh, look. I win."

I t was dark, and Kate was awoken by some scuffling
     sounds. Her bed rocked, and she wondered if she
     were having a dream. Her pillow felt different—not
as cozy as it normally was. More scuffling, a whispered
word she couldn't make out. Someone was in the room
she shared with Nessa. She tried to shake the fog from
her brain, but it was still so thick and her nausea overwhelming again. The cabin creaked with the waves, but
these sounds were louder and coming from the trunk
where the dresses were. She had to wake up.

There was a scrape and a thump as the small traveling
trunk hit the wall.

"Kate?" came a whisper. "Are you awake?"

Only Nessa.

"Yes. What time is it?"

"Early yet. You fell asleep. May I turn the light on?"
The light went on before Nessa finished speaking.

Kate blinked the sleep out of her eyes. The sunset leaking

through the curtains covering the porthole made the wood paneling glow while the room came into focus. The two beds, the built-in wooden vanity, the open doors to the bathroom and the sitting room. "Shouldn't you be at dinner?"

Nessa bounced as she sat on the edge of the bed. "I've got the best news. The captain has invited us to sit at his table tonight!"

A groan escaped as Kate flopped back on the bed. "No food."

"I didn't expect you to come. Nor Babcia. She's almost as bad off as you. But don't you see? The dress is formal attire. I don't have to wait for a ball. I can wear it tonight."

Now Kate gave Nessa her full attention, queasy stomach or not. "You can't wear that dress to a dinner."

"Why not? The men will be in tuxes, the women all wearing their finest. I might stand out a little, but they'll just think I'm enthusiastic about being invited to dine with the captain. They'll just wink over my head at one another and call me a silly girl." She bounded off the bed and knelt before the trunk. "Help me open this thing."

So many thoughts came swirling and colliding in Kate's mind. The foremost was that she'd never heard of anything more inappropriate as to want to wear Cinderella's ball gown to dinner. A dinner! Surely Princess Kolodenko wouldn't allow it.

Kate rolled onto her stomach so she could hang her head over the side of the bed. Ah, that felt better. "What does your *babcia* say?"

Nessa laughed. "I'm not going to tell her. Now, come on. I haven't much time." *Click*. She'd managed to un-buckle the center fastener.

Before Kate could flop out of bed, Nessa had rum-maged through and found the ball gown. She tore off the wrapping and discarded it, unwanted, on the floor.

"Oh, look at it, Kate. Have you ever seen anything more beautiful?" The white and blue silk glimmered in the light as Nessa crushed it to her shoulders and twirled around the room. "Here, help me put it on." Nessa thrust the dress at Kate.

"Right now?" Kate slowly sat up. Everything in her was screaming, *No!*

Nessa slipped out of her dress and stood in her slip with her back to Kate and her arms up. "Ready."

"But you can't wear the ball gown to a dinner."

"Why not?" Nessa turned on Kate, hands on hips. "It is my dress. I can wear it wherever I want." She turned back around. "And tonight, I want to wear it to dinner at the captain's table."

A good dose of adrenaline hit Kate, along with the nausea. "It belongs to your family, not you. And it's my job to make sure it stays safe. It is a ball gown, not a dinner gown."

Nessa's mouth formed a hard line. "You said it your-self—it belongs to my family, which means it *is* mine. Who are you to say where I can and can't wear it?" Her hands balled into fists. "I command you to put it on me. Now."

Kate's mouth dropped. Nessa *commanded* her? Speechless, and feeling a new wave of nausea come over her, Kate did as she was told. She stood on the bed so she could lift the bulky material high enough to get it over Nessa's head. At least dressing Nessa was easier than dressing the manikins at Harmon-Craig. No trick arm that would fall off if you moved it the wrong way.

Her fingers fumbled as she did up the tiny clasps. She was shaking more out of anger than out of awe for the dress. This would not go well. "I'm coming with you."

"Don't be silly," Nessa said, glancing over her shoulder. "You look like you're about to drop over."

Kate started to protest when the boat pitched again, and her stomach with it. There was no way she could smell the fancy food and not be negatively affected. She finished fastening up the dress, flounced the large gathers in the back, and pronounced Nessa dressed.

The stateroom lacked a floor-length mirror, so Nessa bounced and preened as much as she could in front of the vanity mirror. Frowning, she turned to Kate.

"What?" Kate asked, wary of Nessa's expression.

"Is this it?" she asked, lifting her skirts. "I expected, I don't know. More."

Kate raised her eyebrows. "What do you mean, more?"

"Shouldn't it feel magical? I feel the same. Like this is an ordinary dress."

That dress could never be ordinary. Kate tried not to smirk. She didn't know if Nessa understood her warning about the dress's "personality." She watched Nessa fluttering about the room and debated whether or not to remind her.

"Do you have a wand or something you need to wave over me to start it up?"

Kate groaned and rolled over, finding a cool spot on the pillow. The girl would find out on her own.

Sometime later, there was a soft knock on her door. She tentatively sat up, and feeling no increase in ill effects, opened her door. It was Johnny, looking very dapper in a suit coat. Her stomach did a flip-flop. The good kind.

"You're up," he said. "How's the tummy?"

"Better." Kate smiled. *Actually, swirling with butterflies.* She took in the crisp lines of the suit and how it accentuated his shoulders. He looked so handsome. "Did you go to the formal dinner, too?"

He leaned against the doorframe. "Sure did. I'd tell you all about it, but I'm afraid to talk about food in front of you."

"Did you see Nessa?"

Johnny's eyes opened wide as he took off his glasses and cleaned them with his pocket handkerchief. She liked when he took off his glasses. His blue eyes were so striking, but the glasses hid them.

"Did I ever. Was she wearing the dress?"

Kate nodded.

"Whoo-wee. That girl was out for some fun tonight. She paraded through the dining room, stopping to chat with guests like it was an event in her honor. During the meal she spilled her soup when a big wave came along, and made a big fuss about having a waiter come clean it up."

A wave of nausea hit Kate that wasn't caused by the rolling ocean. "That's what I was afraid of. She's calling too much attention to herself and risking stains." Kate put a hand on her stomach. She might be able to handle an appearance and keep an eye on that dress. "I'd better get up there."

Johnny waved his hands, stopping her. "You're making too big a deal about it."

Kate started to protest when he stopped her again.

"Don't worry about Nessa. Everyone thinks she's delightful."

Kate slid her hand from her tummy to her hip. "Did you just call her delightful?"

He laughed, leaning in close. "I only meant that she's got everyone wrapped around her finger. When I left, she was starting in on the captain to push the tables back and open up a dance floor."

Now she was feeling faint. It was one thing to be sitting down to a dinner, but another for Nessa to be waltzing around the room drawing even more attention to herself. "Is he going to?"

"They do every night, apparently. The carpet rolls up

and out comes the band. I had no interest. It wouldn't be the same without you stepping on my feet." He grinned, disarming her growing anger.

"Hey. One time," Kate protested, giving him a playful slap on the arm.

"There's my Sparky. Glad to see you're alive. If I wasn't afraid of setting you back, I'd take you out for a spin around the dance floor."

"Don't say *spin*." She held her hand to her head in mock dizziness.

"We're wrapping up the work we can do on this tin can and I'm hoping to have some fun tomorrow. Will you be up for a swim?"

She nodded. "I think so."

They were interrupted by the *thump, thump, thump* of someone running toward them. They looked down the long hall to see Nessa in her stockinged feet, her shoes in hand.

"Kate, are you well?" she called out as soon as she saw them. "I've got a stain for you to fix."

"What?" Kate narrowed her eyes at Johnny. She knew it. Nessa wrecked the dress. She never should have let her wear it to dinner on a ship that rolled and pitched with the waves.

Nessa pushed them out of the way and tumbled into the room.

Kate turned to see how bad the damage was, but Johnny grabbed her hand.

"Look, I'd better go," he said. He gently took hold of Kate's chin and returned her focus to him.

Kate frowned in exasperation. He just didn't understand.

"I'll check in on you tomorrow morning. Maybe we can have breakfast together." He kissed her forehead. The sweet gesture made her feel like he was tucking her in for the night, and it melted her insides.

She watched him amble down the hallway. Easy for him to walk away. He didn't have a fairy-tale legacy resting on his shoulders. She couldn't mess it up. But he was right, the dress belonged to Nessa's family, and Nessa would have to take some of the responsibility, too.

It would serve the girl right if Kate walked off with Johnny for a moonlit stroll under the stars where they could talk about anything, everything, nothing.

She reluctantly closed the door.

Nessa stood in the middle of the room, studying the skirt. "Oh, I hope it comes out."

"What happened?" she asked, not holding back her exasperated tone.

While turning around so Kate could undo the back, she spilled the story out of her. "I was only having fun, giving my dress a little twirl—the skirt fans out beautifully. And there was a wineglass on the table that tipped and splashed on me. I don't know how it happened. It is not like there was a wave or the tipping of the boat."

Kate's heart fell. She stopped unfastening the dress and

began searching for the wine stain. *The first time Nessa wears it, and she gets a stain.* There it was, on the side, near the bottom of the white skirt. A bright red splotch like a splash of blood on a nurse's uniform.

"You can get it out, right?"

"You're the one who got a stain on it; don't you think you should try to get it out?" she retorted.

Nessa huffed. "It's your job as Keeper."

"You shouldn't have worn the dress in the first place," Kate said. "None of this would have happened if you had worn something sensible to the dinner." Even as the words left her mouth, Kate realized she was being unreasonable. The only way to keep a dress spotless would be to never wear it at all. She didn't know what had overcome her, but she couldn't stop feeling put out, jealous even, over Nessa wearing the ball gown.

In icy silence, they managed to remove the dress. Nessa put on a robe and proceeded to prepare for bed, leaving Kate to figure out how to clean the stain.

Aunt Elsie had given her a special recipe for washing the dress that involved a powder made from lavender and poppies. Kate searched the trunk but couldn't find it. Hopefully it was in her suitcase, which had been put in the hold with the Kolodenkos' forty-six other bags. She shook her head every time she thought about how much luggage they brought with them. Nessa even had ten bags with her in the suite.

Kate dressed and set out to find a bellboy who could

bring up her bag for her. She walked down the corridor, focusing on the wood paneling on the walls so she wouldn't look at the physical bend in the ship that had the odd effect of making her stomach dip. She held on to the plastic railing, fearful of an unexpected pitch. At the stairs she found a man pushing a food cart piled with empty room-service dishes. She stopped him and explained her predicament. "Can you find someone to bring up my luggage?

"No need the luggage," he answered in an Eastern European accent. "I know how to get wine stain out of silk. Follow me." He took her to a cleaning closet and presented her with a bottle of hydrogen peroxide. "Use this, with the cold water," he said.

"Thank you." On a whim, Kate asked him, "Where are you from? You talk like my *babcia*."

"Czechoslovakia," he said.

"I'm looking for a woman named Malwinka. Is that a common name in those parts?"

The man's expression was blank. "If you have lost her, you can ask they call her on the loudspeaker."

"Oh, no, she's not on this ship," She lowered her eyes, feeling foolish. "I'm hoping to meet her on my trip."

"You not know where she lives?" he asked, a small smile playing on his lips. "Europe is bigger than you think." He shook his head as he went back to pushing his cart.

Kate let out a breath. The Burgosov man's instructions were ridiculous. He sent her on a goose chase instead of a shoe hunt. What if the name Malwinka was as popular as the name Smith in America?

By the time Kate returned to the stateroom, Nessa was fast asleep. Kate spread out the dress, looking for the stain. She pawed through the fabric again and again, but couldn't find a mark.

Stunned, she sat on her bed, staring at the clean silk dress, and asked it, "What did you do now?"

TWELVE

By the next morning, Kate had found her sea legs and was so happy to be well and eating, she left all grievances against Nessa back in the cabin. Johnny had joined them in the first-class dining room before having to go to a brief meeting with the movie people, so in all, the morning had been glorious. The two girls sat at the table enjoying the last of their omelets, along with a final glass of orange juice. Princess Kolodenko continued to eat in her cabin, but Kate suspected the elder Kolodenko would probably be feeling better soon, too.

"What was it like growing up for you?" Kate asked Nessa as they left the table. "No one ever told you your royal heritage?"

"Oh, it wasn't like that. I know all the old stories." She led Kate over to the map at the end of the room. It went from pillar to pillar and all the way up to the ceiling. Made out of inlaid wood of various shades of brown, it pictured

New York on one side and Southampton, England, on the other. A hidden light behind the map lit up the setting sun and the crystal ship that slid along a groove, tracking their progress across the Atlantic. "Let's see where we are today." She pointed. "There's our little ship bravely making its way across the ocean."

"We're mostly there," Kate said eagerly.

The girls continued out to the Promenade Deck while Nessa picked up her story. "I was told all about how my ancestors used to be royalty over a small kingdom in what is now modern-day Poland. There was a terrible war when the neighboring kingdom invaded and my family had to go into hiding. Though they made several attempts to take back the kingdom, they never fully succeeded, and another invader came and took over both kingdoms. The two warring kingdoms lost everything because of their feud."

The Promenade Deck was a popular place for strolling. It gave passengers a place to stretch their legs and get some fresh air. Several lounge chairs were pushed up against the wall, and the girls kept walking, looking for two empty chairs out of the wind.

"What was missing was the name Kopciuszek," Nessa said. "Her story sounds very normal, historical even, until you attach that fairy-tale name to it. When I found out *who* we were descended from, I could read between the lines on all those old stories."

"Cinderella changes everything," Kate said.

"Is that the way it was for you, too? Did your family history finally make sense once you knew? Everything taking on a new meaning?"

"We had a small family feud of our own, and so when I found out, the problems between my grandmother and her family finally made sense. She left everything behind when she emigrated to America, and there was always a mystery about the family. She kept me interested in my Polish heritage, though she herself let most of it go. I guess she was preparing me, in case."

They found two deck chairs set apart from the others and claimed them. Nessa lay back and let the sun shine full on her face. "Look at us. We've spent our whole lives thinking we were just regular girls and here we are, the descendants of a famous story." She squinted an eye as she looked at Kate. "And we can't tell anyone. Which reminds me, Babcia wants you to call her by her married name in Italy. She doesn't like to be called *princess* in public. She lets Elsie do it because of their relationship, and we were in America, but it is easier for her not to have to explain to others. At home she goes by her husband's name, De Luca."

"Sure. I understand."

Nessa returned to her sunbathing. "There's one girl in particular I'd like to tell at my old school. She's always acting like she's so much better than me. She's had it in for me ever since we met for no good reason at all. Wouldn't she like to know who I really am."

Kate stifled her incredulity. Nessa was one to talk.

She continued. "You'd probably like to tell Josie, I bet. And Johnny."

Kate just smiled. There was a certain comfort in having Johnny in on the secret. He was on her side, keeping her best interests in mind. *When he isn't getting irritated about my concern for the dresses.*

"You know what? I'd like to test the dress again. Of course, I can't wear it tonight, since I wore it last night, but tomorrow I could."

"Are you joking?" Kate asked hopefully.

"I hardly had a chance to test it out. I need to find out what it does before we're home and Babcia makes you tuck it away again."

"What is there to test?"

"See that boy over there?" she asked.

The boy in question was at the rail staring out over the water. The sun was in his eyes so he raised his hand to act like a hat brim. He might have been the one eating at the table next to them that morning, but Kate couldn't be sure. "Yes."

"I want to see if the dress will make him fall in love with me."

Kate laughed. "It doesn't do that."

"Didn't it make Johnny fall for you?" she asked.

Kate felt her face turn red, not from embarrassment, but from anger. "No. Elsie says the dress only magnifies what's already there, so you can learn people's true intentions."

"Oh. Same thing. I want to learn his true intentions. He winked at me when I was watching the ice sculptor yesterday. I want to know if it was a good kind of wink or a bad kind."

It was not the same thing, but Kate bit her tongue.

Nessa turned and looked at Kate full-on. "What do you hope to find in Italy? With the cottage and everything?"

"If my life were truly a fairy tale, I'd say my dad. But I'd be happy with knowing what happened to him. To find out why."

"The why is the same for you as it was for my sister. They were protecting us. The survivors. Those who die, died for us."

Kate was quiet. In America, she hadn't felt the full brunt of the fear or the brutality of war. But Nessa did. Maybe she put on an act to forget, or to force herself to move on.

"I asked Babcia about Kopciuszek's slippers," Nessa said.

Not wanting to break the magic of Nessa's sudden openness, Kate was silent, holding her breath.

"She told me they were lost to the family," Nessa said.

Nodding, Kate kept her thoughts to herself. She didn't want to tell Nessa everything yet. Maybe she hadn't gotten over the whole dress incident yet. "Did she have any guesses as to where they might be?"

"No, but she hedged." Nessa quirked a smile. "When Babcia doesn't want to tell me something, she only reveals part of the story. I recognize it now."

"The Burgosovs taunted me about the shoes when they wanted me to give them the dresses, but later admitted they didn't have them. My gut is telling me there is so much more to the story."

"Me, too. This can be a secret you and I share, for once. Hush now, here comes the boyfriend who was not in the least influenced by the magic in the dress." She turned and smiled as Johnny ambled over to join them.

"Knew I'd find you here," he said. "We are done for today. You ladies know of any place we could play some deck games?"

Before Nessa could answer, a bellboy came by with a message for her.

"Your grandmother told me I would find you here. She said to tell you she is feeling better, and would you please come and see her."

Nessa thanked the bellboy and went on her way. Johnny slid easily into her vacant chair.

"Are we really alone?" he asked, scooting his chair closer.

Kate glanced down the crowded Promenade Deck. Couples were strolling along, happy to pass the time in each other's company. Two women looked like they were out for exercise and were walking at a brisk clip, and another group walked by carrying racquetball rackets, either headed to or returning from a game. "Yes, we're finally alone." She laughed.

They watched the people and the ocean, content just to be together.

Finally, Kate broke the silence. "How are you? You've been so concerned with me and my stomach, I haven't asked what you think of the *Queen Mary*."

He shrugged. "I've been on here before, but I was just a kid then. Birdy and I played in the children's playroom. I spent hours on the slide, while Birdy couldn't tear her eyes away from the fish in the aquarium."

"You still spend a lot of time together."

He nodded. "More so than with my older brother and sister."

"Maybe she could help you tell your dad you're not going to business school. He probably already knows, and is only waiting for you to bring it up. Trust me, it's better to let them know sooner rather than later."

Johnny reached over and took Kate's hand. "What are you going to tell your brother about the diamond?"

"I see what you are doing here." She waggled her finger at him. "Fine, change the subject, but we're almost in Italy, and you will have plenty of opportunity to tell him which school you are going to." She looked out over the blue-black waves. "I'll tell Floyd that I found it. That's all he needs to know. I'm worried that the shoes might be in pieces. If they're broken up and scattered, they won't be any use in finding my dad."

"From what you tell me, there is only one person who can answer that. Have you figured out how to find her yet?"

"It seems foolish to start randomly asking around for her." Kate laughed. "I mentioned the name Malwinka to one of the porters and he politely made fun of me. I'm assuming she is in Poland, but from what Nessa said, people are being relocated, so she could be anywhere."

"Who could be anywhere?" Nessa asked, rejoining them.

"You," Johnny said, pushing up his glasses. "Are you girls ready for a rousing game of quoits on the Sport Deck?"

⌒ THIRTEEN ⌒

By the end of the voyage, Kate had finally adjusted to the point where she was sad to see their trans-oceanic trip end. The *Queen Mary* was a lovely ship, and everyone felt the first trip in the restored ocean liner was special. It was yet another indicator that the war was over and people were moving on with their lives.

But their travels were not done. After crossing the English Channel on a ferry, they had a long train ride ahead of them through France, and south down the boot of Italy. For the first time, Kate witnessed the physical effects of the war. It was shocking. One moment they would pass a small town of quaint cottages, flower gardens blooming like a postcard. The next moment they'd be traveling through an area where heavy fighting had gouged holes in the earth and reduced buildings to rubble, yet to be cleared.

"Is it like this all over?" Kate asked Nessa.

She replied with a sad smile.

Although the accommodations on the train were nice,

the quarters were cramped, and it was a treat to stretch their legs when they changed trains. Princess Kolodenko had already settled into her new berth, but Kate, Nessa, and Johnny were determined not to get back on the train until the last moment for the final leg of the journey.

They were sitting in a small restaurant, slowly eating breakfast pastries, when a girl with short dark hair plunked herself down in a chair beside Nessa.

"*Ciao,* cousin," she said in a mixture of Italian and Polish, then snatched Nessa's last bite and popped it into her mouth. She leaned on the table with her elbows while she chewed. Her face was gaunt, reminding Kate of the images she'd seen of people during the war. Her clothing was practical—slacks and a T-shirt, and a shoulder bag slung across her chest. Her makeup was heavy-handed, making her dark eyes look bruised.

A look of surprise—followed by disgust? weariness?— flashed across Nessa's features before she composed herself and smiled. She answered in Polish. "You are the last person I would expect to meet here. I thought you were in Germany or some such place. How did you find me?"

The air almost crackled as the two stared at each other.

The newcomer broke the silence first by shifting her attention to Kate. "Are you not going to introduce me?"

Nessa took a deep breath. "Of course," she said in English. "Johnny and Kate, this is Lidka."

The girl, Lidka, jabbed out her hand to Kate. "This is how you Yanks do it, *nie*?"

Her accent was thick, but the girl had spoken Italian, Polish, and English in the space of one minute. Taken aback, Kate shook her hand. How did Lidka know she was American? "Nice to meet you," she said. It never occurred to Kate that the Kolodenkos would have other relatives. How many of them knew of the family heritage? The girl also shook Johnny's hand.

"Are you going home?" Nessa asked in Polish. The way she said it implied the girl was up to trouble.

"*Nie.*" Lidka answered in rushed Polish, speaking for several minutes. Kate understood only bits here and there. She didn't realize how slowly Adalbert and Elsie had been speaking in front of her so that she would be able to understand their Polish.

Nessa, noticing Kate wasn't translating for Johnny, stopped midsentence and switched to English. "Kate and Johnny are my new friends, and I am going to show them Italy this summer. It is such a pretty time of year."

"I hoping you go to villa," Lidka said, smiling triumphantly. "I coming with you."

"*Nie,*" Nessa answered. "You have seen all these places I will show them. It will not be exciting enough for you."

Lidka leaned back in her chair and propped a foot up against the table. "I bring my own excitement. These Americans will have the more fun if I with you."

A waitress walked by and stared at Lidka's foot. Lidka made a grimace at the young girl and she skittered away. "Did they talk about me to you?" she asked Kate.

"No," Kate said, deciding to stick to English.

Lidka continued speaking, not looking at Kate but focusing on Nessa, as if challenging her to contradict her. "We used to live near each other in Poland, before the war. I stay behind and join the resistance, while others run away, leaving us to do the bad works. Is that right, cousin?"

"Call me Nessa." Her voice was tight.

Kate felt the need to speak up for Nessa, but she couldn't figure out what the tension was about. She hoped this strange girl would not tag along. Whoever she was, she was clearly not a friend of Nessa's.

"So, you are cousins?" Kate asked, making an attempt to lighten the mood.

Neither girl spoke. Eventually, Nessa broke the silence. "We are distant cousins. Very distant."

"You hurt my feelings, cousin," Lidka said. "Kate, you would not be hurting the feelings of your family, would you?"

Kate nibbled her pastry instead of answering. This was getting uncomfortable. Johnny reached over and held her hand on the table. Lidka's eyes tracked the movement. How could they help Nessa get rid of this unwanted girl?

That's when Lidka pulled an amber necklace out from under her shirt and absentmindedly began toying with it, like it was something she did often, an unconscious act. Kate's mouth went dry. It matched her own—a sunburst with a round amber stone in the center. Why would this other girl have a necklace exactly like hers? She struggled to keep the surprise off her face. Nessa didn't seem to notice, but Johnny did. His grip tightened.

"We're leaving soon," Kate said. "If you are coming, you should buy a ticket."

Nessa gaped at Kate and shook her head.

Kate understood that Nessa didn't want this odd girl tagging along, but what other choice did they have? The train was going to leave soon, so there wouldn't be enough time to question her about the necklace.

Lidka also jerked her gaze toward Kate. It was like they had been performing a dance, carefully choreographed, when Kate changed the music. Lidka even took her foot off the table and sat up.

"I like you," she said, looking pointedly back at Nessa. "I had few plans when I woke up this morning, and now, here we are." She stood and nudged Nessa. "You could spot me the monies? I had not expected leaving so soon." The bag at her feet suggested otherwise.

When Nessa looked like she was going to protest, Lidka said, "Or should we get Fyodora?"

Kate had been taught enough of Polish culture to know that a good Polish girl should not use the familiar with an elder, especially someone like the princess. It was disrespectful. But Nessa quietly led the way to the ticket office and purchased the fare. Another mystery had joined their little party.

FOURTEEN

By the time the train neared the station at Sora, Italy, Lidka had fully ingrained herself into the group. She never left Nessa alone, so Kate never had a chance to find out who exactly Lidka was, and why she had the power to manipulate Nessa so well. When Princess Kolodenko saw Lidka, the two embraced in what looked like a genuine hug. That, or the princess was adept at masking her true feelings.

Princess Kolodenko asked Nessa to go with her to finish packing her bags, leaving Kate and Johnny alone with Lidka for the first time. They sat watching the fields turn into scattered buildings hugging the base of the mountains, and then they were on the outskirts of town. Everywhere Kate looked it was green and filled with life. The mountains were covered in trees, bushes, and lush grasses. Even the gray skies couldn't take away from the beauty.

After a few moments of silence, Lidka spoke. "Out of America, is your first time?"

"The first that I'll remember," Kate answered.

"I've been to Europe once," Johnny said. "Before the war."

Lidka stared out the window. "Much things has changed since then. The land is different. The people are different. Some things needed to change, but I do not know if we are better off now." She focused on Kate. "You are wondering about me? During the first few days of the war my parents are killed. I am the only child and stay in Poland. Nowhere else to go. The resistance took me in, but a few years later I am captured and sent to work camp as punishment. Every things you have heard or read about these camps is not enough. It was worse."

Kate frowned sympathetically. No wonder Lidka had an edge to her. She'd been through so much.

"When the camp was liberated, Fyodora's people found me instead of her granddaughter. She brought me back to the villa to fatten me up." She laughed, patting her thin cheeks. "At least I am not dead anymore."

"I'm sorry," Kate said.

Lidka ignored Kate's comment. "Nessa was hoping her sister would come home. Not her long-lost *distant* cousin. She and I do not see life the same way. I hoping that will not change how you see me."

Kate shook her head. She lifted her finger to point at Lidka's necklace when Nessa and Princess Kolodenko entered the rail car and interrupted her.

Princess Kolodenko looked refreshed. Her eyes were

sparkling. When the train began to slow down, she said, "It is good to be home. We are halfway between the larger cultural centers of Rome and Naples, but to us, fully home. We hope you love it as we do."

A dark look passed across Lidka's face at the word "home" but was quickly replaced with a smile. Whatever the underlying tension, Kate would try to befriend her. Lidka seemed like she needed a friend.

When they got off the train, Nessa's mother, grandfather, and several drivers were waiting for them.

"Mama!" Nessa called before being engulfed in their hugs.

"Nessa," returned her mother, and whispered several words in Italian, holding Nessa's face between her hands. When Nessa glanced at Kate and blushed, Kate could tell she was talking about the dress. Her mother probably wanted to know Nessa's reactions to it.

Nessa said, "I thought you were still in Paris."

"I can only stay for a few days, but I didn't want to miss seeing you once more before you're gone to America for good. "She opened up her arms for Kate. "And I wanted to meet Elsie's niece. How are you, dear?"

"Where is Nessa's father?" Johnny whispered to Lidka while Fyodora greeted her husband with a kiss and accepted the fresh-cut flowers he had been holding.

"No one has fathers anymore," Lidka said, not lowering her voice. "Nor eligible young bachelors," she added, looking Johnny up and down. "They have all been killed off."

An awkward silence prevailed as everyone took in what Lidka had said. Nessa openly glared at Lidka, while the others fidgeted.

Kate whispered to Johnny, "He died of typhus during the outbreak in Naples. He was a doctor and became infected himself."

Princess Kolodenko's husband, noticing Lidka for the first time, held out his arms to her. "Punia. What a surprise! Glad to see you."

The name Punia sounded familiar to Kate, but she couldn't recall Princess Kolodenko using the name on the train. And from the tenderness with which Mr. De Luca called Lidka by her nickname, Kate wondered if there was any jealousy between the two girls that might explain some of Nessa's coolness.

"I brought you Oscypek," Lidka said, pulling a strange golden brown square out of her bag. It looked like a small loaf of bread with an intricate pattern stamped on it.

"A girl that is after my heart. Thank you." He held up Lidka's gift and said to Kate and Johnny, "Welcome to Italy. Tony De Luca. I am delighted you agreed to come back with Fyodora. Our home has been so quiet lately; it will be nice to have guests once again. And now, thanks to Lidka, we have the good smoked cheese from the highlands of Poland. A blessed day it is."

That's cheese?

Fyodora placed her hand on her husband's chest. "Do

you mean the movie people aren't here yet? But they came over on an airplane."

Mr. De Luca laughed and patted her hand. "Yes, yes. They have arrived safe and sound. You mustn't be afraid of flying, *cara mia*. It is the future of travel. But they keep to themselves in the guesthouse and are busy scouting our lands for places to shoot." He smiled wryly. "A kind of shooting I, for once, don't mind happening on our lands."

"That is the truth," Fyodora said emphatically.

He turned his attention to the men and women gathering their bags into a pile near the princess. "Are these the others?" he asked Johnny.

"Sure are." Johnny introduced the crew before helping them load up the taxicabs to take them to the hotel. Johnny was to stay with his dad and the star actors at the guesthouse near the villa.

Mr. De Luca clapped his hands and smiled at the girls. "Your turn." He surveyed the piles of luggage and shook his head. "This will be two trips. Choose what we take now and we'll come back for the rest."

Kate searched for her small traveling trunk. "I need that one," she said. A baggage porter dug it out for her. "I can carry it." She took it out of the porter's hand and lugged it to the car.

They divided up into the two remaining cars. The driver took Nessa and her mother and the extra luggage. Mr. De Luca drove the other car with the princess in the front and Kate sitting in the back between Lidka and Johnny. Johnny angled his legs, taking up more than his share of space and knocking knees with Kate. She didn't mind.

"If you are hungry there is a picnic basket up here with some bread and cheese and fruit. Anyone like something now?" Mr. De Luca asked. "Maria, our cook, has prepared a feast at home, but insisted we bring you antipasti in case you cannot wait."

Kate shook her head. Her stomach needed more time to adjust to the solidness of land.

As they drove down the road, Mr. De Luca began pointing out the scenes. "We were fortunate in the war to not sustain too much damage. We are a small town, not like Rome or Florence. The Germans occupied until the soldiers from New Zealand drove them out. The roads have all been repaired. Travel is easy again." He laughed. "The tires for our car I had buried under the olive trees to keep the Nazis from finding them and taking our vehicle."

Princess Kolodenko turned around in her seat. "We hid all our valuable possessions as best we could. Even made false walls and hid furniture behind them. Or moved our family heirlooms to the farmhouses most remote from the road. Hid things in barns, but the most effective was burying."

"*Cara mia*, darling, with all the work you did, I expect to be discovering hidden caches for the next ten years."

She swatted him. "I have already dug up everything I buried. You did not even have to do one thing."

Kate and Johnny laughed along with the good-natured

joking, but Lidka stared quietly out the window at the passing scenery, not saying a word.

The sun had begun to set as they left the town and wound around the mountains. The pastoral valleys settled like a green quilt tucked in the folds, so perfect it was hard to imagine a war had ever marred these parts.

Lidka had fallen asleep, her head resting away from Kate. Mr. and Mrs. De Luca's chatter had eased off and the hum of the car was starting to lull Kate to sleep as well. She stretched, trying to stay awake. Fyodora had told her how special the first view of their villa, Avanti, was, and she didn't want to miss it.

Princess Kolodenko turned around. "Our little house is just up ahead," she whispered, glancing at the backseat.

Kate was about to say something to Johnny, but he had also fallen asleep in the last miles of road. He looked so cute with his mouth hanging open and his head resting against the doorframe.

They rounded a corner and drove down into a valley just as the sunset was at its most brilliant. The fiery sky set the clouds aflame, and in the distance, past the rolling hills, stood an old stone castle majestically keeping guard over the land.

"You live in a castle?" Kate asked.

Princess Kolodenko laughed, a soft tinkling sound. "No, dear. That cold, drafty thing is best left for the tourists to wander through." She pointed to the right. "We live in the villa over there."

Kate's gaze followed Princess Kolodenko's directions to a stone mansion, almost as big as the castle. It had a red tile roof, a huge wooden front door, and a line of beveled windows. As they drove closer up the curving road, Kate could make out climbing vines covering half the house and geraniums in terra-cotta pots everywhere there was a nook or cranny. Lights inside started to blaze out in warmth as the sun took its final bow and twilight settled in.

With the others still sleeping, Kate asked the question she'd been waiting days to ask. "Mrs. De Luca, do you know someone named Malwinka?"

The princess stiffened. "I do. And I do not wish to hear her name spoken again." She turned and looked at Kate with a stern expression. "Nor do you need to bring her name up with the girls." Her gaze transferred to the sleeping Lidka.

Kate's heart began to race. "But I have reason to believe she has the glass slippers."

"Malwinka is from the past and will stay there." The princess turned around, leaving Kate at a loss for what to do next.

FIFTEEN

"Lidka." Princess Kolodenko leaned back and touched the girl's arm as the car came to a stop. Three other cars were parked in the wide circular driveway, and Nessa and her mom pulled up beside them.

"Johnny, we're here," Kate said, eager to get out of the car. She nudged him with her knee.

He started to wake up, rubbing his eyes. Mr. De Luca came round to open the car door for his wife. As they all sleepily got out of the car, the oversize front door flew open, and before Kate could register who it was, a man in uniform scooped her up and was twirling her in the air.

"Floyd!" She laughed, letting out an ocean of relief to find him here. "Put me down."

"I got your letter," he said, plunking her down and draping his arm around her. "Your timing was perfect. I had some paintings to deliver to a private collector in Naples. I go back to Germany tomorrow."

She grinned at him. "You're a sight for sore eyes. We've

missed you." *And I can't wait to get you alone and solve the mystery of the diamond.*

Nessa bumped shoulders with Kate, her eyes fixed on Floyd. A big smile on her face.

All the girls like Floyd. She introduced them. "Floyd, this is Nessa."

He reached out his hand, but Nessa shook her head and wrapped her arms around his neck in a hug. "You're practically family," she said. "Kate feels like my sister after bunking with her."

Floyd grinned as he spun her around, too. The adults exchanged amused glances. The rest of the introductions were made, including Mr. Day, who had survived his flight well enough, then Mr. De Luca invited everyone inside.

Kate paused at the front door to touch the family crest carved into the wood. A shield with an eagle, a horseman, and a crown. The Kolodenko coat of arms. Back in New York this symbol had been Kate's first clue that her family was involved in something unusual. It was stamped on Elsie's special steamer trunk, invisible to most people, but Kate could see it.

Nessa's mother caught her eye and smiled.

They continued through the entryway, walking on warm reddish-brown tiles that led throughout the villa. Each room had a thick area rug that anchored the furniture. They passed a family room, a library, and what looked like a study. Eventually they came to a large dining area with a glittering chandelier hanging over a table long enough to seat all of them, with room for more.

Mr. De Luca was not kidding when he said their cook, Maria, had prepared a feast. She served them an antipasti of cold cuts followed by penne pasta and a beef stew that melted in Kate's mouth. A light dessert of fresh fruit ended the meal on a sweet note.

When Maria started taking the plates into the kitchen, Mr. De Luca, said, "You young ones, out to the patio. Is a beautiful night, don't waste it."

Nessa playfully saluted her grandfather, then signaled for the rest of them to follow her.

Nessa's mom followed with a pitcher of cherry *kompot*, a Polish favorite. "I know there is no point in telling you to not stay up too late, so I will just say, enjoy." She squeezed Kate's shoulder. "I am pleased to meet our Elsie's niece."

Lidka, who was still standing near the door, turned and followed Nessa's mom back inside without saying good-night.

"Are you tired?" Kate asked Nessa. She only had tonight to talk to Floyd alone, but with the way Nessa had stuck herself to his side, she knew that was going to be difficult. Even now she was pouring him a drink.

"No, I could stay up all night looking at these stars," she said, pointing to the tiny lights smattered across the black sky.

Kate hadn't seen a view of the stars like this since the

nightly blackouts they had during the war. But even then, the city lights had never gone out completely.

The patio was expertly decorated, surrounded by rows of flowerpots, and beyond those, gardens that Kate would have to wait for daylight to explore. Johnny sat beside her, leaning on the arm of her chair while the perfumed air imprinted itself in her mind. "What are these flowers that I'm smelling?"

"Jasmine," Nessa answered. "Strong, aren't they? They are not the prettiest flowers in the garden, but they make us notice them in other ways."

Kate was sure that whenever she smelled jasmine she would be whisked back to this summer night in Italy. Johnny squeezed her hand. He probably knew she was dying to get Floyd alone so they could talk about the diamond.

Nessa asked Floyd about his work, and that started him talking. Kate had never seen Nessa sit so quietly and attentively before. Whenever it seemed like he was about to slow down, she would ask another question to get him going, all the while gazing at him like he hung the moon.

If Kate didn't do something soon, she'd never have the chance to talk to her brother alone. Of course, Floyd didn't know she was keeping the diamond a secret, so he wasn't catching any of the silent signals she was sending him to stop being so charming and let the poor girl go to bed.

It wasn't until Johnny stood and gave an exaggerated yawn that Floyd even noticed how late it was. "Look at me yammering on so. You all must be tired from your trip," he said, getting up.

Finally.

Kate was about to offer to help clear the dishes when Nessa handed her the tray.

"The dishes go in the kitchen," she said dismissively.

Reflexively, Kate took the tray and started collecting the glasses. When she reached for Johnny's, he held to it. "I don't need a servant to clean up after me," he said.

Kate felt her cheeks grow warm. What if Nessa heard him? "I'm happy to take your glass," she said.

"And normally, I'd be happy to let you," he said, angling his head in Nessa's direction. "But you're a Keeper, not a maid."

"She's not listening," Kate whispered. "So your little lesson didn't work." She strutted past Nessa and her brother and into the kitchen.

Johnny followed close on her heels. "She might have some trouble living on her own in New York," he said.

"I'm beginning to worry she's going to want me to move in with her," Kate said as she ran the water. She could do a quick wash so Maria wouldn't wake up to a sink full of dirty dishes. "You seem to be against domestic help. Don't you have a maid do everything for you?" she asked.

"I plead the fifth."

Kate handed him the dish soap. "Show me what you got."

He cracked his knuckles like he was getting ready for hard labor. "Stand back and be amazed, Kate Allen."

While Johnny started in on the pitcher, Floyd strolled into the room, alone. "Did you get my telegram?" he asked.

"Where's Nessa?"

"She's gone upstairs."

"Yes, I got it. It's the whole reason we're here in Italy."

He looked confused. "Did you find the diamond?"

Kate nodded. "No thanks to your short telegram."

"Apparently a short telegram was all you needed." He grinned. "So why didn't you just give it to Elsie? Why come all the way here?"

"W-what? Your telegram didn't say anything about giving it to Elsie. It could have been a stolen diamond you were recovering for the Monuments Men for all I know."

He laughed. "You always jump to the craziest conclusions. Sometimes a diamond is just a diamond, Kate." He gave Johnny a can-you-believe-her look. "I must have been in a hurry when I sent that telegram. Sorry I didn't explain myself better. Want the full story?"

"Of course."

"I met one of Dad's buddies and he told me about the diamond. He said every time Dad found any Polish refugees he would show them the picture of your necklace and ask if they had any amber on them and if they knew someone who could make the necklace for him. He wanted it to be authentic." Floyd ran his hand over his head. "Some old woman saw the drawing and gave him the diamond. The guy I talked to was eavesdropping and said her English was hard to understand, but that she said something about giving it to an old Polish woman to help her get back to Poland. Since we knew an old Polish woman, it makes sense that Dad took it for Elsie. The woman told him to hide it so no one would take it from him."

Kate gave Johnny a wide-eyed look. At the hospital, it was as if Elsie knew that diamond was for her. She had kept the diamond locked in her hand, hidden from the princess. Someone had been trying to find her, but it wasn't Princess Kolodenko.

"Did you look for the woman who gave your dad the diamond?" Johnny asked, putting a wet, soapy hand on Kate's neck.

She elbowed him and shimmied away, wiping off the suds.

"Naw, what would it matter? It was just some sweet lady trying to help out a fellow refugee."

"And she just presented Dad with a diamond," Kate said.

"You'd be surprised at the kinds of gifts we're given." He rested his hand on his chest. "I've never been given anything so valuable, but I got here after all the danger was past."

Could the woman have been the stepsister, Ludmilla? Kate sat down hard on a stool by the counter.

"What's wrong?" Floyd lifted her chin. "Were you expecting something more? I'd tell you if there was any more information. All we have to go on is what the army told us. There's no conspiracy to keep Dad away from us. It was just some nice woman who didn't have a need for the diamond and thought Dad could help someone who did. An act of kindness, Kate. Not one of your spy movies."

When Kate tried to speak, her voice came out like a sob, and so she stopped to compose herself. *There could be more Burgosovs.* They would have recognized the necklace Dad was showing around, and they could have gone after him, thinking he would lead them to Elsie and the missing dresses. The diamond could be some sort of message, or a warning. Elsie could be in trouble.

"Aw, Kate. You can't still be hoping he's alive?" He looked to Johnny to back him up. "There's no way, you know?" Floyd rubbed his jaw as tears came to his eyes. "I know there are some things that don't add up—like how the army initially wrote that he was in Rome, but then they went back on it and said he was in that building in Florence that exploded when hidden bombs were triggered. But if he were alive, he would have been home by now. I've shown his picture around the area of the explosion. No one recognized him."

She wasn't listening to Floyd. He sounded like a skipping record, repeating the same words over and over. She took a breath so she could calmly think about Elsie without jumping to conclusions. Elsie didn't have anything the Burgosovs wanted anymore. Circumstances had changed since Dad got the diamond, but that didn't mean he wasn't alive still.

"He could be injured and living in one of these out-of-the-way farms. Maybe he has amnesia and doesn't know who he is," Kate argued. *Or the Burgosovs did something.* "We should find this woman."

Floyd bent down to look at her face-to-face. "This isn't the movies. I know Johnny is out here with his dad, and they're working on a story about a soldier coming back to find the girl who nursed him to health during the war. But that's a romantic movie. It's not real life. It's not Dad."

She wanted to change the subject. It was clear her hope was not his after all, and she didn't want him to talk her into his way of thinking. Besides, she knew things he didn't. "It was good to see you." She stood.

"Yeah, it's nice to see you guys, too." He hugged her. "Look, I'll keep an eye out for anything that even hints of new clues about Dad. Just don't count on me finding any, especially since I'm in Germany now." He let her go. "I get to fly the plane tomorrow. Haven't done that in a while. They don't need as many pilots nowadays and since I was one of the last guys to learn . . ." He stretched. "I should hit the hay."

"Right," Kate said. "Come say good-bye before you leave tomorrow."

Floyd took a good look at the house. "Friends of Adalbert and Elsie, huh?"

"Longtime family friends. They go back generations."

He nodded, impressed. "I love the history here. Make sure you check out that castle up on the hill. We just don't have stuff like that back home."

The boys left for the guesthouse, and Kate went upstairs to brood. She didn't know what she'd expected from Floyd, maybe some proof that the diamond was special. But all she got was a lecture. Typical older brother behavior.

When she stepped into her room, she immediately felt that something was wrong. The skin on her arm prickled like there was someone there. She froze, scanning the area. In the middle of the room was her double bed with a rose-covered comforter. The lacy bed skirt could hide a person underneath. A tall wardrobe was on the wall opposite the one with a window overlooking the gardens. A person could hide in there. Oh, she was being silly. "Nessa!" she called out to the bedroom next door.

"What is it?" Nessa sleepily walked into the room. "Everything okay with your brother? I was trying to wait up, but I think I dozed off."

Kate felt foolish. "Sorry, I was just wondering where . . ." She checked under the bed; nothing there. Then in the wardrobe; only her clothes. "Where . . .?"

"Oh, the dresses? I put them in my wardrobe. I figured they could use a good airing out."

"What? They're supposed to stay with me." Again, Nessa was interfering with her Keeper role.

"But they are with you, in this house." She pointed in the direction of her bedroom. "Right down there. What could happen to them?"

Kate was tired, which made her temper short. "We can check with your *babcia*, but I'm pretty sure they should be hidden in the trunk, not airing out in your room."

Nessa huffed as she left the room, but she returned less than a minute later, arms laden with dresses. Kate held her grin. She had Lidka to thank for that trick of threatening to go to Princess Kolodenko.

"What is going on?" Lidka asked. She stood in the doorway, still in her day clothes and looking wide-awake.

"Just making more room in my closet," Nessa answered. "Don't be so nosy."

With her eyes fixed on the clothes, Lidka snapped back, "In the morning you could take care of these things. Some of us are trying to sleep."

Kate didn't think that was quite true, based on what Lidka was wearing, but she wasn't about to argue. She just wanted both girls out of her room. Her unease was gone, and her eyelids were getting heavy. It had been a long day.

"Call me if she gives you trouble," Lidka said to Kate as she returned to her room, leaving Nessa fuming.

After checking to make sure Lidka's door was closed, Kate whispered, "Does she know?"

Nessa shook her head. "No. She wasn't with us in France when Babcia told me, so she couldn't have overheard anything. She's just Lidka. Annoying."

"She got a good look at the dresses."

"That girl has no care for dresses. She wouldn't know that they were special. Nothing to worry about. Not everyone is after the dresses, Kate."

A diamond is just a diamond. Not everyone is after the dresses. Kate began to wonder if she was overly paranoid. She remembered how jumpy Aunt Elsie was when she first came to New York. She thought a Burgosov was hiding behind every taxicab. Was that the way of a Keeper? But then again, in the end, Aunt Elsie had been right to be paranoid.

~o SIXTEEN o~

The next morning, Floyd was off early. Kate dragged herself out of bed in time to say good-bye, and was now sipping Mr. De Luca's espresso in an attempt to wake up. It was shockingly strong. She coughed as it hit the back of her throat. He grinned, sharing a smile with Nessa, who was seated at the table. Nessa had gotten up with the sun, showered, dressed, and then hung on Floyd's every word until he left.

Kate might have thought it cute if she hadn't been so preoccupied with the disappointment over Floyd's lack of interest in the diamond. Apparently he'd heard enough to be satisfied that there were no more leads to follow. He might feel differently if he knew other men were starting to ask Mom out on dates. She could have told him about Neil's interest, but she was afraid he would encourage Mom to go out with him.

"How many eggs?" Mr. De Luca said. He'd been up as

early as Nessa and had already sent Floyd off with a belly full of farm-fresh cooking.

"Two, please. May I help?"

He made a motion for her to sit down. "Is my job and my pleasure," he said. "The women, they cook the rest of the day, but breakfast is mine."

"He loves to make breakfast," Nessa said. "That way he controls the menu."

Mr. De Luca nodded. "It's true. The most important meal of the day. I let Maria do whatever she likes for all the other meals."

Lidka was also seated at the table, nearly finished. She had struck Kate as a night owl, but apparently she was an early riser. She and Princess Kolodenko were deep in conversation about the extensive herb garden behind the house, which they were about to go tour.

While Kate was being served, there was a knock at the door, and Nessa jumped up to get it. She returned to the kitchen leading Johnny.

Kate's heart did a little flip-flop at the sight of him. Wearing his usual T-shirt and jeans, with his hair grown out a little long and a bit of a tan, he looked like he could fit right in with the Italians.

"Funny meeting you here," he said with a grin.

"Have you eaten yet, young man?" Mr. De Luca asked, tying his apron back on. "I can have an omelet ready in a minute."

Johnny nodded. "We had some cold cereal, but an

omelet sounds better. I think I can squeeze it in. Thank you." He slipped into a chair next to Kate and stole a piece of her bacon.

After making plans to meet up later in the day, Johnny went to work. Princess Kolodenko invited Kate to tour the gardens with her and Lidka when Nessa's mom walked in. "If it's all right with the girls, I'd like them to go with Dad and me to the Gadini farm."

"They've got a stalled tractor," Mr. De Luca explained. "It's a beautiful drive."

"Sure," Kate said.

"You don't have to go," Nessa said. "He's terrible on these farms. Has to teach me about every mechanical device there is."

"Don't listen to this one," Mr. De Luca said, grabbing his keys. "A girl should know how to drive a tractor."

Nessa rolled her eyes, but followed him and her mom out to the car.

Mr. De Luca drove slowly over the dusty dirt roads, past fields and grazing cows. He kept up a running commentary on the history of each farm they passed. The crops, the orchards, and the particular brand of wine that came from each vineyard.

"Here we are." Mr. De Luca parked in front of a modest farmhouse. There was a new barn on the property and several smaller, older buildings alongside. Before they'd gotten out of the car, the farmer was halfway across the driveway, his hand outstretched. Mr. De Luca introduced

Kate, then started speaking in rapid-fire Italian, presumably about the tractor problem.

While the men were talking, the farmer's wife opened the door and waved at Nessa's mom and the girls to come in. When they were almost to the door, a scruffy little boy came out of hiding from around the house. He was wearing too-big shorts cinched tightly at his waist.

"You American?" he asked in his choked English.

When Kate nodded, he grinned and ran out to the barn, calling for them to follow.

"Go ahead, girls. Come to the house when you're done," Nessa's mom said.

Inside the empty barn, he climbed a ladder to the loft, chatting in excited Italian. Nessa had stopped interpreting, he was talking so fast. By the time the girls had climbed to the top, he had opened a cigar box and was laying out his treasures for them to see.

"Look, look," he said in English, followed by more Italian.

"He says he collected souvenirs from the soldiers," Nessa translated.

Together they looked through the boy's special collection of military pins, an English comic book (*Fumetti! Fumetti!*), and even a picture of a pretty girl. The boy blushed and tucked it back into the corner of the lid.

Kate thought about what she had on her that she could add to his collection. She'd brought Johnny's sweetheart pin from the war, but she wasn't giving that up to this boy.

She checked her pockets and pulled out half a package of Wrigley's. "Gum?" she offered him.

He snatched it up eagerly and added it to his box. He spoke, and Nessa translated, "This next item is his most special. He has shown only one other, so we are favored." Then he brought out the item he was holding special. It was a set of dog tags.

Nessa exclaimed in rebuking Italian, then repeated herself for Kate's sake. "Where did you get these?"

The boy answered.

"He traded them from some boy from Florence," Nessa said. "I hope the soldier gave them away and they weren't stolen," she mumbled. "But he's got both tags, so the soldier had to be living." She handed the tags back to the boy. He took them from her and insisted Kate admire them, too.

Dutifully, Kate accepted the dog tags, but a quick look made a shiver go down her arms. She read the name out loud. "David Floyd Allen. That's my dad!" How did this boy have her dad's tags? *How dare he?* These tags should be with her dad, or be in the box of his things at home in New York. Not in the crusty cigar box of an Italian farm boy.

"What?" Nessa tried to take the silver tags out of Kate's hands, but she held on tight, like they were a lifeline.

"David Allen." Kate pointed to his name. "And here's my mother's name below it with our address." She pointed to the upper right. "His blood type here, and his gas mask size there." Kate's voice had gone up an octave.

The boy, noticing something was wrong, had quickly started to put back all his treasures. He reached out for the dog tags, but Kate closed her fingers around them in a protective fist.

"No. Tell me everything you know about these," she demanded.

With wide eyes, he looked imploringly at Nessa. They carried on a conversation in Italian for several minutes before the boy slammed the lid shut on his treasures, and he took off down the ladder, leaving one last sad glance at Kate's clenched hand. "*Mi scusi.*"

"What did he say?" she asked, barely breathing. She had listened carefully for any Italian words she might recognize but heard nothing.

"He's a little upset that he is losing his prized possession, but he is happy that they have found the place they belong. He went with his uncle to Florence last year and met a street boy who traded him these tags for all the money he had brought with him." Nessa smiled. "He said since he spent all this money on the exchange, he had to watch his cousins eat gelato lick by lick while he had none."

Kate felt for the boy, but she wasn't giving up her dad's tags. "I'll gladly pay him for his troubles. What else did he say? Where did the street boy get them? From my father?"

Nessa stood and made her way to the ladder. "He said it sounded like a made-up story created to drive up the price of the tags."

"What? There might be some truth in it."

Nessa swung a leg over and began her descent down the ladder.

Kate scrambled after her. "Tell me." She caught up to Nessa outside. She reached out to catch her arm and spin her around.

Looking at the ground, Nessa sighed. "You're not going to like it."

"Tell me."

"You know there was an explosion in one of the buildings. The boy says that an older boy went digging through the rubble and found these."

Kate's breath caught. No, it couldn't be. The military would have found them first. They would have been on her father's body. She had to ask. "Did he . . . Did the boy take them off a body?"

Nessa bit her lip before answering. "He didn't say."

"A boy would know not to take tags off a body, wouldn't he? Then this is our first proof my dad could still be alive." Kate sat, stunned. She allowed herself a small smile. There hadn't been a body.

Nessa looked doubtful. "It's been too long," she whispered.

Kate was getting so tired of everyone saying how long it had been. "Come on," she implored. "You're Cinderella's descendant. Where's your optimism? Look at all she went through, but she never gave up hope."

When they got back to the farmhouse, everyone turned

to look at Kate. The boy must have told them what happened. Mr. De Luca held out his hand.

Kate gave him the dog tags so he could examine them. "Your father's?" he asked.

"Yes."

"This is a surprise," he said.

"A good one, though, don't you think?" She bounced a little on her toes.

Mr. De Luca glanced at his daughter before answering. "I'm sorry we have no answers for you. Only more questions."

They ended the visit with a late lunch. The farmer's wife went out of her way to take care of Kate, apologizing over and over that her son kept the tags. Kate offered to pay the boy, but under his mother's watchful eye, he refused.

To show she had no hard feelings, Kate made sure she smiled as the conversation went on around her in Italian and Nessa tried to interpret the important lines of conversation about crops and food prices. But Kate wasn't listening. She was too busy trying to wrap her mind around this discovery.

The ride back to the villa was a long and quiet one. Mr. De Luca had tried to get the girls talking, but after too many grunts for answers, even he gave up. Instead, he launched into singing folksy songs from his boyhood.

Once the car pulled to a stop, Kate jumped out and headed straight for the front door. She hesitated with her hand on the knob. She could feel the family exchanging looks behind her. She knew they were worried about her, but she needed time to be alone and think things through.

"I'm going to walk around the gardens," she said, turning from the door.

Nessa made a move to follow her, but her grandfather held her arm. He shook his head.

Kate kept walking, through the gardens, following the trail through a field, up a small hill, and ended at the movie shoot in the valley below. When she came up to the crew from behind, she realized she didn't want to be alone after all. If Johnny's strong shoulder was available, she suddenly needed to crumble on it while he stroked her hair and told her everything would be okay.

She quickly spotted him. He was leaning on a card table going over the script. As she approached him, he looked up and zeroed in on her face. He dropped his pencil and pulled her in to his chest. She wrapped her arms around his neck and breathed out, her body shuddering. This whole trip she'd been thinking logically: find Malwinka, get the shoes, find her dad. It had been a to-do list, and a kind of fairy-tale game. But now it felt real. The stakes were high, and she didn't know if she measured up.

"Hey, hey. What's going on?" he asked, pushing her away and wiping her cheek with his thumb.

She held up the dog tags. They dangled lifelessly from her hand.

Johnny reached for them. Recognition dawned as he read the names on the tag. "What? How?"

"Mr. De Luca took us to a farm, and while we were there, the boy showed us his keepsakes from the war. He had a bunch of trinkets different soldiers had given him and some he had traded for. Like these."

Kate stroked her fingers over the stamped letters. She didn't know what to think of the tags. Dad could have dropped them. Soldiers were supposed to wear them, so that a body could be identified and the other person on the tag notified.

She took a deep breath. "The boy said the tags were found in the rubble of a bombed-out building."

"I'm sorry, Kate; that's hard to hear. What are you thinking?"

Her initial reaction had been one of hope, but after her walk, new thoughts had emerged. "So many things. I'm trying to figure out how his tags ended up where they did. Let's assume he was in the building when the explosion went off. If he was knocked unconscious, someone could have rescued him, but the tags should have stayed around his neck, secure under his shirt. Same if he wandered off on his own somehow." She held them up. "Look, the chain's not broken. It didn't fall off."

"So?"

"So then, the tags were purposely taken off. Either by

my dad or someone else. He could have been captured by the enemy and taken to a POW camp."

"But those have all been liberated."

"I know. So I am more convinced he's lost, just wandering around Italy not knowing who he is. I have a picture I can show to people. If we start in Florence where the tags were found and work outward from there, I'm sure we'll find him."

"But Floyd did that already. He got nowhere. And the Italians would certainly notice an English speaker wandering around and try to help him, wouldn't they?"

Kate set her lips tight and crossed her arms.

"Hey, Sparky. I'm not trying to pick a fight, I'm just helping you talk this through."

She put her hands to her temples. "You're right. The tags distracted me. I need to stay with my original plan. I'm here to find Cinderella's shoes and see if they can lead me to my dad."

SEVENTEEN

The next morning, Nessa woke Kate up early and spirited her away. "Come. There's something I want to show you." She handed Kate an apple and led her up a dirt path, going around the back of the castle. The sun rising over the hills revealed dark clouds covering half the sky.

"What do you think of my cousin?" Nessa asked once they were a distance away from the house. She began tossing her apple up and catching it.

Kate relaxed. She had been expecting Nessa to bring up the dog tags again. Last night by the end of dinner, it had become the general consensus that Kate's discovery was a happy coincidence to bring her family closure. She had given up arguing about it, but noticed Nessa watching her closely.

"She's been through a lot," Kate said tentatively, and bit into her apple. She had woken up ravenous and was already looking forward to Mr. De Luca's breakfast.

"True. But so many have. How long should a girl nurse her grievances?"

"I suppose it's different for everyone."

"Did she tell you where Babcia's people found her?"

"A work camp. They were looking for your sister?"

Nessa caught her apple and put it in her pocket. "Babcia was hoping. But my sister was dead before the camp was liberated."

"Do you know what happened to her?"

"To start, she took too many chances. She was a spy and got found out. That was how she was killed."

A spy? Nessa's sister was one of those courageous girls she'd read about. "What did she do?"

Nessa wrapped her arms around her middle, as if comforting herself. "All kinds of things, most of which she wouldn't talk about. She was out at all hours sneaking around. There was a boy. She met him on one of her missions." Nessa sighed. "They went off and got married. Babcia nearly had a fit when she found out." She looked at Kate. "Now that I've seen the family wedding dress, I understand. She gave all that up. She didn't want to wait." Nessa frowned. "Good thing she didn't, either. She was captured just two months later and shipped off to that work camp. Her husband risked his life coming to our place to tell us in person. He was a wreck. My sister had his heart. He still hangs around whenever his job lets him."

"I'm sorry. That's such a sad, romantic tale."

"I guess it is, if I wasn't so close to it. Babcia says she sent him to America to find Elsie after the war, but he had no luck."

Kate sucked in a breath. "In his twenties? Blond, and has a habit of twisting his hat?"

Nessa laughed. "How did you know? My sister was constantly fixing hats for him. Why?"

"I turned someone away once who was looking for Adalbert and Elsie." How different things would have been if Kate had known who he was at the time. "And what about Lidka? You don't seem to like her very much."

"It is that obvious?" Nessa picked a wildflower by the path and twirled it as they walked. "She is hard to get to know. She doesn't let everyone in. She has my *babcia* wrapped around her little finger. Lidka even moved into my sister's room when she came to stay with us. Can you imagine? A whole villa full of rooms and that is the one she chooses. Babcia said it was nice for the room to have life again. Bah. I was happy when she left. She was lazy, wouldn't help with anything. She expected me to wait on her all the day long."

Kate quirked a smile, imagining Nessa playing the part of maid when all she seemed to do was hand off chores to other people. "She had been in a work camp; I've heard about how terrible they were."

Nessa rolled her eyes. "Believe me, I know. It was her excuse for everything. You would think after a year that she would have gotten over it."

Kate was speechless.

"You think I sound cruel?" Nessa tossed the flower into the ditch. "I know she was traumatized. We have a nation of people who have been traumatized, but with Lidka, it is different. She is angry and she continually fuels her anger. Babcia thought she could save her, but then one day Lidka disappeared. We searched for her, but she took her things—and some of my sister's belongings—and ran away. Not even a thank-you to Babcia and Dziadek. It devastated them. They could not fix her, and despite their kindness, she hurt them. I am not happy to see her come back. I know my *babcia*. She thinks this is another chance to save the girl."

From far away, the stone building looked untouched from the years, but as they got closer, Kate saw the pieces of stone that had fallen away, the grass and the weeds that had attempted to reclaim the land to its wild state. They had to pick their way around various obstacles to get to the front door.

"During the war, we hid the Australian soldiers in here," Nessa said as she stepped across the threshold. There was half a wooden door still hanging. "Babcia wanted to repair the door for them, but Dziadek thought it best to keep the castle looking as abandoned as possible."

"Wasn't that dangerous for you?"

"We started small, taking children from the city. Because of the farms, we had food, and there was less danger of bombs. We would hand out provisions to those who were passing through. Hiding a friend, then friends of friends, then strangers. I was the runner who warned them to head to the woods whenever an inspection came through. They got pretty fast at cleaning up their stuff and running."

"And you never got caught?" The air cooled off immediately when Kate followed her through. The light was dim, coming mostly from the open-air windows, though farther inside they entered a room where the roof had caved in and birds had taken up residence. "This seems like an obvious place to hide."

"True, but there is the saying of hiding in plain sight. It does seem obvious, and every time they looked, there was nothing to find. We had a few close calls, but I would sneak around the back way as the cars were driving to the villa. We could see the cars from far away so I had time to slip out. Dziadek let the road to the castle fall into disrepair, and we made it worse by digging big holes."

"Hidden in plain sight," Kate repeated.

"Kind of like you putting the Kopciuszek dresses in the department store window."

Kate smiled. She couldn't tell by Nessa's tone whether she was giving a compliment or a dig.

"This part of the castle is the most run-down, and we let it stay as dirty and smelly as possible during the war. We let it be known wolves frequented it at night. Dziadek even found some animal bones to scatter in here to scare off soldiers who had options, those who didn't need to hide with us. Babcia had it cleaned out since. I think she wanted to erase as many bad memories as possible.

"People were always watching each other. Babcia and my parents helped anyone who was in need. Neighbors, soldiers, partisans. There are several farms on our land. Many hiding places. And we were known for taking in children from other areas where the fighting was the worst."

Kate couldn't help but be impressed. Nessa's whole family had risked their lives to help those in need. Kopciuszek would be proud of her descendants.

"The fresco I wanted to show you is in here," Nessa said, pointing through a wide arch.

The painting was a ballroom scene showing ladies with billowing ball gowns of various soft colors. It was obviously old, with chunks fallen out and cracks splitting the image like shattered glass. Nessa walked up close to it, looking for something. "Ha, I was right. Now that I've seen the real thing. Look over here. It's the Kopciuszek dress."

The white and blue dress was left of center. It stood out from all the others, being the fanciest of all.

"I never paid much attention to this fresco before," Nessa said. "I mean, I liked it well enough and I used to picnic in this room when I was little so I could imagine myself into the painting, but once I saw the real dress, it tickled something in my memory. It took a while for me to pin it to this image."

"Do you think that girl is Kopciuszek?" Kate asked. She gently touched the figure, knowing that she probably shouldn't even be doing that because of her finger oils. Close up it was hard to see any details of the painting. She stepped back to get a better look. The woman in the dress had her hair in an updo and a necklace around her neck, but Kate couldn't tell if it was *her* necklace. She felt the amber to see if it warmed. It did not. "Did she ever live in this castle?"

Nessa joined her, tilting her head as she studied the image. "Don't know for sure, but I doubt it. After they left Poland, I think they moved into Northern Italy first, and this land was a later purchase. I do think the fresco reflects what this room used to look like. Instead of a big set of mirrors to reflect the dancers, they had this scene."

"Look at the shoes," Kate said in dismay. They were faded such that the girl's legs disappeared into the wall.

"No glass slippers," Nessa said. "This might mean the shoes are truly gone. What if the painted shoes faded off the fresco when the real shoes disappeared?"

"Don't say that." The shoes weren't lost, they were just being held by the wrong family. Kate wanted to mention the reason she needed to find the shoes so badly, but Nessa seemed pretty convinced Kate's dad had been missing for too long to be found now. Her hope was so vulnerable she didn't want to risk Nessa bruising it. Kate pressed on despite Princess Kolodenko's wishes. "Do you know who Malwinka is?"

Nessa shook her head. "No. Should I?"

"Your grandmother doesn't want me to talk to you about her. She's from the other line of stepsisters. We've got Ludmilla and her sons on one side tracking down the dress, and Malwinka on the other, who I think has the shoes."

"So they might not be lost. This is great news! All we need to do is find this Malwinka." Nessa smiled.

"Yes, but your grandmother won't talk about her."

"Leave Babcia to me. You know, Kate, the more I think about it, the more I like the idea of trying to find the shoes. You have your quest to find out about the necklace. That's your family's heirloom. I should try to find the shoes. I bet they're linked somehow, anyway. Like how the necklace warms up when the dress is around. The dress could do something around the shoes."

For the first time it felt like Nessa's interests were the same as hers. They were learning to trust each other, despite their tension over the proper handling of the dresses. "Speaking of the amber necklace, why does Lidka have one, too?"

"What do you mean?" Nessa bit into her apple as they wound their way back out of the castle ruins.

"She has a necklace just like mine."

"I didn't notice. Isn't yours one of a kind?"

"I thought it was, at least in its, um, special abilities." They carefully picked their way over the tumbled stones near the entryway.

"I don't know. We could ask her, but she'd only lie. I'll talk to my mom before she leaves today. I can even ask her about—" Nessa stepped out of the castle and left her sentence hanging in midair.

Lidka was standing near the entrance, hands on hips and staring up at the tower.

"Oh, you startled me," Nessa said. She narrowed her eyes. "How long have you been there?"

"Why? Were you talking about me? I came to get you because there is storm coming and Fyodora did not want you getting caught." She cocked her head in Nessa's direction.

Sensing a fight brewing, Kate intervened. "I was asking Nessa if she noticed your amber necklace. It's quite pretty."

Lidka pulled the necklace out from her collar. "Yes, it is, isn't it?"

Nessa stiffened. "Where did you get it?"

"That boy, the same one who had the dog tags. He traded me for it before I left Italy. Cost me a lot, too. He is a shrewd one."

The sun broke from behind a cloud and shone on the amber. The flecks of leaves or insects trapped inside the resin stood out in contrast to the rich honey color. Since that boy had had it, this could be the very necklace Dad had commissioned for Mom. Before speaking, Kate checked to see if her own necklace was hidden, and it was. "My dad was on a mission to have a necklace such as yours made while he was here. I never did learn if he succeeded."

Lidka looked back and forth between Kate and Nessa. She held up her hands. "If you think this is rightfully yours, you may have it." She felt around her neck for the clasp.

"No, Lidka. It's fine. There is no way to know for sure where that boy got it."

Nessa's gaze bored into Kate as if trying to tell her to stop protesting and take it already.

Ignoring Nessa, Kate smiled. Lidka looked like she didn't have many nice things. If she liked the necklace, she should keep it. Besides, it wasn't a necklace they were looking for.

EIGHTEEN

"It's the dress," Nessa said with a deep sense of surety. "It has to be, because otherwise all that's happening is one big coincidence, don't you think?"

Kate nodded absently. They were setting up a picnic near the pond south of the house. Johnny and some others from the movie were supposed to join them. There had been rain after all that morning, so Maria had loaded them down with thick blankets to spread out on the wet grass. Earlier, she'd had some of the crew bring down tables for the food, and they had already spread the red-checked tablecloths. Nessa's mom had left during the downpour, making for short good-byes. She was needed back at the nursing job she'd taken after the war. Her parting words for Kate had been, "Get to know my daughter. You two can help each other understand your responsibilities."

It could be the dresses, but it could also be the necklace. If the magic in the Kopciuszek dress was meant for Cinderella's heirs, then it would make sense that the magic in the necklace be meant for Nadzia's heirs, since she was the first Keeper.

"I asked them more questions about the shoes and Lidka's necklace."

Kate looked up from the blanket she was straightening.

"Babcia told me how everyone said the shoes sparkled in the candlelight the night of the ball. That as Kopciuszek danced, it was as if she were stepping across stars. Everyone knew the shoes were special." Nessa twirled with her blanket in demonstration.

"Did you ask her about Malwinka?"

Nessa shook out another blanket. "I didn't have to. She told me that the stepsister line has grown as ours has, and that from mother to daughter they pass on the need to take what they think they have a right to."

"A need? Like they have to?"

"No, not exactly. It sounded like each generation is taught from a young age to avenge the family name or something ridiculous like that."

"And what about Malwinka?"

"I'm getting to that. She said Malwinka's line dropped out of the hunt, as they say. She has not bothered the family like Ludmilla has, and Babcia doesn't want us stirring them up again."

Kate stood and put her hands on her hips. "But if she has the shoes, we must go to her. Don't you want the shoes back? They belong to your family."

Nessa shot Kate an annoyed look. She spoke in a harsh

whisper. "Of course I want the shoes back. You're not the only one who cares about the legacy. Babcia says they're not glass slippers at all, but diamond ones. They belong with the dress. They belong with me." She finished with her blanket and started arranging the cups and napkins out on the tables. "What makes you think she has the shoes, anyway?"

"One of the Burgosovs told me she did."

"The criminal? And you believed him?"

"Yes. It all makes sense. Malwinka doesn't need to cause trouble because she already has one of the heirlooms. And that's why Ludmilla tries so hard—she doesn't have anything." Kate opened up a food basket and pulled out a large plate of fried chicken. It smelled so good her mouth started watering. She added a plate of cold cuts and a bread basket to the end of a table.

Following Kate's lead, Nessa arranged similar plates on the other table. "Babcia didn't say, but it is likely Malwinka stayed in Poland. If you spend any time with Lidka you will learn that the stepsisters' side rebels against any authority but its own. They think everyone should be equal, except when they themselves can get more for nothing. They have enjoyed the recent change in power. Our family still has property in Poland, but we rarely go there anymore, especially since the Communists took over. Our property is slowly becoming state-owned, anyway. This property"—she spread her arms, indicating the place where they were standing—"used to be a holiday place for us before the war. It *was* one of our secret residences until they brought Lidka here. I don't even know if your aunt and uncle knew about it." Nessa arranged her last plate and put her hands on her hips. "Babcia won't go back home until things change. She says there is nothing for us there, and besides, we were needed here during the war. She says we will have more freedom to act if we stay outside of Communist lands."

Nessa had given Kate a lot of information to process, but there was one revelation that stood out from the others. "Wait. I thought Lidka was your cousin. How could she be related to the stepsisters?"

"*Distant* cousin. Our connection goes way back to Kopciuszek's mother. Lidka is not in the direct line of our Cinderella. She is more closely related to Ludmilla than anyone else. I asked Babcia for clarification on the family when I found out the secret. It is confusing, having to follow the branching lines through the generations, especially since not everyone is told." She frowned. "Imagine if I was never told? I would go my whole life walking beside this fairy-tale legend and knowing nothing. Just glimpses of truth now and then, but none of it coming together to make sense. Such a thing is so far out of possibility I never would have guessed."

"So now what do we do?" The blankets had been spread, the food arranged, but Kate wasn't talking about their idyllic picnic. "Can we go on our own to Poland?"

"Babcia would have a fit. There is no way she would let

us go. I'm sorry. We'll have to think of something else."
She squinched up her face in apology.

Kate couldn't hide her disappointment. Never mind
Princess Kolodenko's unease, Aunt Elsie would be upset
when she found out Kate had come all this way and
never completed the journey. Somehow, she had to convince the Kolodenkos to go to Poland. Sure, Mr. Day was
willing to take her and Johnny when he had a break in the
filming, but it made more sense to have the Kolodenkos
along, too.

Nessa sighed as she looked across their work. "I need
to wear the dress again. Don't you think that will unleash
more of the magic? You say the dress has personality.
What if it gets tired of being locked up in a dresser day
and night, year after year? If we let it out, maybe something will happen."

Always looking for an excuse to wear the dress. Nessa
got to do what she wanted, but Kate had to put aside her
hopes and dreams in favor of the Kolodenkos. If this was
what being a Keeper was, she wasn't so sure she wanted
the job after all. She started to form her arguments as to
why the dress was better left tucked safely away.

Before she could say anything, Nessa continued her
passionate plea. "You've seen Sora," she said, throwing
her hands up. "You've seen my life here at this isolated
villa. When and where can I ever wear a ball gown? It's
going to go to waste."

Kate bit back her initial reply. She had thought these

exact thoughts back in New York before she volunteered to put the dress in the front display window. The dresses called to be used, but the consequences could not be controlled. Although this time, Nessa might be right. And really, what could it hurt? It was a dress. Suddenly, Kate had a creative idea. "How about you model it? Put it on and I'll take pictures of you around the castle. Mr. G would love it."

Nessa's face lit up. "Perfect. There couldn't be a better setting. Kate, you are brilliant."

"And did you ask about the necklace?"

"My mother didn't know Lidka had one, and Babcia said there is no knowledge of another necklace such as yours. Lidka probably has your father's replica. You should have taken it from her. She offered."

"I know." Kate played with the hem of her shirt.

"You feel sorry for her. Don't. She'll betray you just like she did us. I'm not as soft as Babcia. I'm watching and waiting for it to happen."

The first of the hungry movie crew came plodding over the hill, silencing further secret talks. The group had multiplied in the last few days as they were gearing up to have production in full swing. Nessa cheerfully passed out plates and winked at the cute boys. Once everyone had been taken care of, Kate filled a plate for herself and made her way over to Johnny, who had secured a dry spot under a tall cypress tree. She squeezed in next to him. "How's the filming going?" she asked.

"Going well, as far as I can tell. Dad's assigned me to help with the setup crew, keeping an eye on the scenery and props, making sure everything looks good. The director could give Mr. G a run for his money. I don't know who is more demanding." He lowered his voice as he jutted his chin in the direction of a man wearing a straw hat and refilling his plate with more pasta salad. "A bit of a tyrant, but he knows what he wants. How are things at the villa?"

"I thought it was moving slowly, but I may have convinced Nessa to help me find Malwinka."

"What, did you agree to become her servant in exchange?"

"Johnny!" She punched him in the arm. "I'm sure she doesn't even notice when she orders me around."

"Hmm. How did you spend your day, then?"

She frowned at him. "Serving you. Nessa and I helped Maria put this all together."

"And before that?"

"Mrs. De Luca had me out in the garden picking the vegetables, but she just doesn't want me getting bored. She thought I would like it in the garden. And then I helped Nessa hang the sheets outside until Mr. De Luca called her away for something."

"I thought that was you looking all maiderly."

"That's not even a word."

While Johnny laughed at his own joke, Kate discreetly searched for Nessa, to make sure she wasn't in earshot.

She had found a place with the group of young actors. Someone must have had a comedic bone, as they were all laughing, their voices getting louder and louder.

"Well, hang in there. My part should be easing up soon, and then Dad'll take time off for us to do some looking around."

While Johnny was talking, Kate spotted Fran Marshall, model-turned-actress from Harmon-Craig department store. Kate tried to look away, but Fran saw her and made a beeline. She plunked herself across from Kate. "Hi there," she gushed. "It's so nice to see a face from home. Everyone here speaks Italian. I'm dying for someone to talk to." She bit into her bread roll.

Kate blinked. Who was this girl, and what had she done with Fran?

"Oh, don't look at me like that," Fran said, holding her hand politely in front of her mouth. "I've talked to you before."

Johnny laughed and turned his head. "I'm going for seconds." He got up and sauntered away.

Fran watched him go, then said, "Don't worry about the fans hanging around. There's one who keeps trying to catch Johnny's eye, but he's not paying her any attention."

"There are fans?"

"Of course. Every day they stand by the fence and wave at the crew. I used to like him, you know."

Fran's change of subject was dizzying. *Used to?*

"He's a great guy. I grew up with him, since our parents

are good friends. He's really stuck on you. You'd better not break his heart."

Kate didn't know what else to do, so she nodded. It was surprisingly comforting to hear Fran's opinion. But was Fran really so lonely she would be friendly to an old modeling rival? "How is your role going?" Kate asked politely.

"Oh, it's been great. I really enjoy acting. I wrapped up today, so I'll be going home soon. Can't wait. Never realized how homesick I would get, but I miss New York. Don't get me wrong, this place is pretty enough, but I think I'm a city girl at heart."

Kate looked out over the picnickers, comparing the scene to eating at the Automat. Rustic tables, classic checkered tablecloths, heaps of food, and everyone talking and smiling. Beyond them stretched rolling hills planted with crops Kate couldn't name. Fran was right; it was completely different from the city, where the buildings towered over you instead of trees. Where the breeze smelled of cars and buses and ocean instead of flowers and grass and open air. She didn't mind the change one bit.

"Johnny's coming back." Fran stood with her plate and drink. "I'm going to sit with the crew. The cute one near the pond is planning to be a director one day. Remember what I said."

Johnny returned with a second heaping plate of chicken and pasta. "What was that all about?"

"I have no idea," Kate said. *Fran giving her blessing?* "She said her part was finished?"

"That's right. She's done a great job. Dad's pleased. Filming is ahead of schedule, and several of the actors are going home in a few days. Anything you want to send back with her? She could deliver it to your mom at the store."

"I've got a roll of film she could take to Mr. G. I've taken several photos around the villa. Don't want him forgetting about me."

"I wouldn't worry about that; you're unforgettable."

Johnny smiled and her heart did a little flip-flop when she looked into his eyes. Everyone melted away and it was just the two of them, staring at each other.

"Who's up for some baseball?" called out one of the crew members. It broke the spell. Johnny wolfed down the rest of his lunch and ran to join the game. "You coming?" he called back.

Kate shook her head. "I'm not very good."

"None of us are. It's just for fun." He waved his hand, inviting her to come. "Let's see if there are any other girls."

"Kate, where are you going? You have to help clean up." Nessa stood with her arms crossed.

Kate looked around at the people still eating. It wasn't time to clean yet. "I won't be long."

Nessa turned in a huff and started recruiting others for cleaning duty as Kate jogged to catch up to Johnny.

"Are you in trouble?" he asked.

"I'm sure she'll leave me plenty to do."

By the time the teams divided up, it was obviously a man's game. There was no way Kate was going to be the only girl. The fans Fran had been talking about saw that a game was going on in the field, and they had come over to watch.

She waved good-bye to Johnny and started back to help Nessa and Maria return all the picnic items to the villa.

"Wait, you forgot something," Johnny called.

She turned around. "What?"

"This." He kissed her cheek, grinned, then ran back to join the game.

Kate put her hand up to her cheek, her face aflame. Would she ever get used to Johnny Day's kisses?

NINETEEN

The next morning, while the rest of the house was quiet and asleep, Kate and Nessa tiptoed downstairs and into the kitchen to grab a bite of breakfast. They managed to catch Mr. De Luca by surprise.

"What is this? Two pretty ladies come to join me at the break of day?" He held up his coffee. "The stove is not on yet, but there is enough coffee for all."

Nessa kissed him on the cheek, hiding the wrapped dress behind her back. "No thanks, Dziadek. We are up early to take pictures at the castle. Kate is learning to use her camera."

Kate held up the box camera to confirm Nessa's story.

"Go on out to your patio and enjoy the morning," Nessa said. "Babcia should be down soon."

Mr. De Luca nodded and waved them off. "Enjoy," he said over his shoulder as he headed for the back of the house where the sun would be warming a place for him.

The girls exited through the front door and set off

up the dirt road toward the castle ruins. At the top of the hill, they could see the movie crew already setting up for the morning's shoot. Kate wondered if homesick Fran Marshall had left yet. Kate had no itching to head back to New York at all. She was barely getting started exploring.

"The lighting is good," she said. "At least, as far as I can tell." The early-morning sun cast a warm glow to light up Nessa's face, yet created enough shadows and angles to make the black-and-white pictures interesting. Since she had little practice with the camera, she hoped the pictures would turn out well enough to please Mr. G.

When they stepped into the building, all distant noises were instantly muffled through those thick stone walls. It was as if they were crossing into another time, where Kate could leave the real world behind and imagine the fantasy of living here when the roof was intact, the rooms filled with heavy furniture, and the walls draped in tapestries of unicorns and battles.

"Do you mind if we modern girls set up shop?" she asked the vacant building. The castle was quiet, keeping its secrets of the past to itself.

Nessa giggled while Kate spread out a blanket in a private corner for her to change on. She was taking her role as Keeper very seriously. Even though the wine stain had mysteriously disappeared, she wasn't taking any chances of the dress picking up dirt off the stone floor.

The Kopciuszek dress shimmered in the light filtering

through the open windows. The dress took Kate's breath away every time she saw it. Was it the style? The fabrics? Or the fact that Cinderella had worn it to the ball where she'd secured her future?

After Kate helped button up the dress, she stepped back. Nessa truly looked like a princess in the dress, especially since she had put her hair in rag curlers the night before and swept it up off her shoulders this morning. It was too bad there wasn't a ball for her. Nor a kingdom.

"Stand over here by the window. Look out like you are surveying your lands." Kate focused the way Mr. G had taught her. *Click. Wind to the next frame. Click. Wind to the next frame.*

"Okay, now smile. Uh, not so much teeth. A gentle smile. Like you know a secret." *Click.*

They set up in a couple locations where the light was brightest so Kate wouldn't have to use the flash. It helped that the roof was missing in several rooms. Taking pictures was similar to window dressing. Kate had to set a scene in the frame, looking for the best way to show the dress off without letting the striking backdrop overpower the shot. She didn't know if she could wait to take the film back to America for developing. She had already filled one roll and was nearing the end of the second when Nessa made a suggestion.

"Let's do the last ones in the ballroom. I want one beside the fresco."

That room was fairly dark, which meant Kate would

need to use the flash. She had brought the equipment but hadn't used it yet.

"Sure. I'll need to set up a bit first." She went back to the room where she had stored their bags and pulled out the flasholder. After attaching it to the front of the box camera, she screwed in the bulb. If only there was a way to know if she was fixing the settings and connecting the light right. It was disconcerting that you didn't know if you'd gotten the shot until the film came back after developing. At least with painting, you got to see the image as it was being made. Painting with light was a mystery, a contradiction created in the dark.

When Kate returned, Nessa was standing facing the fresco. The dress painted on the wall was an echo of the real one Nessa wore. It reminded her of the sketch Johnny drew of her facing the Cinderella window while wearing the wedding dress.

"What happened to your shoes?" Nessa asked the dancer.

Quickly, Kate held the viewfinder to her eye and snapped a picture. The bulb exploded with light.

Nessa jumped. "Oh, you startled me, Kate. Did you hear me talking to the painting?"

"That's okay. I was talking to the castle earlier. Did it answer?" Kate laughed.

"Like a magic mirror? Wrong fairy tale." Nessa bit her lip. "I'm feeling something. An emotion that isn't mine. It's hard to describe. Maybe frustration? Is this what you are feeling?"

Kate tilted her head as she thought. "No. I'm focused on figuring out how to use this flash, but I'm not frustrated. Is the feeling coming from the dress?"

"I think so. Maybe. I don't know. It's very faint, and I lose it if I concentrate too much on finding it." She waved her hand. "Never mind. I'll think about it later."

After unscrewing the spent bulb, Kate replaced it with a fresh one. "I can see why Mr. G prefers taking photos outside. This could get expensive. Now smile."

When Kate took the picture, there was a responding twinkle out of the corner of her vision. She lowered the camera but didn't see what had caught her eye. After choosing a different angle, she took another flash photo, and again, a sparkle. It was coming from the fresco. "Do you need a break?" Kate asked.

Nessa had started to look like she was drooping. She was blinking her eyes, trying to clear the bright flash from her vision. "It's hard to smile so much," she said. "Even when I'm not smiling." She rubbed her cheeks.

"I'm at the end of my roll, so this is a good time to stop." Kate went to put the camera away. "Besides, someone might come looking for us if we don't show up soon." She peered out the door just to check and scanned the rolling green hills. There was a figure in a war costume by the cluster of trees near the pond. Someone from the movie practicing lines away from the rest, but otherwise, no one was in sight.

The sparkle the flash picked up niggled around the edges of her mind. Thinking there might be something stuck in the wall, she returned to the fresco and ran her hand over the area where she'd thought she saw the twinkle.

"What are you doing?" Nessa asked.

"I think something is stuck in the wall. I saw a sparkle."

Nessa joined her. Together they searched until Nessa cried out, "I found it. It's a piece of glass stuck in here." She picked at the place where Kopciuszek's shoe should be.

Kate examined the spot and, noticing the bevels, her heart started racing. "It's cut too perfectly to be a piece of glass. I think it's a diamond."

The girls bopped heads trying to get a closer look.

"Let's edge it out," Nessa said. "Do you have a knife or something?"

"No. I'll look around to see if anything was left behind by the soldiers."

The rooms had been swept clean. Whoever the De Lucas had hired to do the cleanup was thorough. Kate went from room to room, exploring the old castle, carefully stepping over fresh bird droppings.

She put her hands on her hips in frustration and felt the belt on her skirt. Ah! The buckle. They could use it to knock out the diamond. When she came back to the ballroom, Nessa was examining her fingernails. "Don't try scratching it out," she said, holding up her chipped nails.

Kate held out her belt. "How about this?" She located the diamond and began working on the wall, but then stopped herself. "I don't want to harm the fresco," she said, all Dad's art training kicking in. "Why don't we go get a knife?"

Nessa grabbed the belt. "Let me try." She gently and patiently worked the buckle into the wall until the diamond popped out onto the floor. The girls scrambled, trying to find where it had landed. "Got it!" Nessa cried, holding it up. "I don't think it's a diamond. It's blue. Is there such a thing as a blue diamond?"

Kate gasped. *Another blue diamond.* "Sure. I'll show you a yellow diamond when we get to New York."

Nessa grinned. "We've been surrounded with diamonds lately. The one your brother talked about in his telegram, the shoes, and now one we've dug out of the wall. What do you make of it all? Do you think they are connected?"

This would be the time to tell Nessa that the diamond in her dad's box was also a blue diamond, but she didn't want to share that yet. Besides, she was afraid Nessa would claim it for her family before they even found out the real reason her dad had it.

"Can you picture them?" Nessa asked, pointing to the spot she pulled the diamond from. "Shoes made out of diamonds?" She grabbed Kate's hands and twirled them in a little dance about the room. "They would be worth a fortune."

As Kate stepped out of the dance, she shook her head. "They would be priceless, like the dresses."

"Now why would a diamond be in the painting?" Nessa

asked. "It must be a clue left behind from one of my ancestors. Do you think the glass slippers are made of blue diamonds? How pretty."

Kate avoided answering. "Let's look for more."

"Check the floor, too, in case any fell out. Use the camera flash again. See if anything else twinkles."

Kate set the flash off. "Did you see anything?"

"Nothing."

"No, me neither." The girls scoured the fresco and the floor underneath, but didn't find any more jewels.

"Well, let's get me out of this dress," Nessa said. "I've got to show the diamond to Babcia."

The girls raced back to the villa. No sooner had they returned to the main house than a caravan of movie equipment streamed toward the castle.

"What's going on?" Nessa asked, spinning in the driveway as she surveyed the busyness.

Mr. De Luca sat in his chair out front watching the goings-on with a careful eye. "They are filming in the castle this afternoon. Good thing you girls took your pictures this morning."

"That was close," Kate whispered as they slipped into the house. Everything was quiet. "Babcia is probably changing out of her gardening clothes this time of day." The girls knocked softly on the door, and when they heard "Come in," they burst into the room, both talking at once. Nessa held out the diamond. "It was in the fresco in the old castle. Did you know anything about it?"

Princess Kolodenko didn't look surprised when she reached out for the diamond. "Thank you, Nessa," was all she said.

"But . . ." Nessa looked confused. "What is it? Why would it be stuck in the wall?"

A movement in the corner startled both girls. Lidka was sitting in the rocking chair, and had started a slow rock. Her gaze was riveted on Princess Kolodenko.

"Lidka," Nessa said stiffly.

"Nessa."

"Would you please excuse us, girls? I'd like a word with my granddaughter." Princess Kolodenko waved her hand in dismissal.

Kate tried to scoot out of the house alone, but Lidka followed her to the patio.

"Diamonds are in the walls?" Lidka said.

There was no use hiding it. "One was. We couldn't find any others. We looked."

"Must be nice to be so rich you decorate with diamonds." Lidka ran her hand along the top of a chair.

Kate smiled. "I wouldn't know. Maybe it was left over from the days when the castle was in use."

Lidka quirked an eyebrow. "Maybe."

TWENTY

The next day, Johnny popped in to deliver some news. Kate met him in the foyer. "My dad wasn't able to get our paperwork to go to Poland. I'm sorry, Kate. I thought it would be easy, but with all the changes after the war, I don't know. We'll have to try something else. He's going to see a lawyer and find out what else we can do."

Kate's heart sank. If they couldn't get the papers, how was she to find the shoes? "Maybe if we try filing from Italy instead of America?"

"Maybe. I don't know. We'll try again. My dad hasn't given up. He's curious himself to see what the war did to Poland. Don't be discouraged, okay?"

She smiled, but not fully. It was hard not to get discouraged when they were so close.

"There's nothing to be done today, so let's enjoy Italy while we can. I have plans for you tonight." He winked and was out the front door.

As Kate turned around, Nessa came into the foyer wearing an apron and a scowl. The girls had not been alone since finding the diamond in the castle and had planned to get away to town first thing after breakfast.

"I'm sorry, Kate. I wanted to take you to town today, but Dziadek has decided today is the day for making *giardiniera*. It means 'from the garden.' We pick all the ripe vegetables and can them with vinegar."

"It's my own special recipe," Mr. De Luca said.

Nessa rolled her eyes. "We make it every year." But then she smiled, revealing she didn't mind cooking with her grandfather. "He wants me to have a case of it when I go away to college." Her eyes opened wide. "A case!" She shook her head. "I won't know what to do with that much *giardiniera*. Hold parties, I guess."

"I can take her." Lidka breezed into the room. "I going anyway." She reached up to catch the keys Mr. De Luca tossed at her.

Kate swiveled back to Nessa. It didn't matter to her who she went to town with, although it would have been nice to get to talk alone with Nessa. To take her mind off the recent setback, she welcomed the chance to go out and see more of Sora.

Nessa looked like she was about to protest when Mr. De Luca stepped up beside her and put a hand on her shoulder. "Great idea. You two have fun."

And with that, Kate found herself sitting beside Lidka in the front seat of Mr. De Luca's black convertible car.

Lidka pointed to the glove compartment where Princess Kolodenko kept a scarf. "You need to tie your hair," Lidka said with a grin.

The wind whipped around the open car, trying to pull Kate's hair free as Lidka expertly maneuvered the curves into town. The countryside was beautiful, fields of green dotted with bushes and wildflowers by the road, though marred here and there by signs of war. A house that had been burned down. A crater where a bomb had landed.

Their first stop was for gelato. "Nessa would take you shopping for all day," Lidka said. "You not seem the shopping type to me." She parked in a shady spot. "Here is some advices. Do not allow Nessa push you around. It is not like she is the queen."

"Oh, I don't mind shopping," Kate said, ignoring the comment. "I'm looking for something to bring back for my mom and my best friend anyway." She got out of the car and slung Mr. G's camera bag over her shoulder.

"Is that all? You seem to be looking for something else. Something not small like a tourist souvenir. What else are you looking for?" she asked. "What do you want to find in Italy?"

"Oh, I-I . . ." She groped for words to say. Lidka was uncomfortably direct, and Kate didn't have Princess Kolodenko's skills of deflection. To say she wanted to find her dad seemed foolish in front of this practical girl. One needed a sense of imagination to believe she could uncover the impossible.

She thought about how Josie would answer. "How about love, like every other teenage girl."

"What about this Johnny? With him is it love?"

Johnny's easy grin popped into her mind. He was both serious and playful. Fun-loving and businesslike. He was going to help her find her dad, no matter how much of a long shot it was. How could it not be love?

Lidka pointed at her. "I see already the dreamy eyes. If not in love yet, you are going that way soon. I suppose now is a safe time to be in love."

"What do you mean?"

She shook her head. "Nothing."

They continued down a cobblestoned road until they reached the shop Lidka was looking for. "Still here," she said. "Best chocolate in the town." They placed their order and sat at a small table outside.

Lidka ate her dessert in silence, switching from watching Kate to watching the pigeons waiting for scraps.

"Are you okay?" Kate asked. "I mean, after all that happened to you?"

"What, the torture? The starvation? The betrayal? Which of these things do you ask about?" Lidka's expression turned as cold as her gelato.

"Sorry, I shouldn't pry." Lidka could be direct, but she didn't like others to corner her, apparently.

"I know you Americans are curious about us animals over here. I am, what is the word you use? *Okay*. I learned great skills, which helped me survive after the war. But now it is hard for me to do regular job. I am used to working in black market. It was fun. A challenge to find things that no one else could find. I was good at it. What I am good at now I do not know. Running away, maybe."

Kate was surprised at her honesty. She waited for Lidka to explain further. When Lidka didn't say anything else, Kate pulled her own necklace out from under her blouse. "I have one, too. Are they common in Poland?"

Lidka raised her eyebrows but made no comment. She reached over and compared the two necklaces. "Amber is common. Poland is famous for the amber. I never really liked it, but there is something nice about this necklace." She leaned back in her chair. "To answer your question, I do not know how popular this design is. Where did you get yours?"

"It's a family heirloom."

Lidka looked puzzled at the term "heirloom."

"A family treasure, or souvenir," Kate suggested.

Lidka nodded. "I know your *babcia* and *dziadek* came from Poland. It is good you have a treasure from where you come."

"Yes. It helps to feel connected."

"I am sorry your papa went missing. Tell me about him."

Without intending to, Kate let out all that she had been holding back with Nessa. "And since they never found a body, I have to believe that he was injured and hasn't been able to get in touch with us for some reason. Do you think I'm hopeless?"

Lidka's hard eyes softened. "Hopeful. Nothing is worse than losing hope. Why not should a daughter know what happened to her papa? You should do everything you can to find him."

Kate bit her lip. If Lidka was from the stepsister side of the family, she might help where the Kolodenkos refused. "Do you know who Malwinka is?"

Lidka's expression didn't change. "I know a family member with this name, but I do not know if she is the Malwinka you ask. What is the last name?"

Kate's heart skipped a beat. "I don't know. I was only given Malwinka, but I'm sure she is the same one."

"And what can Malwinka do for you?"

Oh boy. This she couldn't tell. "She has something that I think will help me find my father."

"Sounds a mystery. I see what I can learn for you," Lidka said. "But it seems to me your papa would be in Italy, and the Malwinka I know is in Poland. Poland is not an easy country to get into or out of. Malwinka would need to come to you, which she does not do, or you would need to get an entry permit. Are you not scared to think of going into such a place where not even the Kolodenkos dare go?"

Deep down, a fear was taking root, but Kate didn't know if that was coming from her intuition or from Lidka trying to scare her. The war was over; how bad could travel in Poland be?

"I reading your face," Lidka said. "You already ask the Kolodenkos about a trip to Poland and they have said no, *nie*? It is a different country now, than before the war. Poland is not a bad country for you to visit if you have someone to help you." She held her arms out wide. "Don't I look fine to you? I coming from there and I am in one piece." She stood, adding a final punctuation to their discussion. "You bring your camera. Let us find pretty things to take pictures."

The girls made their way uphill through the small town, until they came to a stone cathedral at the base of the mountain.

"The original cathedral is destroyed in an earthquake centuries ago," Lidka said. "Are you Catholic?" she asked as she entered the cathedral and paused at a shrine to make the sign of the cross.

"Protestant," Kate said. The cathedral was dimly lit with several candles, giving the room a cozy atmosphere.

"During the war in Poland, even the Jews hiding in the open were Catholic. They were taught to cross themselves at each shrine—and there are many in Poland—so they would blend in and not look Jewish."

"The Jews could live out in the open? I thought they all went into hiding if they could."

"Not all Jews look Jewish. These, they needed lessons in acting Catholic and would meet at Catholic cafés. They could go to beauty parlors to learn how to do their hair a different way, and get lessons on how to behave. The people helped."

"I hadn't heard this," Kate said.

"The stories will come out," Lidka said. "A professor of art your papa is, *nie*? Sent here to protect history and religious culture. Come and see what is saved thanks to men like him." She led Kate to the front of the cathedral where candles surrounded an ornate altar. The gold trimmings shone prettily in the glow. A crucifix depicting the suffering Savior was centered on the wall. Kate was used to seeing the empty cross at her church in New York. A pretty statue of Mary was to the left. As they walked closer, Kate could smell the melting wax.

"Many paintings and altarpieces like these were stolen for Hitler's art museum, the *Führermuseum*. Strange how a man who hated God could love the artwork depicting the things of God," Lidka whispered.

"It doesn't make sense, does it? So much of the war didn't make sense."

"Contradictions are life. I have seen people, hurting by their loved one's death, take revenge on strangers, often innocents themselves, with little care to those peoples or their families."

"I don't understand it," Kate said. It made sense to her that if the war was over, everyone should stop fighting. Her views felt childish and simplistic compared to Lidka's. But Lidka was hard-hearted. Kate wouldn't want to be that way, either.

"Maybe if you had been here, you would understand. The people get angry and they do not think about any things other than their anger. It is a terrible thing. But what else can we do? It is the human nature."

Kate didn't know if she shared Lidka's assessment of the futility of human nature. As they were leaving, she glanced back at the crucifix. A symbol of what some would say was their only hope of true peace.

TWENTY-ONE

As the sun was setting, Johnny appeared with a telescope under one arm and a big food basket in the other, packed with help from Mr. De Luca. He held out his elbow for Kate to loop her arm through. "M'lady," he said with a slight bow.

Nessa, who had been hovering, grinned and waved as they left the villa.

"I can't believe we've finally found time to be alone," Johnny said. "What with my dad and work and those girls pulling you in different directions, I never thought it would happen. We owe Mr. De Luca. He's promised to keep my dad busy and his mind off the movie for the night. Did you enjoy your trip to Sora?"

"I did. The town pulls you in with its cheery buildings. They're these lovely shades of white and yellow and rust, and the Italian gardeners have decorated them with flowerpots filled with red geraniums. When you go, bring your sketchbook. We stood on the bridge and watched the Liri

River. The water flows by in sheets, deceptively slow, but when you throw a stick in, you can see how fast it is truly moving. And then we went inside the cathedral. I'd been to Catholic church once with Josie, but their building was nothing like this."

"I had a rush trip into Sora yesterday to pick up some supplies. You're right. Next time I'll have to bring my sketchbook and take my time."

He led her out to the hilltop overlooking the valley where they could watch the sunset shine on the fields, turning them golden. Kate spread out a gray wool blanket, while Johnny set up the tripod and telescope.

"Movie still ahead of schedule?" She tugged at the corners of the blanket so they were smooth.

"We ran into a snag yesterday. Something to do with the costumes, but they're working on it. We're having to swap out our scenes—hence my quick trip to town." He yawned. "We started early, and even though we finished early, it was still a long day." He stood with hands on hips, watching her straighten the blanket.

"But you're smiling, so it must have been a good day." She sat back on her heels.

"It was a good day, but that's not why I'm smiling."
"Oh?"

He held out a hand to help her up. "I'm smiling because I'm out with my girl."

"Oh." Kate lost her breath as Johnny pulled her in for a hug. "Smooth move," she said.

"I picked it up on set. You'll recognize the move when you see it on film. I understand it was effective, Miss Allen?"

Kate laughed as she pulled away. "Yes. Now let me finish laying out this basket of goodies while I still have some light."

Mr. De Luca had sent along a cheese plate, a fruit plate, and some crackers. A carafe of lemonade and two glasses completed the picnic snack. Johnny waited for her to arrange everything before sitting beside her and digging in. "They do know how to eat here," he said between bites. "You know this is just the appetizer—they're expecting us back at the villa for a late dinner. Now, tell me how things have been going at the villa. Do they have you sweeping out the chimney yet?"

"Stop. You know they sent me out to sightsee with Lidka today."

"Yes. And you told me all about the town. Did you two get along?"

Kate twisted her lips while she thought. "She was surprisingly open with me."

"Blunt, you mean?"

"Yes, that's her way. But the big news is that I think she might be the one to help me."

"Lidka?" Johnny ran a hand through his hair. "I don't know about her. She seems a little, I don't know. Hard. Do you think you can trust her?"

"I don't have to tell her about the Cinderella connection. She knows of a family member named Malwinka in

Poland and is going to ask if the woman can help me find my dad. She doesn't have to know how. Besides, she's got street smarts we don't. Connections that she made during the war." Kate lowered her voice. "She used to trade in black market goods."

Johnny's eyes opened wide in mock fear. He pushed up his glasses. "All the more reason to be cautious. You don't know the types of people she's involved with." He reached for her hand. "I don't want you getting hurt." He helped her to her feet. "The stars are coming out. Let's see what I can find with this telescope."

Kate wasn't finished talking. "Nessa doesn't want me to do anything with Lidka. Today, we had a perfectly fine day, but Nessa was in fits that I would go out without her, and especially with Lidka. You saw her hovering back at the house? She hasn't left me alone since I got back. She was sure Lidka wanted to get me by myself so she could ask about the diamond we found in the castle wall."

Johnny turned away from the telescope. "You found another diamond? It's like they grow on trees in Italy."

"Didn't I tell you? A blue diamond was wedged in the fresco at the castle." She shook her head. "We really haven't had any time alone, have we?"

He slid his fingers down her arm until he was holding her hand. "Forces have been conspiring against us, but Mr. De Luca, our very own Fairy Godfather, has intervened. Let's forget about everyone else for now and just look at the stars." He pulled her to the telescope.

But Kate's mind was still churning. "Funny thing is, the diamond never came up. Lidka didn't even hint for me to tell her more."

"I wouldn't worry about it. They have some sort of rivalry going on. You don't need to get pulled into it."

"You still think I let Nessa tell me what to do, don't you?"

"A little." He took off his glasses and squinted into the eyepiece.

"I'm only trying to figure out where I fit in this fairy tale. What I'm supposed to do. How much I'm supposed to push back when she does something I don't agree with. And I suppose it's the same for her. But I don't think she realizes what she's saying sometimes. She's not mean about it, but she's used to getting her way."

"I thought that was a girl trait. Seems like all the females in my life get what they want." He pulled her in for a kiss.

She pushed him back. "I'm serious. She even tried to keep the dresses in her room."

Johnny shrugged. "That's logical. They are her dresses." He went back to adjusting the telescope. "I can't find a star. Let me aim for a bigger target."

Kate's frustration continued to build. "But that's not the way it's supposed to work. I'm supposed to keep them for her. Otherwise, what's the point in my being the Keeper?"

He stepped back from the telescope, his expression

hard to read in the dark. "Frankly, I don't know the point either. Those dresses cause more trouble than they're worth."

Kate was stunned. "Is that how you really feel?"

"Yes. Yes, that's how I really feel right now." He raised his voice. "I brought you up here to get away from everyone. The dresses. Away from your problems. In case you haven't noticed, I'm trying to have some fun with you." He lifted his hands in exasperation and then let them fall, hitting his thighs.

Kate bit her lip and stared at her feet. This didn't feel like fun.

"You can't let this legacy consume your life or you'll end up pushing everyone away."

"I'm not trying to push you away," she said, looking up. Why couldn't he understand?

"You might not be trying to, but you are."

"Look, can we just start over?" There was still time to rescue the date. She forced a smile and pointed to the telescope. "Did you find anything?"

He took in a deep breath, then pushed it out. "Sure." He cracked his knuckles like he was trying to ease the tension. "Come look at this. See if viewing the craters on the moon doesn't change your perspective of life on earth."

She put her eye to the eyepiece. Johnny slipped up behind her and put his hands on her waist.

"Tell me what you see," he said.

"Incoming!" Nessa called from down the hill.

Kate stood, and Johnny buried his forehead in her shoulder. "She has the worst timing."

Nessa marched over the rise with Lidka at her heels. "Babcia sent us up here to bring you a light to find your way home, but really, she's making sure you have chaperones. Dziadek made us wait before letting us go. He said young people need time to fall in love under the Mediterranean stars."

"I like the way he thinks," Johnny said, draping his arm around Kate.

"At what are you looking?" Lidka asked before she put her eye to the telescope.

"The moon. It was the easiest to find," Johnny answered. "The light that rules the night."

"Lidka doesn't like rules," Nessa said. "Or rulers."

"Do not be petty, Nessa. The peoples are in charge now. Like the stars scattered. Everyone is equal."

"But they're not," Nessa said. "That's the problem. Everyone is equally oppressed."

Kate and Johnny exchanged a look.

"You only think so because the rich have been brought down. You have never felt poverty before and you not like it."

"People like you made sure we did. We were targeted."

"It made things right. Restored the balance." When she noticed Kate's expression, she added, "You are not knowing. You were not there."

Nessa looked into the telescope. "And you don't want to know what she was involved with."

"At least I do something. You ran away. Your whole family ran away."

"Yes, and you ran to us and we took you in. You endangered us all with your activities. We still had children to protect."

"Anyone hungry?" Johnny interrupted. He started to pack up the telescope, and Kate folded the blanket.

"Starving," Nessa said, glaring in the lamplight at Lidka. "Just like the people in Poland."

TWENTY-TWO

Dinner was tense, no matter how many silly jokes Mr. De Luca told. Nessa and Lidka sat as far away from each other as possible, and neither spoke unless directly asked a question.

"Lidka, your favorite," Mr. De Luca said, holding up a forkful of risotto like a toast to her. She smiled but didn't engage.

After dessert, both girls immediately went their separate ways. Kate started to follow, but Johnny held her back. "Let them cool off," he said. "Besides, you need to walk me halfway to the guesthouse."

They held hands and wandered through the rose garden, taking the long way. "Thank you for tonight," Kate said. "It was quite romantic."

"Quite," Johnny said, squeezing her hand. "Although I may have shot myself in the foot, as far as dates go."

"What? Why?" *Because we fought?*

"How am I going to top a picnic overlooking an Italian meadow while we gaze at the moon and eat cheese?"

Kate laughed. "I dare you to top it."

"Oh, you don't think I can? All right, Kate Allen. You're on. I'll start working on it now. So you best turn yourself around right here and go back to the villa. I've got some thinking to do." He spun her and gave her a little push.

She turned back. "You might want to work on a better ending," she said, frowning. "This one is lacking."

"Oh, you mean something like this?" He kissed her forehead.

She nodded.

"Or something like this?" He kissed her cheek.

"Better."

"Okay. I'll work on it, then," he said, backing away. "Good night, Kate."

"Hey!"

Johnny laughed. He stepped forward and cupped her face with his hand, kissing her properly this time, until she could feel it down in her toes. "Good night."

Kate wandered back through the roses and ended up at the patio. She wasn't ready to go inside yet, so she sat down in one of the lounge chairs to watch the stars and do some thinking of her own.

"Have a good evening?" Lidka asked out of the dark. She was lying on a lounge in the darkest corner of the patio, as if she were waiting for Kate.

Kate leaned forward. "You startled me. Yes, it was a special evening." Kate lay back.

"I am glad, but do not let the boy distract you too much."

"What do you mean?"

"You came here for a purpose. Do not get distracted. Let me help. Have you not figured it out yet?"

"You're talking in riddles. Normally you are quite plainspoken. Just tell me."

"Your *babcia* married a Burgosov. Do I need to put clues together for you?"

Kate's mind whirled. Grandpa was a Burgosov? A Keeper married a descendant of the stepsisters? Holy Toledo. That's the piece of the puzzle she was missing. Aunt Elsie said her mother gave her the Keeper role because Babcia was being too friendly with some of the Burgosov clan. She never said Grandpa Feliks was the one she was talking about. She sat up straight and swung her feet to the solid ground.

Lidka grinned. "I see understanding. There are more secrets to this family. Keep following bloodline. Is difficult because we follow our mothers and the last names change. But know this. Kolodenkos trace their line back to girl named Kopciuszek." Lidka paused, studying Kate's reaction.

Kate couldn't help but react. She let her mouth fall open in surprise. Lidka knew.

"But it goes back further, to Kopciuszek's parents. When the little girl's mother died, her father remarried, bringing in a stepmother and two naughty stepsisters, *nie*? That stepmother was Kopciuszek's aunt. The father knew he was going to die in battle and wanted assurance his little girl would be taken care of. So before the line split between the current feud of Kolodenko versus Burgosov, we were all one happy family." She frowned. "Well, all one family. It was not a union based on love."

As Lidka handed her pieces, Kate put more of the puzzle together. But the more she saw, the more she became afraid to fully realize the picture that was forming.

"Yes, you, too, are one of us. The stepsisters." She said the word in disgust. "You have Burgosov blood in your body, just as truly you have Kolodenko. Cousin."

"What else?" Kate asked, her mouth going dry. The Kolodenkos thought Lidka didn't know anything, but did they know as much as she did? Oh, but they had to realize Kate was partially descended from a Burgosov. It was the whole reason Elsie became the Keeper instead of Kate's grandmother—because of her relationship with Grandpa Feliks. Nessa was probably unaware, but Princess Kolodenko certainly knew the family history.

"I once was like you. I did not know the secrets. They are all so careful with their secrets. Our families feud, but most of us do not know why. I never knew until I sleep in the sister's bedroom. She had a hidden diary that I found. In the pages of love she had for her boyfriend she write an interesting story of Kopciuszek. Is this what you are curious about?"

Kate licked her lips. "They think you don't know."

"They think what I let them think."

Finally, Kate leaned back in the lounge and rested her head. It felt heavy with the weight of new information. She breathed in the overpowering scent of jasmine while Lidka waited for her to speak. "Why are you telling me this?"

Lidka moved to the edge of her chair where Kate could see a pale outline of her face illuminated from the villa of the Kolodenkos, the true heirs of Cinderella. "It is time you knew, and it looked like no one else was going to do it. Are you not glad?"

"I don't know what I feel." But maybe this information explained why she was having trouble with Nessa over the dress. As Keeper, she was supposed to be protected from the greed associated with it. If she were related, that greed might affect her, too. Did there need to be a Keeper for the Keeper?

"You said you know a Malwinka," Kate added. "She is the one I'm looking for, isn't she?"

"Yes. If you are looking for the head of the Burgosov clan."

Kate took a deep breath. She stared up at the stars and then the moon. She was in real need of perspective.

Lidka said, "I had to find out more about you before I told you. Malwinka is not someone you tease. She is too powerful."

Kate sprang up. "You'll take me to her?"

"You've come all this way."

"Yes."

"Are you going to ask for permission to leave? When I say it is time, we go. *Nie*?" She frowned. "I will talk with Fyodora. She will agree."

While Lidka had been deciding about her, Kate had also gotten to know Lidka during her short stay. She was a girl with an angle. Kate crossed her arms. "What do you want in return?"

Lidka grinned. "You learning street smarts." She picked a leaf from a geranium plant and began to shred it. "I not knowing yet. A favor." She stood and stretched. "Be ready when I say. She is in Poland, and we have to get the proper paperwork before you will be allowed across the border."

"Johnny, too."

"Do you think I am miracle worker? You and me will be hard enough."

Kate held Lidka's gaze.

"I will try," Lidka said. "But do not blame me if something goes wrong."

~ TWENTY-THREE ~

The next day, Nessa and Princess Kolodenko started packing for New York. They were painstakingly going through all Nessa's skirts and blouses, trying to come up with the "coed" look. Kate was sitting on the bed not being much help. Josie was the one with fashion sense, not her. All the outfits looked good, although maybe a little too fancy for college life. Kate figured the first thing Nessa would buy at the college store was a collegiate sweater so she'd blend in with the other coeds.

Kate studied Princess Kolodenko's expressions to see if she could tell whether or not Lidka had brought up the trip to Poland yet. The elder woman smiled easily with Nessa, but did seem to be avoiding eye contact with Kate.

"How warm a coat will she need?" Princess Kolodenko asked, picking up a wool skirt.

"Anything you have worn in Poland should be fine," Kate said. She thought the princess flinched ever so slightly at the word "Poland."

"Like this?" Nessa asked, holding up a fur-lined knee-length coat.

Kate nodded. "Has Lidka spoken to you about a trip to Poland?" she asked tentatively, all patience gone.

Princess Kolodenko stopped folding. "Yes. This morning she said something."

"And?" Kate leaned forward.

"Poland is not like America. If you want to learn, I can tell you all about the land and the people. It will seem like you were there. I have pictures. But for now, let us pack." She finished her folding and stacked the skirt into the trunk. "Next week, Mr. De Luca will take you to Pompeii and Rome. Won't that be fun?"

Disappointment welled up inside. There must be a way to convince the princess. While Kate sat musing, Lidka walked by on the way to her bedroom.

"Lidka," Kate called out. Maybe the two of them could work together to come up with a plan.

Lidka poked her head into the room. "I going into town to pick up the tools for Tony. Kate, you want to come?"

"Yes." She jumped off the bed and mouthed "thank you" when she reached the doorway.

"No, I still need your help, Kate," Nessa complained. "You know New York. I trust you."

Kate was no longer in the mood to help the Kolodenkos. "I know New York department store windows. I can help you match the city backdrop, but I don't know how fashionable you'll be."

Princess Kolodenko intervened. "Why don't we make our selections, then when Kate returns she'll give her approval?"

"I can do that," Kate said.

Nessa waved her hand in dismissal, but she didn't look happy.

"I'll get my purse," Kate said as she squeezed past Lidka in the doorway.

It felt like she was keeping separate sets of friends, but Lidka and Nessa were like oil and water. It was best she spent time with them separately. And right now Lidka was the one with answers, while the Kolodenkos kept standing in her way.

Lidka was waiting by the front door waving the keys. "Let's go." She bounded outside, her shoulder bag bouncing against her thigh.

"Are you thinking about what I said last night?" Lidka asked after they drove past the castle.

"Of course." She'd stayed up half the night mulling it over. Her tired eyes were evidence of her lack of sleep. "And I know Mrs. De Luca said no."

"You are giving up?"

"Of course not."

"Will you sneak away?"

Kate thought of how hurt everyone would be if she up and left after they had paid for her Atlantic crossing—on the *Queen Mary*, no less. An image arose of the princess cabling Mom to say her daughter had run away.

"No. I won't sneak away."

"Then you are giving up."

Lidka seemed to be taunting her. "Why don't you tell the De Lucas you know? Why pretend not to?" Kate asked, trying to turn the tables on her.

"Less friction. You think they would let a Burgosov who knows their secrets stay at their villa? No matter what Nessa thinks, I care about Fyodora and Tony. They took care of me when I did not think I needed help, but I did. Probably saved my life."

"They care for you like one of their own. I don't think you telling will change that."

Lidka took her focus off the road to raise her eyebrows at Kate.

Kate smiled. "Maybe it would."

Lidka laughed. "You are learning." She slowed her speed as they drove into town. "Think of it. You have the same right as any of us over the Kolodenko collection. It is ridiculous what they are doing. You should claim your birthright and take the items for yourself. You can be the one who ends this silly feud."

The Kolodenko collection. Lidka made it sound like a clothing designer's spring line. Did she know about everything in the collection, or was she fishing for information? She didn't seem to know what was special about the necklace, but she could have been faking ignorance. Kate would have to be careful what she said. "It doesn't feel like my birthright..I'm too far removed, not a direct descendant."

"But that is what this family needs. Fresh blood." She parked. "You are intersection of the families. They have been living out the same old merry-go-round for years."

They went into the hardware store with Mr. De Luca's list. The attendant started collecting the items while the girls waited. Lidka leaned back on the counter. "Are you not a little curious what would happen if we changed things between the families?"

Kate shook her head. "I haven't thought about it."

"Like I saying, you are too new. You have no time to scheme like everyone else."

"I don't know that the Kolodenkos are scheming. They're just living out their family history. Trying to do good."

The attendant came back with a wooden crate filled with a variety of tools. Lidka paid, and they were on their way to the car. "I am not ready to go back," she said. "There is popular piazza up ahead. May we stop and order pizza for lunch? I have not had pizza in long time."

"Swell." It was another beautiful sunny day, and the piazza showed promise for a photo shoot. It was too bad she didn't have the camera with her. "I need a shoulder bag like yours," Kate said. "I keep forgetting to bring the camera, but if I had a big enough purse, I could."

Lidka glanced at the tables outside the pizzeria where she wanted to eat. "Not too crowded yet. On the next block is a store that sells these bags. I take you now."

The first bag Kate looked at was perfect. Made of brown canvas, it was the right size to fit her purse and the camera, with a little room left over. Lidka helped her figure out the Italian money, and they returned to the piazza. By the time they got there, the lunch crowd had descended.

"That was fast," Kate said, eyeing all the full tables.

A waitress led them to the only open table, past an old woman dressed in rags. She had matted white hair, tied back in a faded black kerchief. With her gnarled hands, she wound a mass of blue yarn over and over. Once it was a ball, she unwound it and started again. She was muttering something, too quietly to make out what it was, and everyone gave her a wide berth. The waitresses skirted her table without acknowledging her, but they had at some point served her, as evidenced by an empty tea cup.

When the girls passed by, the old woman looked up, her eyes distant. She stopped her muttering and followed them with her gaze. The waitress seated them near the old woman, as the only available was the one closest to her.

"Who is that?" Kate whispered to the waitress, hoping her limited Italian was correct. Something about the old woman interested her.

The waitress bent close and answered in fast Italian.

Lidka translated. "She says, 'I don't know. She is always here, ever since I start working a month ago. She comes early in the morning and my boss feeds her. She leaves before the sun sets. Sometimes she winds her yarn; other times she brings a tatting shuttle.'"

"Ask her what she says," Kate said, not sure why she needed to know.

Lidka translated and the waitress laughed. "She is hard to understand. Some have heard her say, 'The sky is amber.' Others have heard her talking about something she has lost, but no one can figure that one out."

The old woman seemed as interested in them as Kate was in her. She watched them as they ordered, muttering to herself. Then, as they were eating, the old woman pushed herself up from her table and came over to them. She moved slowly, as if her feet hurt her. She reached out a hand to Lidka, her finger pointing to Lidka's necklace.

"Mine," she said. "Lost."

Lidka held up the amber necklace. "This? Is this the amber sky you have lost?"

The old woman nodded hungrily. Her interest in the amber necklace was too intense—it was like she'd seen it before. It was a long shot, but this woman could be the one who gave her dad the diamond.

"Have you seen this necklace before? A drawing?" Kate mimed drawing on a piece of paper.

The old woman ignored Kate and reached out as if to touch Lidka's necklace.

Kate gently kicked Lidka under the table to get her attention. She raised her eyebrows to encourage Lidka to follow her lead.

Lidka pursed her lips. When the woman stepped closer,

Lidka hurriedly unclasped the necklace and draped it over the woman's hand.

"What? No. Ask her why she wants it." Kate resisted the urge to touch her own necklace, hidden under her blouse, in case the old woman would demand hers, too.

By now, they had the whole pizzeria's attention. Everyone was watching to see what the old woman would do. She held the necklace with both hands close to her heart, a smile lighting her face. But then the smile began to fade and was replaced with a look of confusion. She shook her head, muttering, and returned to her corner table. She picked up her things and continued out to the street.

Lidka translated. "She saying something like, 'Feels different, too much time.' Maybe I should not have given her my necklace. I thought it would make her happy."

Later, when Kate was relaying her day to everyone, she told them about the old woman. Immediately Nessa broke in.

"We know that woman. She is the old gardener I was telling you about. I didn't know she spent so much time at the pizzeria. We call her the *babuszka* because when we were growing up she had a set of nesting dolls that she let us play with, and she always wears the kerchief on her head like the *babuszka* dolls."

"The waitress says she's been there every day for as long as she can remember," said Kate.

"Oh dear," Princess Kolodenko said. "I need to visit the *babuszka*. I haven't been since we got home. Tony, did you see her while we were gone?"

"I checked in on her every few days. There has been no change. Her health is frail. I tell her not to go into town every day, but she says the exercise is good for her. I think she is getting lonely in her old age."

Kate remembered the sketch of the cottage. Jeepers, how could she have forgotten one of the clues? "I'd like to go with you," she said, looking meaningfully at Nessa.

∾ TWENTY-FOUR ∾

Kate and Nessa had a great time putting together a food basket for the *babuszka*. They started out harvesting goodies from the garden: romaine lettuce, chives, rosemary, basil, tomatoes, zucchini. They wore big floppy garden hats and took frequent breaks to enjoy glasses of ice water mixed with sliced lemons and cucumbers.

From the kitchen, they added fresh bread, pasta, and two jars of the just-made *giardiniera*. Maria wrapped up some of her pasta and enough jars of tomato sauce until the basket was overflowing. She shook her head and pulled out another basket. "You won't be able to carry it in one basket," she said. "It will break."

When the sun began to set, Kate, Nessa, and Princess Kolodenko followed the path along the woods to the gardener's cottage. Even Nessa, who had previously mentioned being uncomfortable around the old woman, walked in eagerness.

"I found a soldier out here one day when I was bringing the *babuszka* her basket," Nessa said. "He was still as anything, hiding behind a tree. When he saw what I was carrying, he risked making a noise, revealing his hiding place. He was the leader of a band of twenty partisans who were making their way north and they had run out of food days earlier. I gave him the basket and had to go back for more. When I returned, the basket was sitting on that rock over there filled with wildflowers."

"How sweet," Kate said. She imagined the starving men taking the time to pick flowers in gratitude.

They continued down the well-trod path as it wound through a grove of trees. The cottage, just like the sketch, was cute as a fairy tale. It was a squat wood-and-stone building with gingerbread trim along the roof and over the doorway. The windows held flower boxes overflowing with periwinkle, cornflowers, and cosmos. Kate let the other girls walk ahead as she took it all in.

With the addition of the flowers, which were missing from Johnny's sketch, the cottage looked exactly like the watercolor her dad sent her for her birthday. He had been here, all right. But instead of making her feel closer to him, it made her unexpectedly sad. Kate was beginning to understand why her mother was not ready to open Dad's box or come to Italy. This must be how her mom felt when she looked at the box.

Princess Kolodenko matched her pace to Kate's. "It is possible your father was with the group of men who came to collect the artwork we were hiding. I'm sorry that I did not catch all their names. They were not many, but I was busy with all the children and making sure everything at the house was running smoothly. I wish I could help you more. Our villa was so busy at the time."

"I understand," Kate said. Her dad would have spent some time here, getting all the details right. She wondered what drew him to the cottage, and if he came before or after getting the diamond. Perhaps the *babuszka* would know.

No lights were on, and the cottage had the feel of desertion about it.

"Toward the end, we had to take all the children with us into the farms," Princess Kolodenko continued, unfazed by the look of the cottage. "Our main villa was overrun with retreating Germans. They kicked us out—only the best for the officers. Once they left we could move back and assess the damage. They were angry and destroyed much of our lovely house. It has taken us all this time to restore the damage."

"But then the Australians came," Nessa said.

"Yes, they were a welcome sight," Princess Kolodenko said.

"A handsome sight," Nessa said. "All the girls in town were happy to see them. To hear them talk with their funny accents."

Now they were standing in the yard in front of the door.

"I don't think she's here," Nessa said. "She'd have had a light on by now."

Kate pointed to a bicycle leaning against the side of the house. "Does she ride into town?"

"Yes," Princess Kolodenko answered. "Her bicycle was stolen during the war, but it was one of the first things we replaced. I hope she is well." She knocked on the door. "Babuszka. Babuszka, are you in?"

Princess Kolodenko searched the cottage while the rest waited outside. She came out, a worried look on her face. "She is not here. Everything is neatly put away, no fresh flowers on the table like she likes to keep. I'm afraid she has gone."

Nessa pushed her way into the cottage, and Kate followed. Inside was one large room, with a small soft bed pushed up against the wall to the right. At the back was the kitchen with a row of cabinets, a sink, and an old wood stove with its black pipe snaking up through the roof. The floor was spotless wood planks.

"Does she go away often?" Kate asked.

"Never. She had no family apart from us. Oh, dear. Where could she have gone?"

"We could ask the movie people if they've seen her," Nessa said.

Princess Kolodenko nodded. "Great idea. They've already taken an interest in her. They've filmed her several times in the background scenes."

They left the canned food on the table in case they were wrong and the *babuszka* returned. "This is very troubling," Princess Kolodenko whispered as she closed the door tight. "Quickly now, before we have no more light." She led the march back to the villa.

⌒⌒

Late that night as Kate was staring up at the ceiling trying to figure out what could have happened to the *babuszka*, there was a gentle knock at the door. Before Kate could respond, it opened, illuminating Princess Kolodenko's frame. "Are you awake?" came the whisper.

"Yes. Come in."

Princess Kolodenko sat on the edge of Kate's bed. "Do you still want to go to Poland?"

Kate's stomach fluttered. She eagerly rolled onto her side and pushed herself up on one arm. "Yes. Lidka can take me to Mal—" Kate stopped herself. She needed Princess Kolodenko's approval to go and didn't want to remind her outright of who Kate would be going to see. "She thinks she can help."

"I still believe Poland is dangerous."

"She says it isn't."

"Maybe not for her." Princess Kolodenko was quiet for a long time, staring at her clasped hands.

"Is there something else?" Kate prompted.

"I am weighing your safety with your dreams. How your mother would feel for you to travel to Poland this summer. We will have to get her permission."

"Really? I don't think Mom will mind. She took me

there herself when I was so little I don't remember. To come all this way and not see Poland would be a tragedy."

Princess Kolodenko let out a small laugh and looked up at the ceiling. "I have a different view of tragedy." Her gaze fell on Kate. "If the *babuszka* is gone, it means something. I was wrong. You should go." The princess's face was pale in the dim light. She stood, and the concerned look in her eyes before she turned away made Kate draw in a breath. What was the princess not telling her?

∽ TWENTY-FIVE ∽

Kate could still hardly believe they were going to Poland. Princess Kolodenko's only stipulation was that Nessa and Johnny had to go, too. Mr. Day was willing to let Johnny miss work, given that the rejiggered filming schedule was going so well, and they were still waiting on several costume issues to be resolved for the later scenes.

Nessa was less enthused about traveling with Lidka, but after a talk with the princess, she had come around. Now, instead of fussing, she was outlining detailed sightseeing excursions, which completely irritated Lidka. They'd never have enough time for all Nessa was planning, but Kate suspected Lidka's frustrations were the point of Nessa's enthusiastic organizing. Lidka, in her matter-of-fact way, proceeded to arrange for everyone's paperwork to be completed, but was silent on her plans for when they got there.

One evening when everyone seemed to be a little antsy

waiting on their travel plans, Mr. De Luca taught them a popular card game called *scopa*, the Italian word for broom. Lidka refused to participate, instead hovering on the fringes of the group, watching.

While he was shuffling, Johnny said, "That tagliatelle we had for dinner was tasty. I hope you got the recipe, Kate. We could whip up a batch for your mom when we get home."

Kate nodded. "She'd like that." *Cooking with Johnny. Now I'd like that.*

"Just wait until Ferragosto," Nessa said. "You'll have all kinds of new foods to try."

"What is Ferragosto?" Mr. Day asked, picking up his cards.

"Big Italian holiday," Mr. De Luca said, opening wide his arms and punctuating each word with a shake of his hands. "Not as important as Christmas, but big like . . ." He looked to Princess Kolodenko for ideas.

"Like your Thanksgiving? It is a time of celebration that the harvests have come in and it is the start of holiday season."

"Before we lived at Avanti, we would come here for Ferragosto," Nessa said.

"When is it?" Kate asked.

"August fifteen."

Kate raised her eyebrows at Lidka in a silent question of whether they would be in Italy or Poland then.

Lidka looked unhelpfully away. But after Johnny and

Mr. Day had gone back to the guesthouse, she announced they were leaving for Poland the next morning.

"What?" Kate stopped putting away the playing cards. "Why didn't you say so earlier? I need to pack. I've got to tell Johnny." She dropped the cards on the table. Lidka was a hard one to understand sometimes.

Nessa rolled her eyes. "You could have given us some warning."

"I could not get you a permit. Only Kate and Johnny."

"What? Did you even try?" Nessa looked at her *babcia* in exasperation.

"You have a history in Poland," Lidka said. "Kate and Johnny are tourists. They were easy."

Nessa crossed her arms. "Then we'll have to wait until I can get mine."

Lidka shook her head. "I'm going tomorrow morning, with or without anyone else. Six o'clock." She looked pointedly at Kate before leaving the room.

Mr. De Luca took over putting the cards away. "What do you want to do, Kate? Go or wait?"

"I have no choice. I need to go." She frowned at Nessa. "I know Lidka well enough to know she doesn't offer second chances."

Princess Kolodenko sighed. "Run and tell Johnny."

Kate flew out the door. "Johnny!" she called. He was standing in the light of the open door to the guesthouse about to follow his dad inside. He let the door close.

"What is it?" He took the stone path to meet her.

"Lidka says we're leaving early in the morning."

He tilted his head, looking annoyed. "And she just learned this?"

Kate shrugged. "I don't know what her problem is. We have to take her the way she is."

"Can't you wait for me to be finished with this one scene? A few more days would be better timing."

"Lidka is pretty determined. I have to go when she goes. No one else will take me, and she couldn't get Nessa's paperwork."

Johnny frowned. "I don't like it. We're supposed to all go together. How safe is it, where Lidka is taking us?"

"I think it's fine. Otherwise the Kolodenkos wouldn't let me go."

He looped his hands behind his head and walked around, thinking. "Okay. I'll talk to Dad and see what we can work out. Did your mother give her okay?"

"Telegram came this morning. I think she remembers the old Poland. She sounded happy I was going."

"All right. I'll get back to you soon."

He opened his arms and Kate rushed in. "Thank you," she said.

"No problem. But I have ulterior motives, you know." He kissed her neck until she giggled and pushed away. "I want you to be happy."

"You make me happy." She felt the heat rise to her face

at her boldness. "See you tomorrow." She returned to the villa and pulled out her bag to start packing. Nessa crept in and closed the door gently.

"I can't believe Lidka did that," she whispered, standing close to Kate. "She's trying to get you alone. Don't let her manipulate you."

"I think you're overreacting," Kate said. "Johnny will be with us."

"You don't know her like I do. You should not go. Wait until I can come with you."

"I'll be careful." She'd seen Lidka's expression earlier; she never planned to take Nessa with them. When Nessa's visa didn't come in with the others, she saw her chance to leave her behind. But Kate needed Lidka more than she needed Nessa. She couldn't wait. Johnny would be enough to help keep Lidka in line.

Nessa bit her lip, her fists clenched at her sides. "Keep making her speak English. Don't let on how much Polish you know. And if you find the shoes, bring them back. Hide them in your bag or at a locker in a train station. I think Babcia is wrong. The shoes belong with the dress." She lifted her eyes to Kate. "Don't you agree?"

Kate stared back at her. Everyone was missing the point. Dresses. Shoes. The feud. She was missing her dad. The shoes were a tool to help find him. "I don't know what is going to happen. Any decisions will be made in the moment." Kate tried not to bite out her words. She sighed. "The real reason I want to find the shoes is that

I hope they will lead me to my dad. Like how the prince used them to find Kopciuszek."

"Oh." Nessa looked at Kate with sad eyes. "Now I understand."

"It could happen," Kate said quietly. "Fairy-tale magic." She held her hands out as if trying to catch some of that magic.

"Fine. Then leave the dresses here so they don't steal them." Nessa stepped closer to the door.

"They can't just take them, remember? The ball gown protects itself."

"I know. But you might give them away . . . if they trick you."

Kate didn't answer. If she found out her dad was still alive, she would do whatever it took to get him back. She couldn't promise Nessa anything.

"I forbid you to take them." Nessa stamped her foot.

"Forbid me? No wonder Lidka didn't want you along. Everything is not all about you." *Says the Keeper to the Princess.* Inwardly, Kate cringed.

"Wha—" Nessa narrowed her eyes. "Remember at the castle when I was feeling something but couldn't place it? Well, I've thought about it, and I think I was sensing people and what they were thinking. I don't know how else to describe it. Lidka wants to help, but she is conflicted. I don't trust her." Nessa jabbed her finger at Kate. "And neither should you." She huffed, and stalked out of the room.

Kate sat down hard on the bed. She put her head in her hands and breathed out a long, calming breath. She didn't completely trust Lidka, either, but what choice did she have? And of course she thought the shoes belonged with the dresses. She'd do whatever she could to keep them, after she found her father.

She channeled her energy into packing, then went back downstairs to wait for word from Johnny. Mr. De Luca stayed up late with her. He had all kinds of questions about New York and how Nessa would fit in. They both kept glancing at the clock, waiting for Johnny to report back. It got to be so each time one would look, they would both laugh.

"You need to sleep," he said. "Staying awake won't change anything. You'll know in the morning." He got up and started turning out the lights. "*Buona notte.*"

"Good night," she answered back, and went up to her room.

Reluctantly, she turned out her light and lay down. Her emotions were all over the place. She was finally on her way to some answers. But if the Kolodenkos wouldn't even return to their homeland, how safe could it be? Despite Lidka's assurances all would be well, Kate was afraid. If she slept at all tonight, she'd be surprised.

She was finally fading out when a *ping* sounded from the window. *Ping. Ping.* She blinked sleep out of her eyes and looked into the moonlit garden. She laughed. There was Johnny with a handful of pebbles. She waved so he would stop risking breaking a window to get her attention. She hefted up the window and called down, "O Romeo, Romeo, wherefore art thou, Romeo?"

"Nice to see you, fair Juliet," he replied. "Good news. I can come with you. Dad wasn't happy about it, but he doesn't want you going alone."

Kate felt a lightness in her chest. She sputtered something about thanking his dad and how happy she was they'd be going together.

He laughed. "See you in the morning, Sparky."

Excitement replaced the fear in her heart, allowing Kate to relax and eventually drift off to sleep. With Lidka leading the way and Johnny there for support, the task seemed less impossible.

TWENTY-SIX

T oo early in the morning, Kate awoke to an awful clanging sound. She rolled out of bed and popped her head out into the hallway at the same time Lidka opened her door. Mr. De Luca spotted them, smiled, and raised a cowbell above his head.

She and Lidka groaned simultaneously.

"Works all the time," he said. "Come down for breakfast."

Lidka slammed her door. *Maybe she isn't an early bird.*

After changing into her traveling skirt, Kate stared at the packages on her bed. The dresses. What was she going to do? She could leave them in the safety of the villa, but she might need them to make the shoes work. Although if she brought the dresses, she would risk having Malwinka take them.

Standing there, chewing her nail, Kate was torn. This was the hardest decision she'd had to make as Keeper. Harder than deciding to trick the Burgosovs into thinking they had the real dress when she gave them a fake one.

Someone knocked on the doorframe and pushed open the half-closed door.

"Hey, beautiful, what's taking you so long?" It was Johnny, his bag slung over his shoulder. "If you forget something, we can buy it."

Kate stepped back so he could see what she was looking at. "Could I buy these?"

His mouth formed an O. He picked up one of the packages. "What are you going to do?"

"Bring them? Leave them? Stand here until I figure it out?"

He dropped his bag on the bed. "You'd better decide quick. You're the last one to come downstairs. Everyone is waiting for you."

She poked at his bag. "You didn't pack much."

"All I really need is a toothbrush. You girls pack too much. Do you have to bring all three? Why not bring the one? You know." He wiggled his fingers like he was trying to show magic.

She laughed. "Of course." Kate shook her head. "I was making it too complicated. Keeping track of one will be easier than all three, and the ball gown is the one that goes with the shoes. It's the risk I need to take."

While Johnny waited, she stashed the servant's work dress and the wedding dress in the wardrobe, underneath some quilts. Not that she expected them to be there when she got back. Surely Nessa would search the room once Kate left and take them to her own room "for safekeeping."

She started to pack the ball gown, but then raised her eyes questioningly at Johnny. He grinned and nodded. She stuffed the wrapped package into the bag and handed the works to Johnny.

He carried their bags downstairs, except for her new camera bag, which she slung over her shoulder.

At the bottom of the stairs, Princess Kolodenko caught Kate's arm. "May I speak with you outside?" she said.

"Of course," Kate said, and followed her to the patio. The sun was barely beginning to rise, and the morning chill hung like a New York fog. Kate wrapped her arms around herself and wondered if she'd packed enough.

"I have something to tell you," Princess Kolodenko said. "I hope you understand. I saw no need to share with you earlier, but since you will be meeting Malwinka, I want to explain to you all I know." She paced the outside of the patio, checking the potted plants for water.

"What is it?" Kate asked, looking back to the house. She wanted to get breakfast before they left. Mr. De Luca's breakfasts beat any food she'd likely find at the train stations along the way.

"Malwinka does have the shoes you seek."

Kate blinked. She heard the words, but they didn't make sense. "You knew? You said they'd been lost."

"Yes, lost to the family. This is true. The shoes are no longer ours."

"You lied to me."

"I never outright lied, but I let you believe what you

wanted. I said the shoes had been lost to my family, and they have. I have never seen them."

"How did Malwinka get them?"

"My grandmother gave them to her mother. The shoes are important to our family, but not in the way you think. While the legend of Kopciuszek speaks of the prince using the shoes to find her after the ball, it is not like you imagine.

"I don't think the shoes themselves can help you find anyone, otherwise my grandmother wouldn't have given them up so easily. We let Malwinka have the shoes because it keeps the peace. She does not trouble us like Ludmilla does." She held up her hand. "And please, do not talk about these things in front of Lidka. I want her to be free of the family issues. She has enough worries without adding envy to them."

Kate wasn't going to be the one to tell Lidka's secrets, especially after learning the princess had been keeping her own. "Why am I going to Poland if the shoes won't help me?" Kate couldn't keep the despondency out of her voice. She didn't feel comfortable rushing off anyway, and to find out now that the trip was pointless was too much.

"I know you are curious about your heritage. You need to see Poland, and you need to try. I understand that. And for us? I am worried about the *babuszka*. I fear she has lost herself. If she got confused, she might try to return to Poland on her own. I want you to look for her while you're there."

"I've only seen her once. I'm not going to be able to recognize her in a crowd." How could Princess Kolodenko expect her to find their gardener? "Why not send the police to look for her?"

"We have already reported her missing. All I ask is that you pay attention to those around you. Something has happened. Threads are connected. Following one may lead you to another."

Kate rubbed her forehead as if pushing the thought into her head. "Is your gardener so important to you?"

"All our servants are important." Her eyes held Kate's meaningfully. "We found Elsie again, didn't we?"

"Why didn't you tell me what you knew about the shoes when we were in New York?" she asked, her voice barely above a whisper. She was trying not to let the hurt slip out in her voice, but she couldn't hold it back.

"You needed to do something. We hoped having you come to Italy and searching here for your father would be enough to calm your restlessness. Your mother thought this, too."

"That's why she let me come?"

Princess Kolodenko nodded. "Malwinka, while not a friend, is not trouble like Ludmilla. We have made peace through the shoes. Do not upset the peace. Will you try to find the *babuszka*?"

"I'm sorry you lost your gardener, but I'm trying to find my dad." The more Kate spoke, the angrier she felt. "I have to try the shoes, otherwise I'll always wonder."

"Of course. We want you to settle this in your heart. If you try the shoes and nothing happens . . ." She let Kate fill in the consequences. "What are your plans for when you find the shoes?"

"I don't know. I was hoping when I saw them, I would just know what to do." It sounded overly simple, but that was her plan. The dress had taught her, why not the shoes?

"I'm sorry I cannot give you more help. For us, the value in the shoes is in the peace they keep. We have everything else of Kopciuszek's that we need." Princess Kolodenko put her hand in her sweater pocket, pulled something out, and held it to Kate. "Here. Take the diamond you found in the fresco, but don't let Lidka know you have it. Sew it in your clothing and only let her know about it if you are in a bind. She'll know what to do with it. I know my husband has also given you money, but that is easily taken. I'm afraid you will spend much of it for bribes along the way."

Thinking of her father's diamond Kate had already sewn in her waistband, she tried to refuse it. "I can't."

"Please. The diamonds are meant for times like this." She also pulled out a spool of thread and a needle.

Kate took the diamond and squeezed it in her hand. She would have to sew it in immediately before someone noticed. She sat down and began to work.

"Thank you, Kate. Thank you for being kind to Lidka, too. Stay close to her so she cannot leave you if she gets frightened. She is a hard girl, but can be won over with love. She's had so little of it in her lifetime."

Kate doubted Lidka was ever afraid, but she nodded.

The sun was just starting to turn the trees golden on the edges when they went to the kitchen for Mr. De Luca's send-off breakfast. Lidka was clearly anxious to get going. She gulped her food down and spent the remainder of the time fidgeting. She twirled her spoon. She drummed her fingers on the table. She kept looking out the door.

Mr. De Luca calmly observed all this. "I'm glad you came back, Punia," he said, voice heavy with meaning.

She stopped her fidgeting and stared at him. "I try not to be a disappointment. I do what I have to do."

He weighed her words and didn't look pleased. They lapsed into a heated conversation in Italian that Kate could no longer follow. She thought she caught her name once and the word for "safe."

∽ TWENTY-SEVEN ∾

The plan was to take the train through Austria and Czechoslovakia, and from there cross the border into Poland. Once they were across, they'd take the train to Katowice and then find a bus to get them the rest of the way. That was all the information Lidka would share with the Kolodenkos. She said Malwinka lived outside Katowice but would not say where, no matter how often Mr. De Luca tried to trick the information out of her.

"Here are your train tickets," he said. "I will also buy your bus tickets, just let me know to which town."

"Nice try, Tony. You like to keep some of your residences secret; so do they," Lidka said for the final time as they stood near the ticket counter.

Nessa bristled at the use of the familiar name, but she didn't comment.

The train was scheduled to leave soon, so it was time for good-byes. It was strange to be back at the train station so soon and to be leaving the Kolodenkos behind.

Nessa stood with her arms crossed, staring at the roof of the train station. Beside her, Princess Kolodenko unconsciously played with the zipper on her purse. Mr. De Luca was unreadable. After saying good-bye to the girls, he took Johnny aside. Kate strained to listen in, but with all the surrounding noise of the train being prepped to leave, she couldn't hear anything.

Finally, the last call was given and it was time to go. Princess Kolodenko handed Kate the basket she'd brought from the villa. "This should hold you for the trip," she said. Maria had packed them several meals. The basket was heavy like the one they tried to deliver to the *babuszka*.

"Do not look back," Lidka said after they'd found their seats. "It is easier to leave if you do not."

Kate wasn't sure if Lidka said that for her benefit or not. But she had no intention of ignoring the people waiting to see them off.

There was a blast of the whistle followed by a sudden jerk as the train started to move. Kate leaned close to the window and when she saw the Kolodenkos, she gave them a hearty wave. Johnny stood above her and waved as well. Lidka made a noise of disgust before settling into a brooding silence. Kate was glad for the quiet, because it gave her time to think. Johnny held tight to her hand, as if letting go would separate them completely.

The trip would take a couple days if all went well. They had several stops and train changes that could add any number of delays. The car was only half full when they started, but after two stops, several families had boarded and filled in all the empty seats. After sighing several times, Lidka found a newspaper to use as a fan.

They changed trains in Rome, using the between time to have an early lunch, seated knee to knee on a crowded bench. "It's too bad we can't do a little exploring while we're here," Johnny said.

"Do not waste time sightseeing," Lidka said, breaking her silence. "You should plan what to do with Malwinka. She can be intimidating. You need to be prepared."

How can I prepare to meet a legend who strikes fear in one person and fidelity in another? The more Kate learned about Malwinka, the less she knew. It seemed everyone who met her had a different opinion on the woman. It was all so confusing. So she changed the subject. "What did you do after you left the Kolodenkos last?" she asked. She knew it was a point of contention with the family, being the final straw as far as Nessa was concerned. That Lidka had broken Princess Kolodenko's heart by leaving without telling them. Too many people disappeared during the war, never to be heard from again, and it left a person raw.

Lidka eyed her warily. "I went all over the land, looking for my place. It was hard, but you learn. People everywhere are the same. They think they are different, but when they are desperate they are not. They wanting food. They wanting clothing. They have things to trade that they have hidden. We all hide items to protect them during the war." She smiled. "Especially where the borders have changed. The Germans who found themselves in the Regained Lands, now part of Poland, have the greatest need and are under much persecution. The anger is still there. We are all angry."

"Is that why you came back?" Johnny asked.

She quirked a smile. "They are making us go back into our pens. Poles go here. Ukrainians go here. Germans there. Greeks there. And no one wants the Jews anywhere. You would go into villages and people are gone—houses standing, food abandoned, tables with dishes set. Like a life-size dollhouse."

"I don't understand," Kate said. "The war is over. Why can't everyone go back to their homes?"

"The main war is over, but the aftershocks go on, like earthquake. It is getting better." She nodded to the people who were on the train with them. "You see all the women, and children, and old people." She looked at Johnny again. "So many young men have died. Lots of girls are going to America to marry their American soldier boyfriends. Maybe I should go too, eh?" She reached over Kate and playful swatted Johnny's arm. "I joking. I do not need anyone. I will live to be an old maid. I have had enough of soldiers."

At Milan, while Lidka was in the ladies' room, Kate and Johnny discussed their plans. "I'll be honest and tell Malwinka what I need. There is no reason to make up a story or try to steal them from her. I'm sure she already knows why I am coming to see her."

Johnny nodded while he flipped open his sketchbook. The arching steel roof above the terminal had caught his artist's eye and he started to draw. "I agree. We'll just pray she has a kinder heart than we expect her to have. Be honest, but don't tell her everything. Only what she needs to know."

Johnny drew what he could, but soon it was time to board the train. The cars were prepared for nighttime with compartments sectioned off and bunk beds stacked. Lidka smiled. "Thank you, Tony. We traveling in style on this train." She yawned loudly and stretched. "Good, I am tired of cattle cars." She noticed Johnny and Kate were holding hands. "So sorry you will be separated. This is the longest part of our journey, so get some sleep. Good night, Johnny," she said and motioned for Kate to follow her. Over her shoulder she said, "We wake up in Austria, so have your papers ready for the customs people."

"See you in the morning." Johnny squeezed her hand and let go.

Kate smiled and followed Lidka. She didn't like the tone in the girl's voice when she said they would be separated. So when they found two empty bunks, she propped her bag up as a pillow in case Lidka was tempted to dig through her things looking for the dresses once Kate was asleep. "Good night, Lidka."

Early in the morning, the customs agents were waiting on the train, and they quickly cleared Kate and Lidka before moving on to the next car. The girls got off and waited on the platform for Johnny. Slowly, the overcast sky had begun to lighten, but still no Johnny.

"The train is going to leave," Kate said, her voice strained. She craned her neck to see down the row of windows. "I hope he didn't oversleep. Can we send someone to find him?"

Before Lidka could answer, Johnny bounded off the train. "That was close. They had all kinds of questions for me, and it took some time to find an English speaker who was awake." He waved as an older gentleman in a fedora and overcoat walked past. "Thanks again."

Lidka made a noise like *mfff* and marched off to look at the schedule.

When they caught up with her, she pointed. "That is our train. It is not fancy but will take us to the edge of Czechoslovakia where we change to our last train to Poland. Just over half a day more. Are you ready?"

Kate's mouth went dry. "Yes."

The final train through Czechoslovakia stopped at the Polish border. "We get out and walk across," Lidka said, hiking her bag onto her shoulder.

They got in the long line with their bags to cross the border. It inched forward as everyone's papers were

checked and stamped. Finally, it was their turn. Lidka handled the communication. A border guard spoke to Kate
in Polish and she waited for Lidka to translate before answering. He nodded and stamped their paperwork, but
when it came to Johnny, he held up his hand for him to
stop. "*Nie*," he said. The guard wouldn't let him pass.

Kate touched Lidka's arm.

"What is going on?" Johnny asked.

Lidka asked the guard, then translated his answer.
"They not happy with your papers and will not let you
cross. He wants you turn back." She shrugged, looking
unconcerned.

Kate's eyes grew wide. "Our paperwork checks out.
Why doesn't his?"

Lidka frowned. "Maybe it is because Johnny is here for
a movie? They don't trust the Western press."

"He's not the press."

Lidka spoke again to the guard, telling him Johnny
was a visitor, and something using too many words Kate
didn't understand.

This time the guard grew angry. He shook his head and
told Johnny to go back.

Again, Lidka shrugged. "I cannot convince them. Do
you want to return to Italy?"

Kate looked helplessly at Johnny. "We can't leave him
here by himself."

"Fine. We turn around." Lidka started back the way
they had come.

Kate didn't move. She thought of Elsie clutching that diamond. Her hopes were pinned on Kate. Answers were in Poland. The shoes were in Poland. "What is that word the guard used: toe-var-shish?"

"*Towarzysz*. It means comrade or what is English? Partner. He told me his partner said to not let anyone through who does not have proper paperwork, no exceptions." She grinned. "I told him Johnny had chocolate with him as bribe, and that is when he got angry. This one thinks he is honest."

Johnny lifted an eyebrow as if to ask, "What do you want to do?" When she hesitated, he set his jaw. "Can I talk to you alone?" He grabbed her elbow and led her away from Lidka.

"We need to decide now," Lidka said, raising her voice. "They will send all of us back if we stand here blocking the peoples."

"I need to go on with her," Kate whispered. "I've come this far and I'll always have questions if I don't."

"She's done this on purpose. She's trying to get you alone."

Kate stepped closer to Johnny so Lidka couldn't overhear. "I know. But what other choice do I have?"

He took her hands in his. "Wait for Nessa. We'll try again when her paperwork comes through."

She shook her head, watching his posture harden. He was steeling himself against her. "Please don't get mad."

"I'm trying not to, but I think you are being reckless."

"Maybe I am, but we're so close, and we're running out of time. The summer will be over before we know it and we'll be back on that ship."

His jaw remained set.

"What?"

He smirked. "I'm imagining a life where you always choose the Kolodenkos over everything else."

Kate looked at him incredulously. "Is that what you think I'm doing?" She exhaled. Of course that's what she was doing. Would always do. It was one of the reasons Babcia thought the legacy was a curse, not a blessing. If she and Johnny were going to continue, they'd each have to decide what the legacy meant to them as a couple. If anything at all. "Maybe so, but this time I'm also choosing my dad."

The guard walked over to them, arms crossed and face stern.

"Go or stay?" Lidka asked.

Johnny dropped Kate's hands. "I'll cable my dad and then turn around for another bumpy ride back. Send us a telegram when you get there so we know you arrived." He looked at Lidka for confirmation.

"Yes, yes of course. It will be the first thing we do."

Johnny didn't look convinced. He shoved his bag at Kate. "I've got some money and things in there you could use."

Kate refused. "No. You keep it."

"You're sure?" He hugged Kate and whispered in her ear. "Watch your back. If Lidka tries anything funny, go to the police. I'll see if I can meet up with your brother in the American zone of Germany and come round that way." He held her face and kissed her before letting her go. "I will find you."

"You'd better." Her voice carried the tone of an apology. She didn't want to say good-bye on such a sour note. She dug her fingernails into her hand to keep from crying; she couldn't take Lidka's scorn right now. She watched him walk away as long as she could, but the crowd was impatient and they pushed her forward while at the same time swallowing him up, and her heart along with him.

She knew he'd be okay on his own, but would she? A surprising ache welled up inside after he disappeared. They were partners, working together to find her dad. Now she was alone. Just the way Lidka wanted her to be.

~ TWENTY-EIGHT ~

As soon as Johnny left, Kate sensed a change in Lidka. She was more relaxed, like a distasteful task had just been removed from her. It annoyed Kate and made her even more suspicious.

"I have to buy our tickets," she said, heading for the counter.

"I thought Mr. De Luca did that already."

"He could only buy us tickets so far. Now I must purchase more." To the clerk, she asked for two tickets to Krakow.

"I thought we were going to Katowice."

"You must have misunderstood. It is Krakow," Lidka said with her quirky smile. "You will like this city. It is very beautiful as it not get destroyed like Warsaw. There are many old buildings and statues if you like to see them."

Kate clenched her hands. She was sure Lidka had said Katowice. She was changing the location from what she'd told the De Lucas. "We should let everyone know."

Lidka waved her off. "There is no time." She grabbed the tickets and marched to the platform.

Kate hung back, looking for the telegraph window. She could be quick.

"Now. We must board," Lidka said, pointing to the line of people getting on the train.

With one last glance, Kate hustled to keep up with Lidka. She'd have to send the telegram when they got to Krakow.

Once aboard their final train, Lidka gave a big sigh. "This is a good adventure for you, *nie*?" she said. She leaned back and jutted her feet up on the torn seat.

Kate forced a smile. It was a good adventure until about an hour ago. She'd left New York traveling first-class aboard the *Queen Mary* with two princesses and a boyfriend, her heart filled with hope. Contrast that with her predicament now: on a cramped train headed into a communist nation with a girl she'd only known for a few days and a growing fear in the pit of her stomach. *How quickly life can change.*

"Your boyfriend will be fine, if that is what bothers you. Tell me about America. Are the streets paved in gold?"

Kate couldn't tell if Lidka was joking or not. "I live in a small apartment in the city with my mom. She works for Harmon-Craig department store, and when I'm not in school I work there, too, helping set up the displays in the windows."

"This job you like?"

Again, Lidka was hard to read, since everything she

said came with an edge. "I love it. It's fun to set a scene. My boss is one of the best, so I learn something new with every display." She pointed to her bag. "The camera is his. I'm trying to take pictures for him that could inspire unique displays." She looked out the window at the world passing by. New York was so far away now. Mother would be working extra hours to fill in the loneliness—hopefully working and not dating. Josie might be going to the movies with that boy she liked.

"My mom took me to Poland when I was a little girl, though I don't remember it." Kate laid her head back. "I should send a telegram to my mother. Let her know I've made it to Poland." And she could also send telegrams to the Kolodenkos and to her brother. The more people who knew the change of plans, the better.

Lidka closed her eyes. "If we have time." She yawned and let her head fall to the side in relaxation.

Oh, we will make time. Even if I have to sit on the ground and refuse to move, I am sending a telegram.

When they entered the outskirts of Krakow, the train began to slow down. Lidka woke, stretching her arms up high. "Did you sleep?" she asked Kate.

"No. I watched the window." *And imagined every terrible way this trip could go wrong.* Lidka was going home, but Kate was heading into the unknown. Both the Burgosov thug and Uncle Adalbert had warned her about Malwinka, but the Kolodenkos and Lidka showed no sign of fear. Who was right?

"You will sleep on your return trip. Is the same scenery."

At least she is saying I'll have a return trip. When it was their turn to disembark, Kate reminded Lidka about the telegram.

"We can send one later, when you have something to say."

Kate crossed her arms. "They'll worry if they don't hear from us."

"Fine, but we must hurry." She looked at the darkening skies. "We do not want to be caught in the rain."

After locating the telegraph office, Kate composed a note to the De Lucas to let them know of the changes.

Lidka snatched the piece of paper and crumpled it up. "Too long. I write them."

Kate tried to grab the note back, but Lidka tossed it into the trash.

"They need to know where we are," Kate said.

"I tell them. Use fewer words and save money." Lidka wrote: POLAND SAFE. "See? This is all you need." She marched up to the counter.

Frustrated, Kate pulled out another piece of paper. Lidka returned to the table.

"You didn't say anything about Johnny or that we're in Krakow," Kate said.

"Does he not know how to send his own telegram?"

"That's not the point." Although now Kate felt foolish. Of course Johnny would let everyone know he was going on to Germany. "We still need to tell them we are in Krakow."

"Fine. I add word 'Krakow.'" She wrote the word on her message. "Can I send now?"

"Thank you," Kate said, relieved. Perhaps her suspicions of Lidka were unfounded. The girl was abrupt and efficient, but that didn't necessarily mean she was out to cause trouble.

When they exited the station, Lidka stopped short. "Oh," she said, her eyes fixed on a black car waiting at the curb. "Malwinka knows we are here."

A burly gentleman dressed in a suit stood guard over the fancy car. People were giving him a wide berth, but the car was attracting a lot of attention.

Kate's stomach flipped. "Is she in the car?"

Lidka snorted. "She will be at her castle."

"She lives in a castle?"

"*Nie*. She would like to. It is fancy house. Or at least, it used to be before the war. Their belongings were stolen, too. She has tracked down some, but many favorites are missing."

Kate's stomach clenched. She hoped the shoes were safe.

Without smiling, the man opened the back door and motioned to the girls.

"Gustaw," Lidka said with a nod.

Kate followed Lidka into the car. After the uncomfortable seats in the train, the plush interior was a treat, though intimidating. If Malwinka wanted to put Kate on edge with this welcome, it worked.

The house they drove up to was on the outskirts of the city, and it was large. Almost as large as the Italian villa. It was three stories tall and looked like it received no damage at all in the war. The colors were bright, like they had been freshly painted. Kate could feel Lidka's stare, but she refused to acknowledge her.

The driver parked, then opened the car door for them. He walked them to the front of the house and opened that door as well. No words were exchanged, and Kate felt like she was in a gangster movie from the days of Prohibition and Al Capone.

The entryway was tiled with marble, and an oversize oil painting of a woman holding a cat hung from the central wall. The house was silent, like it was afraid to breathe. Kate expected there to be a butler or someone to escort them through the house, but the hall was empty and Lidka marched straight in to the first room and sat on a spindly-legged chair.

Kate followed suit, sitting on the edge of her seat and trying not to faint. Traditional lace curtains framed each window, and the cheery fireplace made for a room far more cozier than she expected to find in the home of the notorious stepsister line.

They waited for ten minutes, listening to the ticking cuckoo clock. While Lidka first sat comfortably settled in her chair, minutes into the wait, she looked as nervous as Kate felt.

"That picture in there? With the cat? Malwinka hates

it. She keeps it to remind her that her favorite painting is missing, and to show anyone who comes into house that she has nothing of value for them to take."

Finally, they heard movement in the hall, and Lidka jumped out of her chair. Kate stood with her, wringing her hands.

A petite middle-aged woman in a flowered shift dress and solid high heels entered the room. A taller, younger woman wearing a maid's uniform and holding a tea set followed her.

Nothing unusual stood out about Malwinka. Kate may have been expecting some outward indicator to let her know if she was in danger or not, but there was nothing. Malwinka was plain in every way except the manner in which she carried herself. She held the posture of someone putting on airs. No, that wasn't it. She didn't seem false at all. She handled herself with the same grace as Princess Kolodenko.

Lidka rushed forward and awkwardly kissed Malwinka on one cheek, then the other, and back again. They spoke hushed words in Polish before Lidka motioned to Kate and introduced her.

Malwinka spoke in Polish, and Kate continued to pretend that she knew very little, waiting for Lidka to translate.

"She says, 'She is pleased to meet the new Keeper.'"

As much as she tried, Kate couldn't keep the surprise off her face. She didn't expect Malwinka to be so forthright, and now it was confirmed that Lidka knew more than she was letting on. Kate felt foolish for thinking she was keeping anything a secret when they all seemed to be one step ahead of her.

Lidka explained, "There is no other explanation for how you, an American and so far removed from our world, would know about Kopciuszek. I am closer and I only found out recently. You must be Keeper. The Kolodenkos speak so carefully. Here you can speak plainly."

"Then she knows why I am here. Can you ask her if she has the shoes?"

Malwinka answered, followed quickly by Lidka's translation. "Tea first."

Kate's stomach was filled with butterflies. She didn't know if she could eat anything on the tray the maid brought out, but she took a sampling of cheese and black rye bread along with her tea.

While they made small talk, Kate sensed Malwinka sizing her up. The woman had keen eyes that focused in on Kate's amber necklace. Self-consciously, Kate tucked it under her blouse.

Malwinka smiled at Kate's discomfiture.

Once the tea dishes were removed, Malwinka's look grew serious and she spoke.

Lidka translated what Kate had already understood. "During the war, we buried the shoes to keep them safe. When people will steal your last spoon, you take care with your treasures. You will see one shoe now."

Malwinka snapped her fingers. The maid scurried over with a wooden shoe box, and after receiving a cool look, retreated to the wall.

With a dramatic flare, Malwinka lifted the hinge.

Collectively, everyone in the room leaned in for a closer look. Even cool Lidka rose off her seat to see the shoe. It was a single glass slipper nestled in a bed of blue silk.

Kate stood so she could get closer.

The diamonds sparkled the way ripples on a lake reflect the sun. *Clear diamonds. Not blue.* It was hard for Kate to hide her disappointment. All this time she had thought Princess Kolodenko had been wrong about the color of the shoes. She was sure there was a connection to her dad with the blue diamond. *Now what are the blue diamonds?*

"Only one?" she asked in English, holding up a single finger.

Malwinka spoke and Lidka translated. "She says you only need one. And she would like to know what you think the shoe will do."

"I was hoping she could tell me."

Lidka translated. "Malwinka's family has had them for years, but the shoes have never done anything for them. They tested out their powers to reunite loved ones, but nothing has ever worked. They tried wearing them and hoping for a pull toward the missing person. They tried one person hiding with one shoe, and another trying to use the other to find it. Nothing. She would like to hear your theories on it, and if you have a good one, will let you test it out to see if you can find your papa."

Kate could feel her necklace warming in response to the shoe. It was authentic; they weren't trying to trick her. But there had to be a catch somewhere. It couldn't be this easy. "I was going to try those very things myself. What if it only works when someone is truly missing? In their tests, the other person was merely hiding, not truly separated. And if I know the story correctly, Kopciuszek and the prince not only were separated but were being kept apart."

Malwinka gestured for Kate to take the shoe.

Kate's initial disappointment had given way to renewed awe that she was looking at the famous glass slipper. Without hesitation, she reached out. The diamond shoe was cold to the touch. Impersonal. She thought it would feel more welcoming. She slipped out of her own shoe and put on Cinderella's glass slipper. Everyone held a breath, eyes fixed.

It was too small.

She waited with her toes tucked in as far as they would go, straining to feel any sort of twinge of magic. Any hint on which direction she should go. A feeling of where her dad was.

It could show up in the form of a dream tonight, the way the dress first invaded her thoughts. But there was always the fear—which she forced herself to pass over quickly— that the shoes only worked to find people who were alive.

She felt her face flush. They were all staring at her so intently but nothing was happening. She gave a nervous laugh and there was a release in the room. Lidka and Malwinka both let out a breath, and then Malwinka began speaking.

"We are to stay here and see what happens. You may keep the shoe with you to see what you can learn," Lidka translated.

TWENTY-NINE

The girls went upstairs to a sparsely decorated bedroom. There were two iron twin beds and a plain dresser between them. Lidka dropped her bags on one bed and indicated that Kate could have the other. So, they would be sharing a room. All the better for Lidka to keep an eye on her, Kate was sure.

Lidka brushed back the lace curtain on the window and looked down. "Does your mama hang lace on all her windows?" she asked.

"Yes."

"We Poles like our lace," she said, making a face and turning from the window. "During the war, as soon as a house was deserted, neighbors would come to take what they wanted. Then the Soviets, then the Germans, and then the Soviets again. As you can imagine, anything of value was stolen, even lightbulbs, and in some cases the floorboards. Though those were likely burned for fuel in the cold winter."

"That's terrible," Kate said.

Lidka laughed. "That is war. We were all trying to survive. If the invaders were going to take it anyway, why not should the people who live here take it first? People were borrowing items until they had to give them up."

Kate thought of Floyd. "But now the artwork, at least, is being sent home."

"From Western powers, yes. Not from East. Art recovered by Soviets is going to their museums and private collections. It is their retribution."

"Aren't they trying to find the owners?"

"Why should they? Art belongs to the people. In the war, it was people who suffered greatly. This is a small consolation for them. To make them feel like they got something out of such a bitter war."

"They might have taken Malwinka's favorite painting to a museum in Russia." Kate tried to prod her, to test if she really thought the art shouldn't go back to the owners.

"They might." Her face was stoic.

Kate held up the shoe. "Had you ever seen this before?"

Lidka looked like she was afraid to touch it. "No. It was one of those secrets I was not told."

"How are you related to Malwinka?"

"I am closer to Ludmilla by blood than I am Malwinka. Malwinka is another distant cousin. She was friendly with my mother, so felt some obligation to me during the war. She tried to get me to leave Poland sooner, to find farm work so I would have food."

"So, she is a good woman?" *The Burgosov in jail implied otherwise.*

Lidka stood and pushed back the lace curtains on the window. "She is like any other woman. She does what she must to survive. Good or bad depends on circumstances."

"And these circumstances?" Kate asked.

Lidka shrugged. "You will find out and then you can tell me."

An unseen weight pressed in on Kate, and she found it hard to breathe. She moved toward the window. The room was too small, and she was tired of Lidka. She longed to return to the open gardens at the villa and moonlit rendezvous with Johnny.

"Does this window open?" she asked. She pushed up and the window jerked open. It was sticky, like paint had gotten into the sliders. The sweet honey-lime scent of the waning linden blossoms wafted in. She leaned forward, taking in big gulps, and reminded herself that as long as she controlled the dress, she had the upper hand. She was sure Malwinka wouldn't harm her because she was the Keeper. She might bluster and threaten, but ultimately, not harm.

Lidka lowered the window. "Not so far, you don't want to fall out." She stepped back. "You are closer to Malwinka's lineage," Lidka continued. "Your *dziadek* was related somehow. You would have to ask someone to draw family tree."

Kate had only thought a little about the implications of her being a Burgosov. To think she was related to

Malwinka—it was an idea she was still getting used to. But her grandparents had left Poland. Neither one of them wanted anything to do with their families, the Burgosovs or the Keeper line.

"Can you do anything with the shoe?" Lidka asked. "Is there something you say or something you do to it? I can understand if you did not want to make it work in front of Malwinka, but you can go ahead now while no one is watching."

Kate snorted. "*You're* watching. But really, it's not an act. I don't know what to do. Aunt Elsie had never seen the shoes herself, and if there was a magic word or something, she never told me. I think I'll need to take it back to Italy. We could start at that building where the boy found the dog tags. Will she let me?"

Lidka ignored her suggestion about Italy. "What about Fyodora? She spoke with you before we left. How did she instruct?"

"She said nothing about how to use the shoes, only that she wanted me to be nice to you."

Lidka frowned, and Kate couldn't decide what that frown meant. Was she disappointed that they knew nothing, or that Princess Kolodenko was focused on Lidka?

"Sleep with the shoe under your pillow and see if you dream about place where papa is."

"Where is the bathroom?" Kate asked. She needed a moment alone to process.

"Down hall, on left."

"Thanks." Kate started in that direction, still holding the shoe, but remembered her bags left unattended. She came back to the room and Lidka smiled at her. She was standing in the middle of the room, closer to Kate's bed. "Excuse me," Kate said, slipping past and grabbing her bags.

After closing the bathroom door, she locked it. At last, she was alone with the shoe.

She examined every inch of it, trying to come to terms with the fact that this was the famous glass slipper. The high-heeled shoe appeared delicate, yet with all those diamonds nestled close together, it felt solid. The diamonds dazzled as if they had their own energy source and didn't need to reflect any light to make them shine so beautifully. No wonder people described Cinderella as stepping on stars as she danced.

She tried it on again, cramming her foot in as far as it would go. The shoe was hard and unrelenting. Well, according to legend, it would only fit the original Cinderella.

She sat down on the edge of the tub to think and the rug slipped, revealing a tiled mosaic on the floor. A shield with an eagle, a horseman, and a crown. The Kolodenko family crest. Kate sucked in a breath. There was only one reason she could think that the crest would be on the floor—this residence used to belong to the Kolodenkos. This was one of the buildings taken from them after the war. No wonder Lidka didn't want to tell them what town she was taking Kate to. Giving her the benefit of the doubt, Kate could imagine Lidka protecting the Kolodenkos by not letting them know who was now living in their old home.

There was a knock on the door. "You okay?" Lidka. *So much for breathing room.*

"Yes. Fine." She opened the door. "I noticed this crest here, in the tile."

"There is another in the dining room, and another in the sitting room. You must have missed it." Lidka crossed her arms and waited.

"Do the Kolodenkos know what has happened to their house?"

Lidka leaned against the doorframe. She looked away. "I have not told them. They know the state has taken much of their property and shared it with others."

"And that doesn't bother you?"

Lidka pushed off the frame and set her shoulders. "Why should it? How many homes does a family need when some of us have none?"

Kate shook her head. "I don't know that you'd feel the same way if roles were reversed."

Lidka shrugged. "Are you feeling things with that shoe?"

It was Kate's turn to shrug. She still wasn't sensing anything. "What if we need someone from the direct line of Kopciuszek to make it work? What if we need Nessa?" *What if I can't do it?*

"It must be you, and you need to figure it out quickly. Malwinka is patient, but she will not wait forever."

⤳ THIRTY ⤳

When the answers didn't come in a dream, Kate began to panic. After three days with the shoe, she had no answers and no clues on how to find those answers.

The prospect of having come so far and risking so much ate at her insides. She could still see the slump of Johnny's shoulders as he blended into the crowd. She missed him. More than when he went away to boot camp. She had taken for granted that he was always there to listen to her problems and help her figure things out. She took a deep breath. If nothing else came of this trip, she'd at least learned how important he had become to her.

And then there was Malwinka. It seemed as if she assumed Kate wasn't trying very hard because she didn't trust the Burgosovs. That was half true. She didn't fully trust them, but she was trying. If only Aunt Elsie could have come with her. Together they'd be able to work out what to do. Even Nessa might have been a help. She knew even less than Kate, but she, at least, was eager to test things out.

Each morning, Malwinka asked her if she'd discovered the secret of the shoes. She hadn't. How long would Malwinka let it go on before she pronounced the experiment a failure and asked for the shoe back?

All throughout breakfast on the fourth day, Kate worked up her courage. The others—the maid who was really Malwinka's granddaughter, and the driver, who was Malwinka's son, chatted in Polish, leaving her out of the conversation. They'd already deemed her a failure and not worth their effort to talk to. Kate was ready to pack up and go home. She'd tried, but Princess Kolodenko was right. The shoes would not help.

There was only one other thing she wanted to try. "What if my dad is too far away in Italy for the shoe to work? May we take it back with us?"

Malwinka's smile disappeared. "You are forbidden to take the shoe to the Kolodenkos."

Everyone stared at Kate as Lidka translated. She could feel the blood rush to her face under the scrutiny. As accommodating as Malwinka had been, she was still from the feuding line of stepsisters. Of course she would not give up any gains she had made.

"I'm also wondering if the shoes only find separated sweethearts, like Kopciuszek and the prince." *And Johnny and me.* She swallowed self-consciously.

Malwinka leaned forward at the name Kopciuszek and

demanded a translation. After Lidka explained, Malwinka shook her head. "*Nie*. Not only young lovers. Kopciuszek gave the shoes to Nadzia the day our family advanced on the kingdom to rid ourselves of the Kolodenkos. Princess and servant used them to find each other many years later."

Lidka piped up. "I know what you are thinking. Your boyfriend is not lost from you. He knows where you are. The shoe will not reunite you."

Kate hoped Lidka was right, but she had her doubts. Her stomach churned with nerves. She was running out of time and couldn't risk a wild rabbit trail. Each passing day brought her closer to their return trip to America.

"Let me know when you have some useful information for me," she said. Even if Kate didn't know the language, she would have gotten the idea from Malwinka's tone. Kate kept her gaze on her plate and finished eating without looking up.

After the table was cleared away, Malwinka stood. "Come, girls. I am going to make some errands that will take us out into the country." Her voice was light, as if she'd already forgotten the tension at the beginning of the meal. "Bring the shoe in your bag, Kate. If it is away from so many people who have lost loved ones, it might work better. The city might be too loud for it."

Kate was eager to get out and see more of Poland. Babcia tried to pretend she had left it all behind, but despite her protestations, she had taught Kate her heritage. She had taught Kate to love the land.

The burly driver was waiting outside for them. He assisted Malwinka into the backseat, then stepped away to allow the girls in. Kate held back, letting Lidka go next. She didn't want to sit by Malwinka, the warnings of the Burgosov still ringing in her ears. Malwinka was being nice, because she wanted something from Kate. Would she stay this nice if Kate couldn't deliver? If she'd learned anything from this family, it was that everyone was hiding secrets.

The rain and cloudy skies that had hovered for days had finally gone away, and the sun had called everyone, it seemed, out of doors. They drove through town on cobbled streets. After passing several buildings labeled *bar mleczny*, Kate asked, "What are those?"

"Milk bar," Lidka said. "Is like cafeteria for the people. The factory workers, they eat for free. For others, is cheap food. Dairy food like milk, yogurt. The government does this new idea for health of the people."

Kate wondered what Nessa would think of a government-run milk bar.

They continued on to the outskirts of town where women were hanging out the wash, past several abandoned buildings, and then through barren fields. Lidka leaned over and pointed. "That used to be village." There was nothing but open meadow and tall weeds. "You have never seen anything like that in America. Sometimes a hatred is so much that a people is wiped out."

Lidka always had to point out the worst in a situation.

The car took them through places that hadn't been touched since the war. Town after town destroyed, with no one living there anymore. No reconstruction. She'd heard of these places, the bombed-out buildings described as skeletons, but to her they were like ghosts. Gray spindles, standing monuments to the lives buried in the rubble or burned to ash in the fires.

They arrived at a farm and Malwinka told the girls to stay in the car while she talked to the farm wife. The woman came out, wringing her hands, and invited Malwinka in. The driver went and stood by the falling-down porch steps.

"What is she doing?" Kate asked.

"Watch." There was pride in Lidka's voice.

There was shouting, then silence. Malwinka opened the door, a cloth-wrapped bundle in her hands, and not bothering to close the door, marched back to the car. The driver opened the trunk, and Kate could feel something land in the back.

"How did it go?" Lidka asked.

"It is done," was the answer.

This strange process was repeated several times, at several different farmhouses. Sometimes Malwinka would take in a package, and other times, carry one out.

"This is last stop. Would you girls like to come with me?"

After watching the process for so long, Kate was intrigued and eager to see what happened behind closed doors. This house looked in worse repair than the others they'd been to as it still bore the scars of the war. A black smudge on the ground a few feet away could have been a barn that had burned down. The only animals they seemed to have were a skinny goat penned in a tiny enclosure, and two chickens meandering the yard. Three pairs of little eyes watched from behind a window frame missing its glass. Kate's heart welled up with pity. She'd never seen such poverty.

Malwinka carried a small package, and when she knocked on the door, one of the little faces from the window came to the door and timidly opened it.

"Your mama, how is she?" Malwinka asked.

The little one pointed inside and let them enter. Malwinka sat by the woman's bedside and took her hand. She spoke quiet words while Lidka made faces at the children. Kate figured she was trying to scare them off, but the kids found the expressions funny and it only attracted them to her more. Kate's attention was divided. She didn't know which Burgosov was more fascinating to her at this moment. She'd never considered Malwinka to be kind before. She didn't realize how suspicious she'd been, always on the lookout for a trick.

When Malwinka opened the package to reveal a music box, the woman on the bed burst into tears. Her frail hands reached up to take the box, and she called her young ones to her. She opened the box and a Chopin sonata filled the room. In such a setting it was both strikingly beautiful and sad at the same time.

As they left, Malwinka spoke in halted English. "I want you to see acts I do." She continued in Polish for Lidka to translate. "The people here do what I say. I work to restore the peace. Now you trust me?"

Kate nodded, although trust wasn't exactly what she would call it. Lack of fear, maybe.

Lidka pulled her arm and whispered. "She sets things right. People are afraid of her. She can make people return what does not belong to them. Same as with Kolodenkos."

It was late when they got back to the house. The timid maid was waiting in the foyer to see if anyone wanted a warm milk before bed. Lidka gave her a withering look before marching past her and up the stairs. Kate would have followed Lidka if it weren't for the hurt look on the maid's face. She nodded and followed the young woman into the kitchen.

The maid slammed a pot onto the stove. Then she marched to the icebox and grabbed a bottle of milk. Kate slid onto a chair at the table, wishing she had followed Lidka. Something had angered this woman, more than just a snide look from Lidka. After she sloshed a mug in front of Kate, she dumped the pot in the sink and marched out of the room.

Kate touched the mug and drew her hand back. *Well, what in the world?* She'd have to wait for it to cool. She stood and paced the room, examining the Kolodenkos' former home. The kitchen was tiled in white, as was the counter. The cupboards, also white, were carved with roses. The curtains over the window provided a bright splash of color with their red flower print. As Kate circled the room, she noticed a door at the far end and wondered if it led to a pantry. She went to open it when she heard low voices. It must be a servant's passage, not a food pantry. The maid's angry voice, followed by Malwinka's calm one, came through the door.

"It's not working," the maid said.

"Did you put the glass slipper in the same room?" Malwinka answered. "Where the father can't find it?"

"I'm not an idiot. But everyone is getting restless. They're wondering if we should do away with him. Even if the daughter does find him, then what? We let them go?"

Kate's ears began to burn.

"Be patient," Malwinka said. "She's hardly had time. We've had the shoes for years; she has had only days."

"But he needs a doctor before it's too late. We can't keep him like this much longer."

As realization sank in, Kate's legs went limp. She grabbed for the counter to steady herself. They were talking about her dad. They had him, and he was in trouble.

"Everyone will be patient," Malwinka said. "We've worked too hard to quit now."

"You need to talk to them, then. I'm not going back there. I'm done. I don't want to be a part of this anymore."

"Fine. If this is the way you talk to your grandmother,

then you are truly done. Leave. Tonight. May I never see your face again."

The maid cried out, "But I have no where to go."

"There is no place here for you. I only kept you this long for your father's sake. No more."

There was a sound of a door shutting, followed by a sharp sob.

Kate grabbed the mug of milk and drained it down the sink. She needed to get up to her room before she saw either Malwinka or the maid. As Babcia used to say, *fear has big eyes,* and she needed to pull herself together. Uncle Adalbert was right: Malwinka had finally revealed her true nature.

Kate had to figure out how to make the shoes work— and fast—before it was too late.

THIRTY-ONE

Kate heard every sound in the house, from an irregular water drip somewhere near the back of the building, to the creaking, settling noises caused by a shift in winds, to Lidka rolling over in her sleep.

Dad is alive.

Tears of joy soaked into her pillow. This changed everything. Before, she was merely hoping, but now she knew for sure and had a way to find him. Even if she couldn't get the shoes to do anything, Malwinka knew where he was.

And he needs a doctor.

Thoughts of Malwinka twisted up her stomach. What was this woman's game? Not only were these Burgosovs selfish and devious, they were malicious. She had to get away from them, but they were the direct link to Dad. She could escape tonight and go to the police, but according to Lidka, Malwinka had some kind of power over them. She would have to get farther away, but then how would she ever find her dad?

She was trapped. The only way out was to give them what they wanted. She had to make the shoes work. She reviewed everything she knew about the Cinderella story. Stories always had a glimmer of truth in them, even if they got some details wrong. With dismay, she realized she didn't know that many details of the true Kopciuszek story. There were two versions she'd read in fairy-tale books. One where Cinderella's mother died and a tree planted over her grave gave Cinderella the gifts of the dresses. And the other where there was a fairy godmother who took care of the details.

Now, what did either of those stories have to say about the glass slipper? Something about Cinderella having to leave by midnight and the magical items returning to the objects they were created from. She knew that the dresses didn't disappear, so that part of the story had changed with the retelling.

One shoe was left behind when Cinderella ran from the ball as the clock was striking midnight and her magical items began to transform. From what Elsie had told her, she already knew the prince, so why would he have her try on the shoe to learn who she was? He wouldn't. He would know her when he found her.

Malwinka had put the other shoe where her dad was. It was as if she was trying to replicate the scenario where one shoe was left behind for the prince to find, and the other remained with Kopciuszek. So if she could find the shoe, she could find Dad.

"Where is your partner?" she whispered to the shoe.

There was a flash. A glimmer. Kate sat up in bed and looked out the window. It was as if a flashlight had swept past the window and caught the facets cut into the shoe. She slipped out of bed and padded across the cold floor. The yard was dark, darker still near the linden trees where someone could hide and watch. She tried to open the window, but it wouldn't budge. She pushed harder, remembering how sticky the sliders were when she opened it last, but she couldn't do it. Then she noticed. It had been nailed shut.

Shaking, she backed away from the window and returned to her warm bed, clutching the shoe. She curled into a ball as the gravity of the situation filled her. She was a prisoner, too. Now, what did that make Lidka? Was she innocent or was she Kate's personal guard?

Thoughts tumbled and tumbled as she raced for a way out. But as the night wore on, her body relaxed as it grew used to the night sounds of the house, and she began to get sleepy. Her thoughts loosened and she started to let go when an idea floating on the edges of her mind drifted into center. She blinked herself awake and pulled out the shoe again.

"Where is your partner?" she asked it. *Flash*. It wasn't an outside source causing the sparkle.

It was the shoe itself.

It had responded to her question. She asked it again. *Flash*.

"What are you doing?" a groggy Lidka asked.

"Nothing. Sorry. Go back to sleep." She stuffed the shoe under the quilt.

When Lidka's breathing relaxed into a regular deep in-and-out, Kate dove under the covers with the shoe. "Where is your partner?" The flash was slow this time, the light sparkling from toe to heel. She flipped the shoe over and tried again. "Where is your partner?" The shoe answered, this time with the light sliding across the shoe, from side to side. Kate experimented a few more times, trying to decipher if the shoe was giving her Morse code. It wasn't. Finally, she realized the line of light remained the same, no matter what angle she held the shoe. Kate covered her mouth to stifle a laugh. The shoe was like a compass. In the same way a compass needle pointed north, the light pointed in one direction. When she turned the shoe to match the light, it glided down from heel to toe, showing her the direction to go. That must be how it worked. Clever, that fairy godmother.

If Kate could sneak out tonight, she could find her dad and rescue him. She knew he wasn't in the house because the maid had to go somewhere she didn't want to go. But if Kate did leave, the first place Malwinka would look would be where they were holding her dad. She would be no more ahead than she was now. No, the better play would be to continue to pretend she didn't know they had her dad. She'd show them how the shoe worked, and then after she and her dad were reunited, together they would escape. If Johnny was able to get to her brother in Germany, and if the Kolodenkos told him the change in location, help might already be on the way. And if all that worked out, she had no idea how they would meet up. *That's a lot of ifs.*

She'd take it one step at a time. First, her dad.

Gustaw was wearing an apron the next morning at breakfast. There was no mention of where the maid was, and Kate realized she didn't even know the young woman's name. If Gustaw was upset with Malwinka over how his daughter was treated, he wasn't letting it show as he dished out scrambled eggs.

Malwinka didn't ask about the shoe. Maybe she was upset over last night, or maybe she was tired of Kate giving the same answer. But Lidka noticed something had changed.

"You are different, why?" She narrowed her eyes. "You have secret?"

Malwinka looked up from stirring her tea, realization dawning. "You have done it?"

Kate forced herself to look at Malwinka with steady eyes. "The shoe lights up, pointing in one direction. I think I should follow it and see what happens."

Lidka translated. She and Malwinka shared a smile.

How much does Lidka know?

"Show me," Malwinka said.

"It's up in my room."

"I will get Gustaw to ready the car. Pack your bags, girls," she called over her shoulder as she left the room.

"Why do we need to pack our bags?" Kate asked, growing nervous. She thought her dad might be in Krakow, somewhere close where they could keep an eye on him. Lidka looked up sharply at Kate's quick answer to Malwinka, and Kate realized her mistake. Hopefully Lidka would think Kate was naturally picking up new Polish words.

"The shoe may lead us far away. Is best to be prepared," Lidka said.

Later, standing in the entryway with her bag at her feet, Kate sheepishly took out the shoe. Last night, alone in the dark, talking to the shoe felt natural. But now in the daylight in front of the Burgosovs, it seemed off. Her instincts were to take the shoe and run, but she still needed help getting around Poland. When the time came, she'd need to be ready to outsmart Malwinka.

"Where is your partner?" she asked the shoe in Polish. A flash.

Malwinka grabbed the shoe out of Kate's hand. "How did you know to speak to it?" she asked.

Lidka waited, hand on hip, instead of translating.

"Well?" Kate asked.

Lidka rolled her eyes and said in English, "How did you know to speak to it?"

"I didn't. I asked in frustration last night. Remember, you taught me the Polish word for partner. The flash is brighter when it's dark."

Malwinka repeated the phrase. No flash. She said it again, and when nothing happened, shoved it back into Kate's hands. Jaw set, she marched them outside.

"Should you not—"

Malwinka raised her hand, interrupting Lidka. "What I do is my business. You do not have to worry about me." She patted Lidka's cheek. Lidka turned away, looking annoyed.

Kate felt a twinge of relief to see that Lidka and Malwinka weren't as unified as they seemed. If Kate needed her support, Lidka might take her side.

⤳ THIRTY-TWO ⤳

The shoe pointed them south out of town. The driver couldn't always go in the exact direction the shoe was indicating, but like using a compass, it would get them there eventually. Kate played along, even though it felt silly and a waste of time. She had to hide the fact that she was onto them so she would have an advantage.

It was dark now, but Kate insisted they continue. "It's easier to see the shoe at night," she explained, and no one questioned her.

Now they were driving up into the mountains, around curvy roads with sharp drop-offs, and she'd seen Gustaw's head nod a few times as if he were getting tired. Eventually, the drone of the car put her under, and when she awoke, she was alone in the car, which was parked in front of a hotel. In the dark, she could make out Malwinka speaking to Gustaw, illuminated by light coming from an open door. There was no sign of Lidka. As Kate pushed herself up from her slouched position, the door opened, and Lidka said, "Tonight we sleep here."

"Where are we?"

"Zakopane in the Tatra Mountains."

"Do you think we're close?" Kate swung her legs out of the car.

Lidka looked at her curiously. "Maybe."

"No, we have to keep going," Kate said, standing and rubbing her eyes. The sooner they got to him, the sooner the game would be over and he could get the medical help he needed.

"Ask the shoe," Lidka said, yawning.

"Where is your partner?" Kate asked. The shoe flashed in the direction of the mountain.

"See? The mountain. We're out of road. We have to wait until light."

Breakfast was a lavish affair in the dining room. They were the only guests, but you couldn't tell based on the spread laid out before them. The owner hovered like a hummingbird, flitting here and there around Malwinka, as if afraid to leave any comfort to chance.

When they entered the foyer, backpacks were lined up and waiting for them by the door.

"What is this?" Kate asked.

"Like I said, we cannot go by car," Lidka said. "The

shoe is pointing into mountains where is no road. We have gone far as we can."

Kate eyed the equipment skeptically. The only hiking she'd ever done was climbing the stairs between floors at the department store. "How steep are these mountains?" Her oxford shoes would be ruined by the end of it all. "Is there a first aid kit in there?" she asked. "With bandages and medicine?" What would her dad need?

Lidka laughed as she slung a pack on her back. "Do not have worries. If Malwinka can hike it, so can you."

Kate glanced to see if Malwinka had heard, but she was talking to the driver.

"Have a lovely hike," said the owner of the hotel. "I've never gone up myself, but my guests say the views are spectacular."

The hotelier was correct. The mountains were beautiful. Being a city girl, Kate wasn't used to such natural majesty. Sure, the beach and the ocean were lovely, especially during a sunset, but there was something about a mountain towering over you to put you in your place, to make you feel small, to give you perspective. Just like Johnny had said when they were looking at the moon and the stars.

Oh, Johnny. What would he say if he knew the predicament I've gotten myself into? He'd been nothing but loyal to her, keeping her best interests in mind. He wanted her to do whatever she needed to find her dad, even if he had to let her go. She hoped he'd gotten to Germany safely and sent word back to Italy. But even if he came to look for her, he wouldn't think to search in the mountains.

It had been hours since they'd seen the last hiker, and the sun had already disappeared behind the tall peaks, threatening to take away the last of their light. She snacked on the nuts from her bag as she contemplated her sore muscles. "Does this trail end at another town?" she asked, eyeing the dirt path dubiously. They'd left the main trail around noon and she was being generous calling the path they were on a trail at all. "It's getting late."

"No. There are no more towns," Lidka said. "But there are caves."

They're keeping my dad in a cave? A gust of wind blew through, and she shivered.

Gustaw muttered something, and Malwinka laughed.

Lidka explained. "He says our family has been using the caves for centuries. These were the bandit hideaways. Have you heard the famous name Janosik?"

Kate shook her head.

"He was like Robin Hood. He would steal from rich, but he would share."

"Let me guess. He was a distant cousin?"

Lidka grinned her answer. "He was a highland hero until he was killed. Or, maybe more so after he was killed. The men dance the *zbójnicki* in his honor."

Gustaw put down his pack at a somewhat flat spot. He called out in loud Polish, "Hey boys, let's dance the *zbójnicki*." Then proceeded to prance in a circle. Lidka clapped to provide him the music. He started jumping these wild, high-knee jumps that made Kate think he might fall off the edge or twist an ankle if he wasn't careful. But he smiled and laughed, cracking his stoic face and looking like a regular guy instead of Malwinka's bodyguard.

"Enough," Malwinka called. "It gets dark." She waited for Gustaw to put on his pack and take the lead.

"We're really going to sleep in a cave?" Kate asked Lidka.

"Is not so bad," she said. "We have blankets in Gustaw's pack, and there are warm sweaters in our bags."

"Are you always this prepared when you follow the shoe?"

Lidka, misunderstanding Kate's sarcasm, looked at her funny. "We have never followed the shoe before."

Did they really think she was so naive? Hopefully, that meant they missed all the branches she snapped once they got off the main trail. She'd marked their path as best she could without causing too much attention to fall on her.

Gustaw lit a lantern, and then ducked into the mountainside, followed by Malwinka.

Her heart skipped a beat. *Maybe Dad is in this cave.* "Where is your partner?" she asked the shoe. It glimmered in the direction away from the cave. *Oh.* "Shouldn't we keep going?" It was so frustrating to not know her dad's condition. He could have an infection and need that new penicillin that had saved so many soldiers during the war. All they had were basic bandages. He could even slip into a coma or die while they were camping overnight.

"We need sleep," Lidka said. "Tomorrow we start fresh."

"Is the cave safe?"

"Safe for now," Lidka said. "Watch your head and do what you're told."

"What do you mean?"

"Nothing," she said as Malwinka returned, effectively cutting off their conversation.

They quickly set up camp on the dirt floor. Kate was glad for the extra sweater in her bag and the warm wool blanket she was handed. If they were worried about her keeping warm, they still wanted something from her, which meant she wasn't in immediate danger. But was her father? They could have him in another cave somewhere, barely protected from the elements. If he were close to death, a cold night like this could do him in. She wouldn't be surprised if they awoke to frost on the ground.

Though she tried to stay awake to listen in on any more conversations, her body didn't seem to care she was sleeping on a cold, hard floor. As her muscles melted into the rock, content to have stopped climbing, she drifted to sleep.

She bolted up to the smell of fire and took in her surroundings. She was in a large cave. On the side of a tall mountain. And Gustaw, in his thick plaid shirt, was looking like a lumberjack cooking breakfast. He was roasting some kind of animal over the fire, but Kate didn't ask what it was. It would taste better if she didn't know. By the side of the fire he was cooking some of the wild garlic that grew under the trees. When she joined him, he handed her a cup of hot tea. She wrapped her cold fingers around the mug and sipped. After his dancing yesterday, she wasn't as intimidated by him as before.

This morning, with a clear head, she analyzed her situation while the others finished eating and packing up. She glanced at Lidka as she folded her blanket. They acted so helpful to her, yet they were the ones holding her dad hostage.

As they got in hiking order, this time with Malwinka leading the way, Kate tried to make conversation with Lidka. After receiving several grunts for answers, she gave up. She'd wait until the sun warmed Lidka's frosty edges before trying again. She wanted to find out how deep she was involved in this. The Kolodenkos would be heartbroken again if Lidka betrayed them.

They rounded a corner, and in the distance a castle rose out of the ground like it was a part of the rock itself. The early morning sun shone, catching the monument in a spotlight against the deep green pines. The castle had multiple turrets, crowned with a cross on the tallest peak. Its hidden setting added a fairy-tale-like quality to it, as if Kate had turned a page in a storybook and there it was.

"What is that?" she exclaimed, digging out Mr. G's camera.

"The castle," Lidka said, finally speaking. "Kopciu-szek's."

Kate sucked in a breath. So that's where they were going. Cinderella's real castle was maybe an hour's hike in front of her. She snapped a picture before directing her attention to Malwinka, feeling bold at the revelation. "You knew the shoe was pointing this way. How?"

"Easy. There is nothing else here."

"Oh." Kate lapsed into silence as they marched on with renewed energy. Her attempt at leaving a trail of bread crumbs would have to suffice to get her and her father back down the mountain in the right direction.

As they got closer, it became evident that the castle had been abandoned to the elements for many years. The outer wall had been breached in several places, and the stones were now covered in green moss. It was in worse shape than the abandoned castle in Italy. Piles of rotting timber indicated where the stables might have been, and the courtyard itself was a mass of weeds and wildflowers. They climbed the steps up to the front door, and Kate paused. The Kolodenko crest was etched into the lintel above the door. "This really was her castle," she whispered.

Malwinka nodded. "Kopciuszek moved in after she married the prince." She snorted. "But they didn't stay long."

Kate looked down the valley. "The village is gone, too. Has another taken its place farther down?" She needed to know how far away the closest help was.

"*Nie*," Lidka answered. "No one comes this far up mountains. People not like this place. It gives the bad feelings."

The empty valley reminded her of the razed village Lidka had pointed out earlier. It struck her that so much could change over time. Here was evidence of a once-strong power, and all that was left of it now was a crumbling stone building. "But the land is so pretty." She pictured Cinderella looking out a window surveying this valley with its tall mountains bordering the rolling green meadow, the wildflowers, the distant forests. Kate tried to imagine fairy-tale cottages and lanes and people milling about selling their wares.

Gustaw stepped out and signaled for them to come in. He had gone through the main rooms lighting wall sconces. *And no doubt alerting those within.* The entryway was a narrow hall with open doorways on either side.

Once in the castle, Kate, with a flutter in her chest, asked the shoe again. "Where is your partner?"

This time when the shoe flashed, all the light centered on the bottom of the shoe. Her heart caught in her throat. He was so close, underneath them.

"This way," Malwinka said, taking a torch off the wall and then continuing down the long hall.

"Who owns this castle now?" Kate asked. She ran her hand along the polished marble wall.

"It is state-owned," Malwinka said through Lidka's translating. "But once upon a time, the Burgosovs owned it."

"I thought it was Kopciuszek's castle?"

"Once upon a time," Malwinka said, "it was. Our ancestors fought terribly over it. Now it belongs to the people."

Whereas Lidka used the phrase "belongs to the people" with a touch of reverence, Malwinka said it with irony? Disgust?

Malwinka led them past several rooms, down a staircase, and along another corridor, until Kate was completely lost. She had been trying to create a map in her head, but there was too much to remember, and many of the rooms and corridors looked the same, empty of furnishings, decorations, life. There wasn't even a nest of field mice in any of the rooms she peered into.

They went down another level, where it was even darker and colder and the stone walls were no longer polished marble. The light from the flickering torch cast strange shadows, and Kate was actually glad Gustaw was with them. Finally, Malwinka stopped at an end room that had a small square cut out in the door. She stretched up on her toes to look in.

"Give me the shoe." She held out her hand.

"Why? What if I still need it?" Kate said, gripping it tight.

Malwinka wrenched it from Kate's hand, leaving behind a burning sensation.

Kate's palms began to sweat, despite the cold air. It was either Dad on the other side of the door or the Burgosov accomplices. And if it were Dad, what condition would she find him in? Would he still be alive? Her senses were on alert.

Malwinka took out a key, swung the door wide, and invited Kate to look in.

"Dad?" she called out tentatively.

THIRTY-THREE

It was him. His hair was a little thinner. His cheeks were hollow. His clothes were not his. But it was him. He was alive.

Kate called again, louder. "Dad?"

Even though finding him was exactly what she'd hoped for, it seemed impossible that she was staring at him now. A lump formed in her throat, and she swallowed.

Sitting at a rough-hewn table, wearing someone else's too-big khaki pants and shirt, he tilted his head as if trying to make sense of what he was hearing. Of course, seeing Kate in Poland would be one of the last things he would expect.

"Dad!" she called out louder, her voice bouncing off the stones. Forgetting everything else, she ran for him. "It's me, Kate."

He was standing before she reached him. "Is it really you?"

She hugged him tight, but when he hugged her back,

his arms were loose like a child's, even though she suspected he was squeezing her as tight as he could.

Then he touched her face as if unbelieving.

"Don't I still look like me?" she asked, laughing. She'd done it. She'd found her dad. "Are you okay? Let's get you out of here." She examined him for signs of illness. He looked like he was well. There were dark circles like bruises under his eyes, and his cheekbones were more defined than she remembered, but he was standing. He could use a shower with a good, strong soap. Maybe the maid had been exaggerating when she said he needed a doctor before it was too late.

"I don't understand. Why are you here?" His voice was raspy, unused.

"To find you. We thought you were dead, but we didn't know for sure, and then I had the chance to come to Italy to look for myself." She raised her hands. "It's going to take a while to explain, but first, let's get to a phone so we can call Mom."

As Kate said this, the door was slammed shut and locked.

She whirled at the sound. "No! No. No. No." She rushed to the door and turned the handle uselessly. She had been so caught up in seeing her dad she forgot to keep an eye on the others. She pounded. "Lidka! Open up." There was no answer.

When she turned around, her dad was tracing the edge of the rough-cut table with his fingers and fumbling for the wood stump where he had been sitting. She watched him for a moment, the way his eyes seemed vacant. She waved her hand and he didn't respond.

"Dad?"

"There is another stump here," he said. "Sit down and tell me everything. We have lots to talk about." His vacant eyes looked somewhat in her direction.

Kate remained standing. She needed to stay by the door so she would be ready when it opened. They couldn't be finished with her yet. She still had something they wanted. "Why did the maid say you needed a doctor?"

"There was an explosion. I was following a tip on a stolen painting, but the building hadn't been properly swept yet. I think I set off a bomb. The only thing left to heal is my eyesight. There was a doctor. At first. He said it might heal, but I'd need surgery that he couldn't do, and the sooner I got it, the better my chances."

"What?" Her knees felt weak. "Are you in any pain?" She searched his face for the truth.

He shifted in his seat. "I'm fine. But please, I want to know how you got here. Is your mom here, too? Floyd?"

"Just me. Mom's still home and Floyd is in Germany."

"Germany?"

"He is following in your footsteps, working as one of the Monuments Men. He's cataloging all the stolen artwork and finding the owners."

Waves of differing emotions crossed his face, one after the other. "I don't even know how long I've been here. At first, I was unconscious more than I was awake. It's all so jumbled." He rubbed his grizzled face like he was trying to wake up.

"You say the Burgosovs found you after the explosion?" She rattled the door handle once more. "They're keeping you here as a prisoner. Do you know why?" She was getting frightened that they wouldn't open the door. The conversation she overheard with the maid jutted into her thoughts. *Even if she does find him, then what? We let them go?*

"No, I haven't been with these people that long. As I said, I was hurt and unconscious for most of it. I remember waking up in a farmhouse. We had fresh milk. I was in so much pain when I came to, I went under again. Next memory I have is being in the back of a wagon. The jolting woke me up but knocked me out again. Gradually, I came to. Someone was helping me. They said they knew who I was, and they'd try to get me home soon."

"How could they know who you were when you didn't have your dog tags? A boy in Italy had them in his treasure box. He said he traded them with a boy who found them in the rubble."

Dad frowned and shook his head. "I don't know. It was all hazy. It seems I slept for weeks. And then I had to learn how to walk again. My legs were badly damaged." He rubbed his right knee. "I lost the lower part of this leg." He lifted his stained pant leg to reveal a prosthesis.

Kate held back a gasp. "You said someone was helping you. Do you know who?"

"I don't know. The doctor. I haven't seen him since I stabilized. I figured he got called away to patients worse off than me. Then one day, a few months ago, maybe, I woke up here." He cleared his throat. "More about me later. Why are you here?"

"To find you."

The corners of his mouth curled slightly. "I wish you hadn't. It appears now that we are both prisoners."

The word "prisoner" made Kate pound on the door again. "Lidka. Let us out!"

"You know these people?"

After pounding at the door a few more times, Kate sank back onto the seat opposite her dad. "It's a long story. It all started when Aunt Elsie and Uncle Adalbert showed up on our doorstep with an old steamer trunk." Kate searched the room for another exit. There was only the one door and one barred window up high on the wall. She stood on the stump to see if she could reach it. What she saw made her skin prickle. The matching shoe was hidden on the high windowsill. This must have been where the maid had put it. Malwinka had forgotten to ask for this shoe.

"Go on," Dad said. "Help me fill in the blanks."

How much of the story will he believe? She stretched for the shoe, her fingers barely able to grasp it and pull it down. She'd hide it so the Burgosovs wouldn't have a complete set. After what they'd done, she had no concerns about upsetting the peace Princess Kolodenko thought the families had formed.

She searched for a place to hide the glass slipper. "Aunt Elsie and Babcia grew up with a famous family—royalty from another time. During the recent war, they were separated, but Elsie had something of theirs, and they came to New York to get it back. They have a daughter close to my age, who invited me to come to Italy with them for the summer."

"Are we still in Italy?" Dad asked. "Based on the language I figured they'd moved me to Poland. Communication hasn't been easy. I can pick up a few words here and there that Babcia used to say."

"You guessed right. We're in Poland."

He pressed his hands on the table as if holding himself back.

"On our way to Italy, I met another girl, Lidka. She helped me follow the clues to a woman named Malwinka. And here you are."

He shook his head. "Those are some big dots to follow. I still don't know how you found me."

She stashed the shoe in a dark corner and covered it with a blanket. Not a great hiding place, but there was nowhere else, except her bag, and that seemed obvious. She grasped his hand. "It's complicated, but those are the highlights. The good news is it wasn't only me." She cleared her throat. "My, uh, boyfriend is also here somewhere. We were separated at the border, but he planned to come through Germany."

"A boyfriend, huh?" He smiled a little, the first evidence

of the teasing man she remembered. "I see we do have a lot to catch up on."

"Oh, you'll like him. He's . . . he's . . ." How to describe Johnny? "Reliable. And artistic, so you'll like that about him."

"Does he have a job?"

"Dad!"

"Well?"

"Yes, and he's going to art school in the fall."

Dad got up and walked to the wall. His gait had a decided limp. He stood under the window with the light warming his uplifted face. "I've missed so much. I pretend this window looks out over our street in New York. I think of you all, picture you sitting down for breakfast. Arguing over whose turn it is to do dishes. I'd love to be back in my classroom this fall." He made a noise like a laugh, but sad. "But now that I can't see, I won't be much use to my students."

A lump formed in Kate's throat. He sounded so unlike her dad. He sounded like he'd given up. "You won't know until we get you home and you see your doctor. Who knows what's causing the blindness. It could be fixed with a simple procedure."

Dad didn't say anything for the longest time. They had run out of words, even though they hadn't seen each other in so long. This wasn't how she expected the reunion to go.

"Does your mother know I'm alive?"

"The army sent us a letter saying you were missing, and then they told us you were presumed dead. They also sent your personal effects."

He turned slightly away from the window. "What was returned?"

"Not much. Your sketchbook with a surprise inside."

Now he turned around fully. "You found it?"

"Mom refused to open the box. So when Floyd sent me a telegram telling me to look for a diamond, I opened it. You had a good hiding spot. I almost missed it. What was the diamond for?"

"I was going to give it to Elsie when I got home. She could have sold it to pay for passage back to Poland."

So Floyd had the correct story after all. But what was it with all the blue diamonds? Elsie had acted like she knew exactly what the diamond was. And Princess Kolodenko had acted funny about it, too. There was still a mystery to uncover; Kate had to look harder. "You can give it to her yourself. I brought it with me." She opened her bag to take out her mini sewing kit.

"Shhh. They may be listening outside the door. We might need it as a bribe later."

Kate proceeded to pull the stitching out of her waist-band near the hidden diamond. No sense in her keeping two. She reached for his hand and put the diamond in it. "There you go. I can sew it into your shirt collar if you'd like. That way you'll have it to give to Elsie when you meet her."

"Going home is one hope I haven't given up on," he said.

"My hope now is that we don't give Mom a heart attack. Can you imagine her surprise?" Kate pushed back the thought that Dad might be the surprised one if Mom had started dating again.

Dad chuckled. "She'd faint if I just showed up and knocked on the door. 'Hi, Deb, what's for dinner?' We'd better call her first and ease her into the idea."

She laughed with him. It was good to see Dad's humor returning. "I also got the watercolor you sent me for my birthday. The one of the fairy-tale cottage."

"Did you like it? Such an interesting little place I stumbled across. The architecture made it so different from the other villas. How did Floyd know about the diamond?"

"He met one of your buddies, who told him about you getting the diamond from an old lady."

"She was a strange one. Didn't look like she had much, and I tried to refuse her, but she insisted I take it. We were in one of the piazzas and she was sitting all alone at a little table, mumbling things. Everyone avoided her. But she caught my eye and waved me over to her. I thought she might have some information for me. You never know who has a masterpiece hidden in their barn."

Kate's mouth went dry. *Of course. Threads are linked.*

"I met her, too," Kate said. "They call her the *babuszka*. It was her cottage that you painted, and it's on my friends' property, the Kolodenkos."

"Is it now? Huh. I can't remember which happened first—the watercolor or the diamond. If she saw me painting her place, that could be why she singled me out. We didn't spend much time in that town."

"Did she know you were asking about the amber necklace?"

"Oh, uh. Maybe. Why would that matter to the old woman? Wait. That was the same day I picked up the necklace. She might have seen me." He rubbed his temples. "My memories are all jumbled. It's hard to keep things straight."

"That's okay, Dad. What matters now is that we get out of here."

THIRTY-FOUR

In the morning, Gustaw brought their breakfast, a selection of smoked cheese and crackers. He escorted Kate to the primitive bathroom up a level before locking her in while he led her dad to do the same. Before leaving them alone, he did a quick search of the room and quickly retrieved the shoe from her not-so-swell hiding place in the corner. He appeared unfazed at the dark look Kate gave him. She should have thought to smuggle it out to the privy.

"We need to leave today," Kate said after the man had left. She put the plate on the table. "If I lead the way, can you walk okay?"

Her dad rubbed his knee. "I can manage. What I was missing was a good pair of eyes. I'm glad you came. I know I didn't sound like it last night, but I was worried for you." He sat down. "I still can't figure out why they want me. If the war is over, what's the point? There had been talk of me looking at some paintings for them, but when my eyes never healed, they still kept me."

"Sometimes people get so deep into trouble, they don't know how to get themselves out of it again. Instead of owning up to their mistakes, they keep on going." She was thinking about Lidka. "Maybe they didn't know what to do with you."

"I'm blind. It's not like I can identify them."

"Let's work on getting out of here," Kate said, changing the subject. "We can figure out the Burgosovs later."

While they ate, they talked over several plans. The hardest part was how to break out of the room without arousing suspicion. Once they escaped the castle, Kate may not be able to find the exact trail they took, but as long as they started down the right side of the mountain, they should reach a town eventually. They'd need to leave at night to have the longest lead time.

Midafternoon, Lidka came for her.

"Are you fine?" she asked as they walked up the dim passage.

Maybe Lidka hadn't betrayed her, but had been as shocked as Kate was. Lidka was new to this crazy family secret. She didn't know all the history, or could have been told one very skewed version.

"Yes," she answered, hiking her bag up on her shoulder. She was going to try to steal the key and needed a place to quickly hide it. "I am happy to be with my dad again. When can we leave?"

Lidka shook her head. "I not know what Malwinka's plans are." She shone the light back the way they had come. "But the shoes worked. I am a person who needs to see something to believe. Since I had never seen the dresses or the shoes, I thought maybe they were merely expensive items and that was their worth. I have seen people fight over less."

The light from Lidka's flashlight skittered on the stone walls as they walked through the winding passageways. Kate counted turns and made note of doors. If she were to escape with Dad, she could afford no mistakes, no hesitations.

"I played along with everyone about Kopciuszek being real, but I did not think it was true," Lidka continued. "I knew that Malwinka wanted to meet you and offered to help. And you wanted to meet her. She knew about you even before you left New York. It was nice of you to ask Kamil on the ship about a Malwinka—an American girl asking questions—since until then we were not sure exactly when you would come. And look, everyone got what they wanted."

Kate stopped, her anger flaring. "Meeting us at the train wasn't a coincidence. You knew we were on our way to Italy, so you made it seem like you stumbled across us. I remember thinking it was odd you had a bag with you, but justified it because I never considered something so devious. What is wrong with this family?"

"Is not like that," Lidka said. "We do what is needed. Sometimes we have to play game to get there. You are not playing game? Pretending you do not know Polish when

I know you do?" She switched from English to Polish to make her point.

Kate looked away. "Does Malwinka know?"

"I not tell her everything. She is smart and will learn on her own."

Lidka pulled her along, maintaining a tight grip on her arm.

Kate stopped again, straining against Lidka's grasp as she made another realization. "Holy Toledo. The cheese we had for breakfast. It was the same kind you gave to Mr. De Luca; you'd just come from here. I was hoping you didn't know about my dad, but you did. The whole time. Back in Italy you could have told me."

"Keep moving. The stepsisters not like waiting."

"They're not stepsisters like the original ones were," Kate corrected her in irritation.

Lidka laughed. "You can call them the stepsisters— they all do. It helps fuel the fire." Lidka brought her into a large room with a black-and-white-checked marble floor. Great arches spanned the roof and frescoes of cherubs and angels filled the ceiling. The room must have been the great hall back in the days of Kopciuszek. Kate's attention went from the paintings to the group waiting for them.

There was Malwinka and Gustaw, and another woman with her bodyguard. The other woman wore her white hair pinned up at the back and reading glasses strapped around her neck. She wore a crisp dress and heels that had Kate wondering how she got to the castle. Her own shoes were covered in dirt.

Lidka brought her into the middle of the room and waited, not letting go of Kate's arm.

The new woman slowly circled Kate, examining her from head to toe. She spoke in English. "So this is the girl who sent my boys to prison."

Kate swallowed her gasp. *Ludmilla.*

"Such sweet boys, they are. Loyal to their mama. They tell me things about their trip to New York. How there was a girl who is the new Keeper. How she was willing to give us the dresses in exchange for her papa."

She stopped circling Kate and stood in front of her. "Is this true? You were willing to give us the dresses in exchange for your papa?"

Kate's confusion held her tongue. The Burgosov in New York had told her he made up the story about the shoes.

"Yes, my boys tell me before I know what Malwinka's plans are. She did not admit she finds an American man looking to make an amber necklace to match a family heirloom from Poland." She frowned at Malwinka, an air of distrust circulating between them. "But sometimes families—even stepsisters—have to work together to get what they want. You see we have your papa. Now all we need is the dress. Where is it?"

Kate glared at Malwinka. The dress didn't belong to her; it never would. It wasn't right for Kate to hand it over to her, but she had prepared for this possibility. As Lidka had said, Kate was developing street smarts. But Princess Kolodenko, on the other hand, thought she and Malwinka were at peace. Her family had relinquished the shoes for nothing. The descendants of the stepsisters were still working together to get what didn't belong to them.

Kate hated the idea of giving up the Kopciuszek treasures, but there was no doubt in her mind this time. She was ready to go home and take Dad with her. "Fine. You can have the dress. I'm done with being the Keeper."

Ludmilla smiled smugly at Malwinka. "I told you it was a good idea," she said in Polish. "Bring it to me."

"I don't have it," Kate answered, quickly realizing her mistake when Malwinka tilted her head and studied her. She'd answered in Polish. She'd been distracted by the surprising arrival of Ludmilla and had dropped her guard.

Ludmilla, not noticing Kate's slipup, narrowed her eyes and stared at Lidka. "You said she packed it."

Lidka stared back. "She did. I heard her talking to her boyfriend."

Ludmilla tried again. "You are Keeper. I know you would have brought the dress to try with the shoes. It was the missing piece Malwinka did not have. Where is it?"

"I don't know," Kate answered this time in English, and less boldly, avoiding Malwinka's gaze. "Maybe in Germany. Maybe in Italy. You can check my bag. I don't have it."

Lidka whispered, "Where did you hide dress? I know you brought with you."

Kate crossed her arms, wrenching her elbow out of Lidka's grasp. "It was in Johnny's luggage, not mine. And you got rid of him."

Lidka let out a tiny gasp, suggesting to Kate her suspicions were true. Lidka never wanted Johnny to go with them. She had purposely done something to his paperwork. At the time, Kate wasn't sure she was doing the right thing, sending the dress with Johnny, but she was glad now that she had listened to her gut.

"That will be all, Lidka," Malwinka said, dismissing the girl.

Lidka exited without looking at Kate.

The two women consulted at the far end of the room. Kate could hear the angry whispers, not the actual words. Malwinka spoke calmly, but Ludmilla was animated, forceful in what she was saying. Kate didn't know which woman scared her more. While they were busy, she took out her camera. The lighting was poor, but when else would she get another chance? She adjusted the settings, then, *click*.

"Put that away," Ludmilla said.

They consulted a little longer before the two separated. "Come closer, girl." Ludmilla spoke, but it was clear the way she kept looking to Malwinka for approval who was in charge. "You will have the dress brought here if you want to free your father," she said.

"How will I do that?" Kate asked. "I don't know where it is." She crossed her arms, in part to show her defiance and in part to hold herself together.

"Tomorrow morning you girls and Gustaw will hike back to Zakopane and contact this boy. He is to bring the dresses he has stolen. You will not mention that we have your papa, and you will get him to cooperate without involving the Kolodenkos. *Nie*?"

"He didn't steal them," Kate argued.

"They are not his," Ludmilla said with a glare strong enough to send a chill down Kate's neck.

"He doesn't have the correct paperwork. He got stopped at the border, remember?" She tried to sound indignant, but the waver in her voice betrayed her.

Ludmilla smiled. "That is the easy part. And once we have the Kopciuszek collection, you are free to go back to America."

Kate clenched her jaw. How could she trust the Burgosovs to let them go? Malwinka had done nothing but lie to her, and Ludmilla had done nothing but maneuver to get the ball gown.

"I see you don't believe Ludmilla," Malwinka said in Polish. "There is nothing we can do to convince you of our sincerity. But since you have no choice, you will do what we say and hope for the best. You Americans are always so positive, are you not?"

Kate's eyes flashed. She couldn't believe these people were her blood relatives. "I'm not leaving without my dad. We can all go to your house. It will be easier and more comfortable." She looked around the large stone hall. It was like the hint of a dream. If only the walls were covered in tapestries, and thick velvet curtains hung from ceiling to floor over the windows, or even if a robust fire was built in the fireplace, it would be a lovely place to stay. As it was now, it was sad and abandoned, and being used as a prison.

Ludmilla's face became even more stern. "You do not choose how this happens."

Kate ran through her options. She could sit down and refuse to move. An image of Gustaw looking like a lumberjack flashed through her mind. He was strong enough to sling her over his shoulder and lug her down the mountain like a sack of grain.

"Fine," she said in a way that meant it wasn't fine, but she would agree anyway. Besides, they'd be gone long before morning. She'd find a way.

Malwinka cleared her throat and looked meaningfully at Ludmilla. Ludmilla twisted her lips like she didn't agree with her. "One more thing," Ludmilla said. "Tell us about the blue diamond."

Lidka. Kate's palms began to sweat. She felt the urge to check her waistband for the hidden gem but scratched her cheek instead. "What blue diamond?"

Ludmilla raised her arms as if to say "I told you so" to Malwinka. Malwinka jutted out her chin.

"You found one in the fresco at Avanti. We know there are more, and they are tied to Kopciuszek's treasure."

Kate shook her head. She could honestly say she had no clue how the blue diamonds related. Elsie seemed to think they were part of the shoes, but Kate had seen the shoes. They were clear diamonds exactly as Princess Kolodenko had described.

"The Kolodenkos betrayed Malwinka. She thinks they did something to change the shoes. What did they do?"

Again, Kate had no idea. "The shoes worked. I found my dad. What could the Kolodenkos have done?" They stared each other down until Kate looked away. She was so tired. All she wanted to do was return to Dad.

Malwinka rang a bell and Lidka hurried into the room, somewhat out of breath. "Take her away. You will go to town with Gustaw early in the morning."

Kate glared at Lidka's back as she followed her out of the room.

"Ludmilla is after ball gown. Are you going to give it to her?" Lidka whispered.

"Yes." *No, we're escaping tonight. I just need to get the key from Lidka.*

"Do not you want to think about it?"

Kate didn't say anything.

"I did not know what they were planning." This time Lidka sounded apologetic.

Kate huffed.

"I speak the truth. I thought they would let you go."

"For someone who is so street smart, why would you think they would let us go?"

"Malwinka told me things. She thinks she safe because you are from another country. We send you on ship and you go back. Ludmilla change her mind, I think. I am not like that."

"Not like what?" As far as she was concerned, the Burgosovs were horrible people. All of them. She may have a shared bloodline, but she refused to get pulled into their mess.

"I am not like them. I do not want the Kopciuszek pieces for myself. They should be for the people. In a museum so everyone can see. Do you not believe that, too? You put the dresses on display for the people of America. You did not keep them for yourself."

Kate didn't know what to say. In a way, Lidka made some sense. When treasures were on display at a museum, more people could enjoy them. But the war had shown the conflict over both the private and public collection of art, who got a say in what was displayed, and where. Adolf Hitler had been trying to build the greatest art museum in the world, and he systematically attacked countries and looted them for the objects he wanted. People had no say. They were not given the option of donating or selling their possessions. The public had only rumors and stories of the Kopciuszek collection's existence. It did not belong to the public. But should it? And who was to decide?

Every generation of Cinderella's descendants had to wrestle with these thoughts. But the Kopciuszek dresses were unique in a way other art was not. The fairy-tale magic set them apart. Made them dangerous to be known in the public. If a painting could not be kept safe in a museum, how could a magical ball gown? No, Kate would not be of the generation to expose the collection to the public. She would fight to keep it private, whether owned by the Kolodenkos or the Burgosovs. But first things first.

They had cleared the main part of the castle and were headed down into the dreary corridor. "If what you say is true, you need to help us escape. Tonight."

THIRTY-FIVE

"Yes. I know where we can run away," Lidka said. "Not 'we.' I just need you to leave the door unlocked and distract Gustaw."

"No, you need me. Remember *babuszka* in the piazza? My amber necklace I gave? I see her again."

The *babuszka*. Princess Kolodenko's request popped into Kate's mind. *Find her.* "When? You didn't tell us."

Lidka gave her smirk. "Like you, I do not tell everything. She was hard to understand, but she told me go to the forest near Gryfino. To a cottage."

"What good would it do to go there?"

"Malwinka does not know about it. She would find me wherever else I go. We cannot cross the border, or her people will hold us for her."

Kate touched her necklace. The *babuszka* had wanted Lidka's amber necklace, but it wasn't the necklace she was expecting. Deep down, Kate had a feeling *her* amber pendant was the one the *babuszka* wanted. "Where did you really get your amber necklace from?"

"You already know this."

"I know one story. I want the truth." Kate slowed her steps. She didn't want her dad to overhear what Lidka had to say, if it was what she suspected.

"Ludmilla already told you words spread about American man looking to make sunburst amber pendant like family heirloom. I trade in jewelry during war and helped Malwinka locate this American man. He had necklace when Malwinka found him." Lidka's gaze fell. "She gave to me to get you to trust me."

"Swell," Kate said, crossing her arms. And was what she was telling her now another ploy to earn her trust?

"And my dad's dog tags?"

"That I do not know. I suspect Gustaw left them behind when he took your papa so they could travel with an un-identified man."

Kate paused to let it all sink in and decide if she should trust Lidka now. "Let's say we make it to this cottage. We're just supposed to hang out in the forest, for how long? We have to go home. My dad needs surgery before it's too late, and my mom doesn't even know he is alive. I don't want to be part of this game."

They had arrived back at the prison room.

"Gustaw does final check on you tonight. I will come for you after that." Lidka picked up a bundle lying outside the door and shoved it into Kate's hands before locking her in again.

Dad jumped to his feet as soon as Kate entered. A soft light was glowing from a single candle on the table. "That girl you came with brought you candles. The room didn't need to be lit when it was just me."

"Don't give her any credit," Kate said. "She's with them." She upturned the bundle on the table. Several items spilled out, but all Kate saw was Cinderella's shoes. Lidka had stolen the shoes back for her. "Dad, we're escaping tonight with Lidka's help."

"Good. But I've got one condition. You don't take any risks. If we're caught, I'll do what I can to give you a chance to run—and you run."

She agreed in order to make her dad happy, but there was no way she'd actually leave him behind. Not after all she'd gone through to find him. He was too precious.

Kate watched the light fade from the window until it was completely dark outside, and then she lit another candle. Time seemed to drag on forever, and Kate considered leaving without Lidka. Except she wasn't able to steal the key. She'd learned a lot from Lidka from their time together, but not how to be a good thief. Their backup plan now consisted of her dad hiding behind the door and tackling the next person who came through.

"Maybe she couldn't make it work," Kate said. "I'm sorry to get your hopes up."

Then the door opened. "Now," Lidka said. "Follow wall with hand. No lights."

They went a different direction than they had been following into the castle. This way sloped downward. Kate hoped they weren't headed into a dungeon.

"This is how Nadzia escaped," Lidka whispered. "The Burgosovs not find this passageway until years later."

"What is all this about?" Dad asked.

"Explain later," Lidka said. "First, we have to make one stop on our way out." She turned another corner and brought them to a short hallway with a wooden door at the end. When she opened it and shone her flashlight inside, Kate couldn't conceal her surprise.

"I don't believe it." The beam of light bounced off gold trinkets, paintings, statues—row after row of them. "Dad, it's filled with art. It's like one of those treasure storehouses Floyd talks about."

"I discover it yesterday," Lidka said. "This is where Malwinka hides everything. She acts like she is helping her neighbors, but she is biggest thief of all." Lidka made her way between the rows to a side table filled with crates of smaller objects. She grabbed a small figurine of a servant girl carrying a basket of laundry. "The maid used to sit on windowsill in kitchen at Malwinka's house. It belongs to Kolodenkos." She put it in her bag.

"This must be the art they wanted me to evaluate," Dad said. "I'll contact the proper authorities when we get down this mountain."

"Let's go," Kate said. She cared less about the art and more about getting away. She led her dad back into the hall while Lidka exited the room and closed the door.

Soon, the passage lost its brick floor and became packed dirt. The air grew cooler and the space smaller. "We are in the tunnel now," Lidka said. "I've never gone this far. We can only hope there have been no cave-ins."

The dampness soaked into Kate's skin, sending chills down her back. She pushed away feelings of panic. She'd never truly been claustrophobic before, but the weight of the darkness was heavy, and it made the walls seem closer than they really were, throwing off her sensibilities. She didn't like walking with such little light, and she still didn't trust Lidka. The girl had shown no real loyalty to anyone but herself.

The path stopped at a rock wall with a wooden door. Lidka tried to turn the handle, but it was locked. She took out her keys and tried several in the lock. Nothing worked. "Ideas?" she asked.

Kate's dad felt the door, then slammed his shoulder into it. "Oof. That's pretty solid. Shine your light around the frame and see if there is a weak spot."

Lidka traced the door with the flashlight, looking for rotting wood or a crumbling stone. "Is well built to survive all these years," she said.

"Go back to the lock," Kate said, her pulse quickening. She'd noticed it was an odd shape, not your standard thin keyhole.

With the light illuminating the surface, Kate bent down and took out her necklace. She smiled. If she was right, someone had been very clever. She slid the amber necklace sideways into the slot. It was met with resistance, but she pushed until there was a *click*. She turned the handle, and woodsy, fresh air rushed into the stale passage.

"You did it," her dad said.

They stepped out into one of the caves. At the low entrance, Lidka shut off her light. "We walk in darkness," she said, ducking out.

Lidka moved like a panther. Kate and her dad, on the other hand, lumbered like injured prey. It was one thing for Dad to walk in the smooth passageway. It was entirely another to hike down the mountain without being able to see where he was stepping, and having to walk on his prosthesis. The trail was impossible to see in the dark, and they kept stumbling. Kate felt the scratches from the tree branches trying to trap her and hold her back for Malwinka.

"One step at a time, Kate," Dad whispered. "That's how I learned to walk again. Focus on the next step. It's all you can control."

They talked as little as possible, aware how far a voice can carry in the silence. They hiked downhill for what seemed like an hour before they risked speaking.

"How far is the nearest town?" Dad asked. "We should go directly to the authorities."

"No." Lidka said. "They would give us back to Malwinka. We talk to no one until we get to the *babuszka*."

"And how do we do that?" Kate asked.

"We get on first train going west. We have to be on that train by the time Malwinka discovers we are missing."

THIRTY-SIX

Despite the hazards, the trip down the mountain had been faster than the struggle up had been. Once the sun had taken away the darkness, their path was even more sure. The train station was packed already with travelers waiting for the first train.

"Tourists," Lidka said. "Zakopane is nice vacation town."

"Do you have enough money?" Kate asked.

Lidka nodded. "Tony was generous."

They stood in line to buy tickets. Lidka handled everything, and it reminded Kate of the last time she'd let Lidka handle everything. This time she stuck by her side and tried to understand as best she could the fast Polish being spoken.

They managed to be among the last set of passengers allowed on the crowded train. Kate smiled as she settled into her seat. "We made it."

Lidka stared out the window. "We got on train," she

whispered. "That is all we have done. We are last passengers, but here we sit not moving." She never took her gaze off the platform.

Dad crossed and uncrossed his legs. He shifted back in his seat.

"You two are making me nervous," Kate said.

Ten more minutes went by before Lidka stood. "We getting off." Lidka grabbed their bags and shoved them at Kate. She took off down the aisle and started banging on the locked door, yelling to be let off, that she was sick.

"What's happening?" Dad asked.

"I don't know. Follow me."

By the time they had made their way to Lidka, everyone was staring. There would certainly be enough witnesses if Malwinka started asking questions.

"When they open door, we rush out. They not stop us all. Get lost in crowd, then meet me at corner near boy selling papers. The porters are so used to hearing boy's voice they ignore him. If they take you, leave behind something from your bag and I will know. I will try to contact Fyodora for help."

The door opened and Lidka tumbled out, purposely crashing into the porter. Kate jumped out, then spun around to help her dad down. As soon as her father's feet touched the ground, she pulled him into a trot, keeping her hand in front of him to push people aside. Lidka kept the surprised porter occupied, but a second porter noticed Kate and her father.

Taking her cue from Lidka and using her best Polish, Kate called back, "He's going to be sick," hoping that would make the man pause. It did, but only long enough for Kate and her dad to duck into the nearest building and try to blend in. She spotted an abandoned newspaper on an empty chair as the porter outside pushed his way through the door.

"Sit here, and pretend you're reading the paper. If we separate, he might not notice us. I'll be back." Kate worked her way toward the ladies' bathroom. Inside was a girl standing near the sink tying her hair back in a red-and-blue kerchief.

"That is pretty," she said in Polish. "Will you sell it to me?" She held out what she hoped was a reasonable amount of money.

The girl's eyes brightened, and she handed over the kerchief. When the girl left, Kate could see her father tucked behind the newspaper and the man who was chasing them working his way through the room. It looked like he had already passed by Dad.

Agonizing over each second, Kate waited until she couldn't stand it any longer. She casually walked out of the room with her new kerchief tied over her head. There was no sign of the porter. "Dad, I'm back," she said, standing at his side.

She had never felt so lost in her life. It must be worse for her dad, who knew even less of the language than she did and couldn't see any danger until it was too late. Her heart pounded so hard it was a wonder she wasn't calling more attention to herself.

If only she had never noticed the royal crest on Aunt Elsie's steamer trunk, how different her life would be right now.

"Let's go to the corner so she can find us."

Lidka was already at the rendezvous spot. She was pacing back and forth and running her hand through her hair. She motioned for them to follow her down the street and around the corner, where she slowed and let them catch up to her.

"I overheard men talking. Malwinka got to them. They are checking all trains. I could maybe blend in enough to pass, but an American girl who speaks such little Polish and blind man who speaks none will be easily caught. We have to find another way. I used to have some contacts in this place. It may take some time to find them again." She turned her back, looking for something. A safe place for them to wait, maybe.

Dad cleared his throat meaningfully, and his hand went to the spot she had sewn in the diamond.

He was right, but she wasn't going to let him give up Elsie's diamond. That hospital she was in was expensive. "I have something that might help us."

"What can the shoes do for us now?"

"Not the shoes." Kate lowered her voice. "I have the blue diamond."

Lidka's eyes grew wide. "You telling me this now?" She sounded angry.

Immediately, Kate's ire shot up. "I couldn't trust you before. I barely trust you now."

"Show it to me."

"No. Decide what to do with it first. I won't let you have it until the last minute."

Lidka made a face. "Fine. Come with me to *bar mleczny*. You can eat while I take care of the things."

The milk bar was extremely plain, just tables, chairs, and bare white walls, but it was well-frequented. They sat at a cramped table near the back where they could keep an eye on the door. After Lidka left, they bought omelets and two glasses of milk. They came with straws.

"This is not how I imagined vacationing in Poland," Kate said, taking a sip.

Dad chuckled. "It's not how I expected to end my time in the war, either." He took a bite of his omelet. "Mmmm. That's surprisingly good."

"A good appetite needs no sauce," they both said at the same time. Kate grinned at her dad. This was what their reunion was supposed to feel like.

Kate continued to fill him in as she watched customers come and go. The Burgosovs would have had time to hike down the mountain by now. If they got hungry, they could walk through the doors and see them.

"I think I should try to send Floyd a telegram," she said to Dad. "He can contact Mom, and I'll let him know where we are. Will you be okay to stay here?" She tried not to think of how scary it would be to not see who was coming in the door, to not know you were found out until it was too late. "I'll get you a paper before I leave. That seemed to work well in the train station."

"I don't trust that girl, either. Do what you need to do."

Kate scanned the room and saw a man get up, tucking a paper under his arm. She went to him and asked in Polish, "Are you finished with the paper?" He nodded and handed it to her. "Thank you."

Dad taken care of, she wound her way back to the train station. She hoped she could find it again and not get lost. The next obstacle would be to not bring attention to herself.

THIRTY-SEVEN

With a purposeful stride, she followed the streets she thought led to the station until she found it. There were even more people queued up than earlier this morning. Checking the trains was causing a backup. People were sitting on their luggage, like they had been waiting for a long time.

Compared to the crowd waiting to get on the train, the telegraph line was short. Kate composed her note to Floyd while standing in line and was ready by the time she got there.

IN ZAKOPANE ON WAY TO GRYFINO.

DAD TOO. MEET US.

It was a risk, but what else could she do? It was in English, so the operator might not understand it. Or, it might raise his suspicions and she'd be detained. But she couldn't risk sending it to Floyd in Polish because he was a little rusty.

She slid her slip across the counter, biting her lip as he

read it. He scratched his cheek, nodded, and tapped it out for her.

There. No matter what happened now, her backup plan had been enabled. Floyd would know the two locations they could be if they didn't show up. And he'd know she'd found Dad. She left the counter with a light step. Until she noticed the porter who had chased her earlier. He wasn't looking her way, so she wound her way around the other passengers, tucking herself in with a family. The mother was struggling with herding twin toddlers while holding a baby. Kate held her hands out for the baby. "Can I help?" she asked in Polish.

With a grateful smile, the woman passed her the baby and took a hand of each of the boys. Kate helped her lug their bags and the kids outside, where they found a place to camp out. It looked like they were moving, as Kate caught glimpses of lace curtains and photos tucked in with their meager clothing. Kate cooed with the baby before handing the chubby darling back to the mom. She waved at the boys and jogged back into town.

As she pulled open the door to the milk bar, she happened to look down the street and see the broad shoulders of Gustaw. Their eyes met, and Kate's heart lunged into her throat. She held her breath as she quickly reviewed her escape routes. Then he blinked, looked away, turned around, and ambled down the street. Did he see her or didn't he? He had to have seen her. She'd felt their gazes lock. She thought back to the day Nessa chided her for her paranoia. *Not everyone is after the dresses, Kate.* Maybe Gustaw, like his daughter the kitchen maid, was done. She could only pray.

She continued into the milk bar. Her dad wasn't at the back table. No, no, no. He had to be here. Several men were bent over papers. One turned a page and Kate saw his face. Dad. He had changed tables.

"Why are you over here?" she asked him. "I about had a heart attack." She decided not to tell him about seeing Gustaw. It would bring up more questions than she could give answers. Her guess was that Gustaw was upset about his daughter and was rebelling against Malwinka. She hoped it was that and not a trap.

"Sorry, I heard them get up and thought it was a better location. It's near the kitchens and there must be a back door. How did it go?"

"Done. Floyd will know we're together and where to meet us. Still no Lidka?"

He shook his head. "Want to read the paper to me? I've gone through it all but haven't learned a thing."

Kate laughed. "Sure." She translated what she could but kept her attention on the front door should Gustaw change his mind.

By late afternoon there was still no sign of Lidka. Kate's heart skipped a beat every time the door opened. They bought some kind of meatless cabbage stew and some yogurt and continued to wait.

"I'm beginning to think we should try to make it on

our own," Dad said. "The longer we sit, the greater the chance they will find us again."

"Let's give her ten more minutes."

"Why do you think we should wait for this girl? She tricked you into coming here."

"I think she is trying to make up for it." Kate looked out the window. "I hope."

Dad drummed his fingers on the table. "I still can't figure out what they wanted with me. This whole time I thought maybe a civil war broke out and I was being kept by a remote family who didn't know what to do with me once they had me. At the beginning they asked me lots of questions, but I was never tortured. It was as if they realized I was giving truthful answers and didn't know anything of importance. When they found out I was an art professor, they started asking me questions about art."

"Two of them got caught in New York for art smuggling," Kate said. "They were traveling throughout Europe stealing things. They tried to take the Kolodenkos' heirloom dresses from the Harmon-Craig display, and that's when they were caught."

"Hmm. It could be related."

"The two families have been feuding for centuries. You got caught in the cross fire."

"The Hatfields and the McCoys. Feuds don't end well."

Finally, Lidka opened the door of the milk bar. She motioned for Kate to come.

Relief washed over Kate. "She's here. Let's go."

Lidka was already partway down the block. "I have friend who can get us on train after inspections. They are going through the trains all day long." She sighed deeply. "I am surprised they did not find you here."

Kate looked away, not wanting to tell Lidka about Gustaw in case she would want to change the plan again. Sneaking on after inspections sounded like a great idea to her.

"You give me diamond now?"

Kate nodded and started looking in her bag for her sewing kit.

Lidka produced a knife.

"Oh. That'll work." Kate eyed the knife with suspicion. Of course Lidka would have a knife. "You'll need to cut into my waistband."

"You are more clever than I gave you credit for," Lidka said. She sidled up to Kate and, with a quick motion, cut the place Kate indicated.

Kate worked the diamond out. With a pause, she handed it to Lidka. "Thank you," she said, hoping her words were also interpreted as, *I trust you, but I don't trust you, so please don't make me regret giving you the only item of value I have.*

With a nod, Lidka led the way back to the station. They worked their way along the outside edge, crossing the tracks ahead of the station, then sneaking back between the trains. Kate wished sunset would hurry up, but the summer sun was holding strong.

A tall, skinny man was hanging out by the train closest to the station. He stood by a pile of crates. Lidka shook his hand.

"Punia." He dipped his head in greeting, then piled up the crates so she could climb into the open window.

Something about the way the man said Lidka's nickname struck a memory. Kate watched the girl disappear through the window, and the memory went with it.

It was Kate's turn next. Lidka made it look easy, the way she hopped up and was in. She must have been used to getting into places in unusual ways. Kate was used to following the rules, walking in the door with a ticket in hand. The first attempt, she came back down on the guy's head. He grunted but gave her more of a shove the second time, sending her flailing across the rough opening and into Lidka's arms, who then dragged her through the window. Last was Dad.

The passengers already inside looked away as if nothing unusual were happening. Since they had already been waiting for hours to go, one more inconvenience wouldn't bother them. Especially with the cold stare Lidka gave the few who turned for a second glance. Folks slid over to make room for three more people.

The man outside raised his hand, his fingers pinching something as he nodded to them. Lidka must have slipped him the diamond when they shook hands.

As the train started to move, Lidka crashed back into an empty seat. Soon she was soundly sleeping, leaving

Kate to wrestle anxiously through their plans on her own. Kate could hash things out with Dad, but the less she said the better. She didn't want him asking too many questions. They had to find some way out of Poland, beyond Malwinka's supporters. Surely they could cross at a remote location on the German border. Kate smiled reassuringly at her dad before she remembered he couldn't see her. She reached for his hand instead and gave it a squeeze. While Lidka slept, Kate had to be the eyes for all of them.

✌ THIRTY-EIGHT ✎

Kate didn't know how Lidka could sleep. The seats were uncomfortable, and the passenger car was heating up with all those bodies inside. Not to mention that Kate was expecting to get thrown off the train at any moment. She looked down and saw that her clenched hands were white, she was squeezing them so hard. She let go and wiped the sweat off her palms. She looked out at the scenery, reminding herself she was in Elsie's beloved Poland. She should check on Mr. G's camera after that ungraceful leap into the train, but the furtive glances she was getting now that Lidka was asleep changed her mind.

She couldn't help thinking that they got away too easily. After spending the entire day at the milk bar, it seemed unlikely no one would think to look for them there. She pictured Gustaw turning away from her and hoped that he was on their side, not that they were being pushed into another trap.

They arrived in Gryfino early morning. The sky was beginning to light as if it were only waking up itself and needed more time asleep. They stepped down from the train, directly to the track level, just like in Zakopane, as there were no platforms. Several others got off the train with them, carrying odd assortments of items. These were definitely refugees.

"Why are all these people leaving?" she asked Lidka. It's not like the war was forcing them on.

"Operation Vistula," she answered.

"What is that?" she asked.

"The Ukrainians were supposed to leave Poland after the war, but some did not. Now the border is closed and government of Poland is spreading them around country so they become diluted. They want them to forget they are Ukrainian."

Kate couldn't tell if Lidka approved or disapproved. "Why can't they stay where they were living?" Kate whispered.

Lidka lilted her head, like she was tired of explaining the simplest things to Kate. "They are making us go back into our pens. Germans are over there. Ukrainians there. Poles here. Is for good of the people. Poland is for Poles. Is not America for Americans? Is reason why you did not allow refugees to go to America?"

Kate didn't know how to answer that one. She had learned a lot about politics over the years, but it didn't always make sense.

The thin man standing closest to them scowled at Lidka. "I *am* Polish. I've never lived in Ukraine. I was kicked out of my home in Poland and only allowed to leave with what I could carry. That is, after they took anything of worth."

Lidka merely shrugged and turned away. Kate stared wide-eyed and tried to offer a sympathetic smile. Once again she was witnessing the aftershocks of the war.

"It is nothing that has not happened before. Kolodenkos were forced to flee to Italy. It worked well for them," Lidka said, marching down the sidewalk.

Mention of the Kolodenkos reminded Kate about Lidka's nickname. "How did you get your nickname? I thought it was Mr. De Luca's name for you, but that other man called you Punia, too."

"During the war we all had nicknames. To survive, you either had to lose your identity or risk having it stolen from you. 'Punia' is Polish word, meaning is bush kitten. Wild cat."

What a fitting nickname for Lidka.

A milkman was making deliveries, and Lidka stopped him. "Do you know where Babuszka lives?" she asked. "She is new to town."

The grizzled man laughed. "We're all new."

They carried on, asking everyone they came across. They all shook their heads. Kate wasn't surprised, since the question was the Polish equivalent of walking down the street in New York asking if anyone knew where the old woman lived.

"I thought someone would know," Lidka said. "This is a small place and she is unusual."

They entered a restaurant, and at the warm smell of breakfast, Kate's stomach growled. She hadn't eaten since the milk bar. A waitress with a little girl clinging to her leg showed them to a table.

"Don't mind her," the waitress said. "She lost her first tooth this morning and the blood scared her a little. She won't leave my side. Good thing the owner is my papa and he spoils his little granddaughter."

After the waitress took their orders, Lidka said, "We are looking for Babuszka. She would have arrived a couple weeks ago."

The waitress shook her head. "We've got so many people coming through, I can't keep them straight. Some stay, some move on."

But the little girl's eyes opened wide and she stared at Lidka. *She knows something.*

Kate crooked her finger at her. "Let me see your tooth," she said in Polish.

The little girl shook her head but came over to Kate and pointed to the empty space in her mouth. The mother returned to the kitchen, but the girl stayed behind.

"Oh, look at that," Kate said. "You have a cute space in your smile." The girl smiled even wider, showing off the new gap. "Have *you* seen the *babuszka*?"

She nodded enthusiastically and pointed down the street in the direction they had been walking.

"She lives that way? What color is her house?"

Shake no.

"No house?"

Shrug.

The waitress stopped by. "The girl won't talk, but if you don't mind her sitting with you, she likes to draw."

Lidka made a move like she was going to protest, but Kate scooped the girl up and sat her on the empty chair. The girl grinned like she was privileged to sit with them. The waitress plunked some paper and crayons down before greeting new customers.

Immediately the girl started drawing a tree. Lidka rolled her eyes.

Many trees later, the girl drew a woman wearing a kerchief deep in the middle of the trees. She patted Kate's arm and pointed to the woman.

"She lives in the forest?" Kate asked.

The little girl nodded.

"What else?"

The girl drew a building at the top of her page and pointed to herself.

"We are in the building?" Kate asked.

Another nod. Then the girl drew the river. She put her finger on the restaurant, then followed the river south before pointing to the forest in her picture.

"Thank you, sweetheart." Kate wished she had something to give the girl.

Lidka was already extracting the young thing from her

chair, but before sending her on her way, she handed her a candy. The girl clutched it and ran back into the kitchens.

"You are more kind than I expected," Kate said with a smile.

"So, we know where we're going?" Dad asked.

"Into the woods," Kate said. *Where all fairy-tale characters seem to end up.*

They followed the river out of town until they came to an opening in the trees that looked like it might be a path. The pine trees were young, and there was little undergrowth. "Let's try it," Kate said.

The path meandered through the forest and disappeared at several points. If they weren't so determined, they would have given up and gone back to town. They continued deep into the forest until the path ended at a clearing and a familiar storybook cottage.

"Dad, you remember the sketch you drew of the cottage in Italy?"

"Yes."

"Well, it's right here in front of us."

The only difference from the place in Italy was that someone was home at this cottage. An old woman nestled into the rocking chair out front like she was part of the forest, and had been resting there comfortably for years. A small fire had been set a respectable distance away from the cottage and was now reduced to glowing coals that were warming a large stewpot.

"It's the *babuszka*," Kate said.

The woman beckoned them to come to her.

Lidka hiked up her bag farther on her shoulder and quickened her pace, leaving Kate and Dad behind. By the time they got there, Lidka had already gone inside.

"Hello," Kate said, and she introduced herself and her dad, reminding her how they had met in Italy.

The *babuszka* smiled and nodded. Smiled and nodded. But didn't speak. She looked tired.

"Come in," Lidka said. "There is food."

Kate helped her dad navigate the door and settle into a chair at a small table. A platter of meat and cheeses and bread was waiting. Lidka had already started eating.

"Shouldn't we invite the *babuszka* in?" Dad asked.

"I will," Kate said.

The *babuszka* had moved off the rocking chair and was now stirring the pot hanging over the fire. "Thank you for the food," Kate said. "Please, come eat with us."

The *babuszka* said nothing, just continued to stir. Kate came closer and watched the long-handled spoon go round and round. The stew she was making smelled delicious, the scent of rosemary rising from the pot. Kate took her eyes off the stew and looked at the *babuszka*. A dawning look of recognition spread across the old woman's face. "You," she said in a dry voice. "You are the Keeper."

Surprised, Kate nodded.

"Do you have it?" The old woman let go of the long spoon and shakily started forward.

Kate reached out to hold her steady. The *babuszka* could mean so many things, but Kate knew she was asking about the amber necklace. The real amber necklace. She felt the weight of it around her neck. She pulled the pendant out from under her blouse, surprised that in all her travels, no one had tried to take it from her.

The *babuszka* motioned with her hands that she would like to hold it.

Kate unclasped the necklace and handed it over with complete trust.

The old woman closed her eyes and lifted her head to the heavens. "What was lost is found."

✑ THIRTY-NINE ✑

Early in the morning, Kate found the *babuszka* at the side of the house. She was tilling the soil, a variety of garden tools at her side. She looked like a picture, with her layered dress, shawl, and kerchief over her hair, tied under her chin. She also wore the amber necklace.

Kate took out her camera and focused. She framed the *babuszka* to the left of center, her hoe crossing the center line of the frame. She paused. The *babuszka* looked different. Refreshed. *Click*.

"May I help?" Kate asked in Polish. She put her bag down on the edge of the rectangle of soil the *babuszka* was tilling.

"Of course," she answered in clear English. "I'm planting my pumpkins." The words came out unmuddled, but from a voice that was dry and unused.

Kate blinked. Her English was excellent. And where was the tired old woman from yesterday?

They'd all bunked down after sunset, but the old woman had stayed out by her fire all night. The stew she had made them tasted as good as it smelled. Lidka had finally relaxed in the cozy cottage, convinced Malwinka wouldn't find them here. But Kate had trouble sleeping. She kept picturing Gustaw looking right at her and then walking away.

"A little late this year," the *babuszka* continued, "but I know a few tricks to get them to grow. I remember another year I was late planting my pumpkins." She smiled. "And what a year that was."

"You've been a gardener for a long time?" Kate asked, marveling at the woman's transformation.

The *babuszka* nodded, then demonstrated how she wanted the soil broken up. "This will be my first pumpkin patch in this kingdom."

Kate glanced at her, wondering at the reference to a kingdom. Did she know she was in the modern country of Poland?

"Why did you leave Italy? The Kolodenkos are worried about you."

The *babuszka* stopped tilling. She braced her hands on the tip of the handle and examined Kate. "I was never meant to stay. I was only there to be close to Fyodora. The war took its toll on my health, and it was time for me to return. I thought I had the necklace to get me here."

Kate's face burned. She should have given it to the woman at the piazza, but at the time she didn't know who she was.

"But you didn't return to your first home," Kate said, testing her guess that the *babuszka* once lived near the castle.

She nodded and returned to her tilling. "You have seen the beautiful valley, have you not? It is quiet, like here. But it has sad memories. People stay away. They are afraid of the place, though they don't know why." She looked up and waved her hand to the forest. "I am needed here, now. These people who live beyond this place are in turmoil. I can be a servant to them."

"How old are you?"

The *babuszka* turned her back as she continued working. "I stopped counting years long ago. Now I count girls."

Did the *babuszka* suffer like Aunt Elsie? Confusing words without even knowing it?

"You are not curious what I mean?"

"Yes."

"Your *babcia* is Katja Petrov?"

"Yes."

"I knew her. And Elsie, her sister?"

"My aunt."

"I've known them all." She looked deep into Kate's eyes. "And now I've met you. The next Keeper."

Kate was not exactly surprised, but to be here, with her fingers getting chilled in the early morning air, and talking with the woman who could answer all her questions, did leave her in awe.

"Are you . . ." Kate couldn't say the words out loud. *Fairy godmother.*

"My friends call me Esmerelda. But I have grown accustomed to being called Babuszka. This is fine." She patted her kerchief. "I look the part."

"You are different from when we first saw you," Kate said, trying to be tactful. How do you tell someone that you once thought she was walking on the edge of insanity, but now she seemed normal?

Esmerelda cackled. "I feel so much better now that you are here and have brought the amber necklace. I never realized how much of me was in there until your *babcia* took it so far away." She hobbled over to the pile of tools and dropped her hoe. "You know, I felt the very day it set sail. I knew then that I had to stay close to the Kolodenkos if I were to ever see it again. That family always has been kind. Each person makes a life for themselves, but it does help to be taught right from wrong early on. The Burgosovs still pass down hatred and wickedness in their family." She dug around in her pocket and pulled out a folded paper filled with seeds. She handed some to Kate. "You are both Burgosov and Kolodenko. You are also Keeper?"

"Yes."

"You are the first." Esmerelda demonstrated how to plant the pumpkin seeds.

They worked in silence. Kate suspected Esmerelda was giving her time to reflect. So much had happened on her trip, she hadn't had time to process it all. Finding her dad had overshadowed everything else she had learned, particularly her connection to the Burgosovs, and by extension, the Kolodenkos.

What a strange position to find herself in, at the point of union between two feuding families. She was the official Keeper through her family line, but using the Burgosovs' logic, she could lay claim to the Kolodenko treasures, too.

Of course, Lidka told her she was more Burgosov than Kolodenko because Kate wasn't a *direct* descendant of Cinderella, only a relation. She didn't want to take sides in a feud; rather, she liked it when she thought she was outside of the conflict, keeping the collection safe while they battled it out. For her, the stakes had been ones of family pride, a heritage of service. Did that have to change now that she knew who her grandfather really was?

"You are still you," Esmerelda said, as if reading her thoughts. "When you find out something about where you came from, it does not change who you are or who you are becoming. Nadzia was like you. She was an orphan girl, left on my doorstep when she was a baby. Someone had gone to great trouble to bring her to me. The people in the village always thought I was strange. I preferred to live in the mountains by myself. But when I heard that baby cry early one morning, well, my life has never been the same."

"She was left in a basket on your doorstep? I thought that only happened in stories."

Esmerelda smiled. "I was used to quietly helping people, staying in the background, doing my bit, and then leaving. But now I had a girl come to live with me. I thought about giving her away. Finding a nice family to leave her with—on their doorstep as I had found her on mine. But the mother who left Nadzia with me must have had her reasons. I thought maybe she might return, and if I moved on or gave the girl to someone else to raise, the mother would never know. Her planning would have been for nothing, and how sad she would be."

Kate finished planting her final seeds and, standing, brushed the dirt off her hands. "Did the mother come back?"

Esmerelda shrugged. "Perhaps. Whenever we went into town I studied the faces of the girls. Did any of them follow from afar? Did any try to get close to us? I never could tell with all the strange looks I got anyway, showing up with a baby all of a sudden. I'm sure the people thought I stole her." She wiped her face with a kerchief. "Have a drink?" she asked, her eyes squinting against the light.

A gourd filled with water sat on a stump near the house. Esmerelda poured them each a drink in little tin cups. By now, the sun had fully come up, touching the soil and warming the seeds.

"How did Nadzia end up at the castle?"

"Kopciuszek came to us. Poor, wretched girl. She was being mistreated at home and would escape to the mountains, like me, whenever she could. I grew herbs that her stepmother liked, so it was a good excuse for her to come visit me. The stepmother would get first pick of the herb garden, which made her happy, and Kopciuszek would get a few hours of freedom. She and the younger Nadzia became good friends. When Kopciuszek's fortunes changed, she invited Nadzia to go with her."

"How did her fortunes change?" Kate asked, hoping for the magical tale.

Esmerelda cackled. "Oh, that is a fun tale, but one to be saved for another time." She grew serious. "All you need to know is the blessing doesn't have to stay the way it is. I bound Nadzia to Kopciuszek so the girls would look after each other. I didn't realize the trouble it would cause in future generations. If you want, I can release your family."

Esmerelda called it a blessing. Kate had only been Keeper for such a short time. Did she want it to change? Should it change? Now that they were safe again, could she walk away from the dresses?

FORTY

They were interrupted by Lidka, running out of the house, eyes wide. "They are here. The stepsisters. They found us. Babuszka, where can we go?"

Kate's heart began to race. Once again, they were in a secluded location. She never should have listened to Lidka. She and Dad should have gone straight to the border and claimed their American citizenship, and then zipped him home so he could see a doctor about his eyes. Or there might have been an embassy in the capital city. Why didn't they think to look?

Esmerelda shook her head, her eyes focused on the forest past the cottage. Sure enough, there were shadows moving furtively among the trees. Kate's instincts had her looking for a hiding place to duck behind, like a futile game of hide-and-seek. But her dad was still in the cottage unawares. She couldn't get separated from him again; whatever happened would happen to the two of them.

The stepsisters emerged from the forest and surveyed

the setting. Malwinka and Ludmilla, alone. When they spotted Esmerelda and the girls standing beside the cottage, they began walking with renewed purpose.

The descendants of the stepsisters were halfway across the clearing when there came a sound from behind.

"You!"

Kate whirled around to see Princess Kolodenko and Nessa emerging from the forest. They were dressed in hiking gear and carrying backpacks. Heart pounding, Kate searched the trees for Johnny and Floyd, but apparently the Kolodenkos came alone.

"Isn't this lovely," Malwinka answered. "A family reunion."

As each side advanced, Kate realized they were going to have a showdown in the middle of the pumpkin patch.

"Stop," Esmerelda commanded. She did not yell or even raise her voice, but everyone froze on the edges of the freshly turned soil and waited. "Each side will be heard, but you are not to speak to each other. Kolodenkos, you stay on that side of the yard. Burgosovs on that side. The cabins are comfortable and have everything you'll need for your stay."

Two cute cabins were placed back in the trees on opposite sides of the yard with the fairy-tale cottage in the middle. Kate hadn't noticed the matching buildings until Esmerelda pointed them out. By the confused look on Lidka's face, she hadn't noticed them, either.

"You are tired from your journeys. Go and rest. I will

visit you later." She waved them off like she was shooing little children to run and play.

"What do we do?" Kate asked. Lidka hadn't moved, either.

"You can choose a side or remain at the cottage."

"What about my dad?"

"Oh, dearie. He is resting peacefully. Nothing could wake him right now."

Meanwhile, the Burgosovs and the Kolodenkos were eyeing each other as they slowly made their way to their respective cabins.

After checking in on Dad to confirm that he was very much asleep, Kate received permission from Esmerelda to talk to the Kolodenkos. She knocked on the door of the little cabin.

Nessa answered and beckoned Kate in. The cabin was a central room with two twin beds on the right, a sitting area on the left, and a kitchen in the back. "This is cozy," Kate said.

"There's an outhouse out back," Nessa said. She did not sound impressed. "I'm sorry we had to leave your brother and Johnny behind, but you can see why we couldn't bring them. We suspected *they* would show up."

"How is Johnny?"

Nessa laughed. "Like a charging bull. He's just crazy trying to get to you. I'm sure he's spitting mad we left without him this morning."

Kate's heart warmed.

Princess Kolodenko stopped her pacing to welcome Kate. "He contacted us immediately after you were separated," she said. "We met with your brother and he showed us the telegram you sent him about going to Gryfino."

"So they're close?" Kate held her breath. She couldn't wait to see him again.

Princess Kolodenko nodded. "Back at the hotel in the town of Szczecin. Floyd is eager to see his dad. You found him; how is he?"

"Malwinka had him as a prisoner. He's recovered from his initial injuries except he is blind."

"Blind!" Nessa exclaimed.

"He's alive," Princess Kolodenko countered. "Kate, I'm sorry I didn't take your search more seriously. We didn't believe your father survived. And to think I sent you to Malwinka." She put her hands to her chin like she was praying. "I should have gone myself."

"She thinks she's been betrayed. She asked about where the blue diamonds come from. I had no idea what she was talking about."

For the first time, there was a crack in Princess Kolodenko's stately demeanor. She started to speak, then faltered and looked away.

Nessa saw it, too. "What is it, Babcia?"

Princess Kolodenko sighed. "I didn't think they knew. Well, it is all going to come out now. Esmerelda will see to it. Where are the shoes, Kate?"

"In the cottage."

"And describe them to me."

Puzzled, Kate answered, "They are made from beautiful clear diamonds. Sturdy, with a strong heel, yet delicate enough to wear with the ball gown."

"Tell me how they worked," Nessa said. "They helped you find someone you loved."

"Yes, they did. Malwinka had one shoe hidden in the room where they kept my dad. She gave me the other. I didn't know what to do with it. Finally, in frustration one night, I asked it, 'Where is your partner?' and it lit up, pointing the way."

"Oh, I'd like to see that," Nessa said.

"Interesting," Princess Kolodenko said. "My family was not aware. We were taught that Kopciuszek was able to find her servant Nadzia by tracking the use of the blue diamonds." She smiled, a faraway look on her face. "The story-book legend had always been that the prince found Kopciuszek using one shoe. It never made sense to me before, but now I understand how he did it."

Princess Kolodenko sat at the table. "The shoes have been altered, Kate. Originally they were not the plain glass slippers you used to find your dad. They are missing their heart stones. The blue diamond clasps formed into the shape of hearts. These are what make the blue diamonds. We are unclear how they are created, but when we need a diamond, one becomes loose and we can pluck it out. Over time, another appears in its place."

Kate made a plucking motion with her fingers. "Aunt

Elsie, back at the hospital. That's what she was trying to say." That's how Elsie recognized the diamond.

"The Keepers didn't need to know about the diamonds. I never should have shown her. This is truly what the Burgosovs have been after all these years. They want the heart stones."

⤬ FORTY-ONE ⤬

The air fairly crackled with the tension growing among the three buildings in the woods. In Esmerelda's cottage, Lidka sat at the window keeping watch, Dad was fast asleep in the bed in the corner, and Kate sat at the table observing them both. Esmerelda had gone out to talk with each side and told the girls to wait.

"What do you think is going to happen?" Kate asked, breaking the silence.

Lidka shrugged. "Doesn't matter. I'm leaving anyway."

"Where are you going?"

She didn't answer but stood, hands balled at her sides.

"Girls, come on out," Esmerelda called.

She was stacking up firewood near the burning coals as if she were getting ready to cook everyone dinner. It was not a happy family reunion, however, as the Kolodenkos and the Burgosovs stood apart from each other, eyeing the other side with distrust. Oblivious, Esmerelda shuttled about, adding sticks to the pile and humming to herself.

Finally, she sat back down in her rocking chair, and said, "Let's begin."

"Your family gave us worthless shoes," Malwinka complained, taking a step toward Princess Kolodenko. "There is no wealth here. Something is missing."

Princess Kolodenko remained silent, her lips set.

Esmerelda, ignoring the outburst, motioned to Malwinka. As if hearing a silent command, Malwinka pulled the shoes out of her bag and placed them before the *babuszka*.

Openmouthed, Kate looked at Lidka. She refused to meet Kate's eyes. "How could you?"

"You got your dad. Everything could go back to the way it was," she said, crossing her arms.

Next, Esmerelda turned to Ludmilla and tilted her head. Ludmilla produced the wrapped ball gown. Esmerelda unwrapped it, and, smiling, draped it over her knees.

Nessa's eyes opened wide and she riffled through her own bag. "When did she steal the ball gown? I brought it with me. Kate had given it to Johnny for safekeeping. I've had it with me this whole time."

"There is a reason you need a Keeper." Ludmilla grimaced at her and stepped back, bowing and sweeping her arm in an arc, inviting Nessa to go next.

Nessa lifted her chin and marched over to the waiting *babuszka*. She draped the servant dress and then the wedding gown on top of the ball gown. With one last longing look, she turned away and set her back to the Burgosovs.

Next, Esmerelda raised her eyebrows at Princess Kolodenko. When the princess came close, the *babuszka* gently cupped her face. Reluctantly, Princess Kolodenko took out two sparkly blue objects and placed them in Esmerelda's hands.

Malwinka and Ludmilla gasped, then whispered to each other.

"What are those?" Lidka asked.

"The heart stones that give us the blue diamonds and are the source of our wealth," Princess Kolodenko said. "When we are in need, we can pluck out a diamond. Over time, a new one replaces it. This was Kopciuszek's secret. It was our secret. But now that Esmerelda has taken everything back, it doesn't matter anymore."

Esmerelda bent over the shoes and fixed the blue diamond heart clips to them. There was a hush of sadness about the meadow as the sun sat low in the sky. Centuries of feuding had led to this. It was like they were children and the *babuszka* was taking all their toys away.

Just then, Lidka darted through the circle they had formed. Before anyone could react, she grabbed the pile of Cinderella's treasures. Stunned, everyone stared as she ran toward the fire pit.

Kate's body reacted before she even realized what Lidka intended. She lunged after her. "No!" she yelled. "You don't understand what could happen. That dress has power."

Lidka stood with the items held out over the coals. "I have to. I am tired of this feud. Is time for it to end. Once these are gone, we will have nothing left to fight over."

"Wait!" Ludmilla approached slowly and steadily as if trying not to spook a cornered animal. "We can work this out. You don't need to destroy anything."

"Yes, we're all here," Malwinka said. "We can decide together what must be done."

Lidka set her lips into a determined line. She dropped the bundle into the coals, and everyone gasped. For a moment nothing happened.

Kate searched for a long stick, something she could use to pull out the items before they caught fire.

The servant's dress caught first. A small flame licking at the years of grease stains embedded into the fabric.

Ludmilla lunged and tried to reach into the pile, but she shrank back from the sudden heat.

Next went the wedding dress, and Kate's heart fell. Such a beautiful gown.

Her attention moved to the ball gown. What was Cinderella's dress going to do? For the longest time they all stared, waiting. Waiting.

BOOM!

The ground shook, and Kate was knocked flat. She couldn't see for the smoke, and her ears rang with a high pitch that blocked out all other noise. Instinctively, she crawled away from the fire, coughing and gasping for air. The smoke burned her throat. She moved far enough away that she could stand and look back. A cloud covered the area, hiding everything from view. Where was Lidka? Did she make it out? Where were the others?

Close to her, a figure was stumbling, a shadow lost in the smoke. Kate took a deep breath and rushed in to help. It was Lidka. Kate caught her by the arm and helped her get to the clear air. She collapsed moments later. Her clothing was charred, shredded, and her burns were difficult to look at. She smiled at Kate before closing her eyes in pain. "It's over," she said.

"Help!" Kate called, blinking cleansing tears out of her eyes. The smoke stung. "Help. We're over here." *Where is everyone?* She didn't want to leave Lidka alone, but she had to find help. Lidka needed to get out of this smoky air.

From out of nowhere came Esmerelda.

"Come on, dearie," she said tenderly to Lidka. "We're going to get you to bed. Can you stand?" She brushed back Lidka's hair from the side of her face not burned.

Lidka's eyes fluttered open, but she stared emptily back at Esmerelda.

"Help me, Kate. Take her other arm."

Both arms were burned, and Kate hesitated to touch her.

"Under here, like this," Esmerelda said, demonstrating. "She's not hurt there."

Together, they got Lidka to her feet and led her back to the cottage. The others had also found their way to the door and watched with mixed expressions. Once they had Lidka lowered into her bed, Esmerelda shooed them away, including Kate.

Kate found the others shook up from the blast, but otherwise unharmed. They waited silently outside while a soft wind blew away the smoke layer by layer. When the air completely cleared away, they were all left in shock. There was a crater where the fire pit used to be, which was to be expected. But the surprise was what happened to the forest.

The tree trunks for as far as they could see were bent at right angles like the blast had burst through them on its way out. It was the strangest sight Kate had ever seen.

It was as if the trees were trying to kneel.

Princess Kolodenko shook her head as she surveyed the bent trees. "There must be hundreds of trees out there. No one will ever believe the truth, even if they were told."

FORTY-TWO

Ludmilla had found a stick long and sturdy enough to pick through the ashes, and had started poking and prodding the smoking remains. Malwinka hovered beside her, overseeing the search. "Look over there," she directed. "There is a lump that could be a glass slipper."

Ludmilla poked the spot, and the pile of ash collapsed. Malwinka slapped her arm. "Be careful, you fool."

Meanwhile, Nessa had joined the search with her own stick. Ludmilla took one look and began to poke around faster. Ash rose up from the pile like a thundercloud until they were all covered in cinders.

"It's your fault we've lost everything." Malwinka continued to berate Ludmilla. "It's better to have a sparrow in your hand than a pigeon on the roof. If you hadn't been so greedy, we would still have the shoes. But no, you had to have the dresses, too."

"*I* didn't have the shoes, you did, and you were keeping them a secret." She kicked up a poof of ash toward Malwinka.

If Kate wasn't so worried about Lidka, she would have laughed at the pair looking more and more like cinder-wenches themselves.

With a heavy heart, she turned away and returned to the cottage. There was no point searching the ashes, because she knew there would be nothing to see. The ball gown didn't just burst into flames like it did in the display window at the department store; it exploded. The remnants of the dress would be scattered all over that forest.

Princess Kolodenko hovered near the door of the cottage. "You must think me strange to care so much for a girl who keeps running away," she said.

Kate shook her head. She felt the same about the girl who was playing her.

"During the war, I learned to notice individuals. To see each person's struggle. If I tried to help the masses, I was overwhelmed. But I could help the person in front of me. My daughter lost her husband and one of her daughters, and now she is off in France, learning to cope by working. Nessa is about to leave to start a new life in America. Tony—you've met him. Tony is Tony. He is strong. But Lidka? She is the one in front of me now."

The door opened and Esmerelda came out. "Your Lidka will be fine," she said. "The wounds are healing, but there will be scars."

"May we see her?" Princess Kolodenko asked.

Esmerelda opened the door wider. The princess motioned for Kate to go in first, but Kate declined. "You go," she said. "I'll watch them." She indicated the gathering around the ashes.

Malwinka had found the hoes and, together with Ludmilla, had spread the ashes into a wide circle. "Look for something sparkling," she directed Ludmilla. They were still searching for the heart stones.

Nessa came and stood by Kate. "Everything is gone," she said.

"Mmm," Kate replied.

Nessa shifted slightly. "What?" she whispered.

"Nothing."

"That 'mmm' did not sound like nothing."

"Wait and see."

The Burgosovs picked through the ashes long enough to satisfy themselves that Cinderella's legacy was gone. With nothing to fight about, it seemed they had nothing to talk about, either. After a long moment of silence, they wandered off, not even saying good-bye or waiting to talk to the *babuszka*. The matriarchs of each line of stepsisters marched into the woods, presumably back to civilization and to remake whatever life for themselves they planned, as so many others were doing postwar. Neither of them waited to see how Lidka was faring. Not the side she was born to, nor the side she defected to.

"They didn't even check on Lidka," Nessa said. "Babuszka and Babcia take care of her while the ones who should be looking out for her search for the treasure." She toed the dirt in a circle. "While *I* searched for the treasure. I'm sorry I have been so bossy," Nessa said as she watched them go. "I'd like to say it was all the influence of the dresses, but that wouldn't be completely true. I got caught up in being descended from royalty but forgot the best kind of princess is one who serves."

"I'm glad you noticed," Kate said with a smile. "Apology accepted. And I'm sorry I was so possessive about the dresses. They are—were—your family's belongings, not mine. A Keeper is not an owner. "

"We've learned our lessons. Too bad we learned them too late." After watching the stepsisters leave, the girls went into the cottage.

Esmerelda had done wonders with Lidka's burns, and the scars, though still noticeable, were not too shocking.

Kate looked over at the sleeping form of her dad.

"I will wake him in the morning. Do not worry. He will not know how long he has been sleeping, but he will be refreshed. I don't know about his eyesight," she said, answering Kate's unspoken question.

Princess Kolodenko held her hands out to the wounded girl. "Come back to the villa with us."

"*Nie*." Lidka blinked and stared out the window into the darkness. "I will wander until I find my own place. Perhaps in Russia. So many have died or left, there will be room for me."

Lidka's words, though not harsh, were clearly not what Princess Kolodenko was hoping to hear.

"It is late," Esmerelda said, pulling out a pile of blankets. "Everyone go to bed and we will talk more in the morning."

FORTY-THREE

The next morning, Kate woke early. It was dark in the room, but she could make out someone moving around, trying to be quiet. The door opened, and Kate realized it was Esmerelda leaving the cottage. Minutes later, a shadow crossed in front of the window. *Nessa.* Curious about where the girl might be going, Kate wrapped a blanket around herself and slipped out after her.

Esmerelda stood over the ashes of the fire pit as if waiting for the girls. Kate sidled up next to Nessa, who reached for her hand. They waited in the cool morning, feet wet with dew and their hearts expectant.

As the sun rose, giving their faces a youthful glow, the *babuszka* spoke. "It is down to you two."

The girls smiled at each other.

"Nessa, you are wondering who I really am. If I am the fairy godmother you hope for."

Kate felt Nessa squeeze her hand.

"Kopciuszek was a lovely girl. She had a harsh life, but the choices she made and the attitude she kept were what made the difference. I could not have helped her if her heart was pointed in another direction. She had faith and sought the good."

Esmerelda turned to look at them full-on. Kate's heartbeat sped up.

"What is it you seek?" she asked them.

Kate's mind raced on how to answer. What did she seek? Now that she had found her dad, she couldn't think of anything else she wanted. Her family was safe and would soon be back together. She wanted to be with Johnny, but she didn't need a fairy godmother's help for that. According to Nessa, he had come to Poland to rescue her. All she needed was two minutes to tell him how much he meant to her.

She tried to think bigger. She'd thought with the close of WWII that the world was at peace again, but having seen what she had and seen how it had affected Lidka, she wasn't so sure. People seemed to have a leaning toward strife. Despite the terrible acts that had taken place, the aftershocks of the war continued. While some chose to forgive and move on, others insisted on seeking revenge. Her thoughts turned to the Kolodenkos and Burgosovs. If families couldn't even get along, how could anyone expect nations to?

She looked at Nessa. The young princess was wrestling with her own wants.

"I cannot make sweeping changes," Esmerelda said, as if reading their thoughts. "But I can give tools to help. I gave Kopciuszek these tools: a ball gown to wear so she could be seen worthy by those who judge outwardly, and the magic shoes so she could have the diamonds to help those around her." The *babuszka* grinned. "I tossed in a few extras—the special qualities of the dress and shoes. For the dress, Kopciuszek would be able to tell the intentions of those around her, their emotions magnified. And the shoes, as you discovered, will reunite loved ones who have been separated. She did not ask for any of these things. Sometimes we don't know ourselves enough to know what we need, only what we want."

As she was speaking, she motioned for them to follow her into the forest. They walked until they couldn't see the cottage anymore. The sun was higher now, and in the distance, the rays caught a glimmer. Something sparkly was draped on a tree, right where the bend was.

It was Cinderella's dress.

Nessa ran first. She had scooped up the dress before Kate even reached the tree. "And here are the shoes," Nessa said. She tucked the dress in the crook of her arm while she retrieved the shoes at the base of the next tree.

"Where are the other dresses?" Kate asked, searching the forest for a pile of white silk. "The servant outfit and the wedding dress?"

"Life isn't without consequences. Those are gone. This is what remains."

Kate felt the loss deep down, and it surprised her. When she'd first seen the glimmer of the dress through the trees, she'd assumed Esmerelda would return everything to the way it was.

"Does this mean we can keep it?" Nessa asked.

"If that is what you want," Esmerelda said. She looked expectantly at both girls.

Kate let out a breath. She wished she had more time to think. No one ever plans to meet a fairy godmother.

"Please, Kate?" Nessa said. "I have the feeling we are meant to decide together about this."

Esmerelda tilted her head, examining Kate. "The role of a servant is what you make of it. The world would be a better place if we all served each other more. It is a quiet responsibility and one that should be chosen, not forced, to make the greatest impact."

Here was a chance to break the legacy. To separate her family from being a Keeper of the Wardrobe to the Kolodenko royal line. It was what her *babcia* wanted once. It was what Lidka tried to do.

Or should she request a share in the dress? She dismissed the thought before it was even fully formed. She was not a direct descendant. It wasn't fair to even bring it up. Nessa was looking at her with a pleading face. Again, Kate felt the weight of centuries of history on her shoulders. She thought of the efforts of her dad, and now her brother, with not only preserving the world's artistic treasures but also of ensuring they remained with the families who owned them.

What would be better? To see these treasures destroyed and the fighting end? Or to protect them and see what good could come of their existence?

Her face must have given the answer before she could say it, because Nessa broke into a grin and attacked her with a big hug.

Esmerelda, looking younger still, said to Kate, "Your instincts are good. You must work with Nessa. Help each other, girls." She reached out her hands, and they formed a circle. Sparkles started falling like snow, making the air shimmer with magic. Kate and Nessa grinned at each other. *This is the best part.*

"I bound your families together all those years ago, with the hope they would make a difference. You have benefited from their history. You know the challenges. You know the rewards. These gifts are meant to be used. Nessa, look for opportunities as they arise. Kate, don't feel like you are accepting a lesser role. It is equally important, merely different. Nessa cannot do her job without you. This is what you have chosen."

Esmerelda placed the ball gown and shoes in a homespun bag before handing them to Kate. But when Esmerelda reached behind her neck to unclasp the amber necklace, Kate held up her hand to stop her. "Are you sure? Don't you need the necklace?" Esmerelda looked so young now. So different from the odd *babuszka* at the piazza.

"Yes, but I'll be seeing you again," Esmerelda said as she fixed the necklace around Kate's neck and adjusted it so the sunburst pendant was centered.

"Thank you," Kate whispered. When she held the amber pendant, it warmed to her touch, and she breathed in the pine scent. Her throat caught, and she blinked back tears. It felt right to have it back. For the first time, she felt like the necklace and the role of Keeper were truly hers, like she had earned them. All her doubts and regrets about the choices she had made vanished.

"A fresh start," Esmerelda. "Just you two. No one else to know."

Back at the cottage, Nessa continued on to the cabin to check on Princess Kolodenko. Kate and Esmerelda went inside to begin preparing breakfast. It was still dark with the curtains over the windows, but Esmerelda pushed them aside, shining morning light on Lidka. She screwed up her face and flung her arm over her eyes. Dad was still sleeping soundly in his dark corner.

"Are you ready for him to wake up?" Esmerelda asked. Kate nodded.

The *babuszka* touched his forehead. "Wake," she said. Dad took a deep breath. Stretched. He opened his eyes and turned his head as if he was getting his bearings. Kate smiled, but there was no reaction. He still couldn't see. She was hoping that since Esmerelda helped Lidka's burns, she could heal his eyes.

"Hi, Dad."

"Good. You weren't a dream," he said, sitting up. "That's the best night's sleep I've had in a long time. Even my headache is gone. I was so used to having it, I didn't realize how good it feels to have a clear head."

"I'm glad, because we are on the move again today."

He swung his legs over the side of the bed. "I thought we were going to camp out here for a while." He rubbed his eyes and blinked several times.

"What is it, Dad?" Kate hopefully asked.

He shook his head. "Hmm. I thought for a minute there, but no. Nothing."

So close. Maybe the healing would take time. "While you were sleeping, the Kolodenkos came with good news. Floyd got them through the German border, and he is back at the hotel in Szczecin. It's near. We can leave today."

"You're kidding?" He stood and reached for her, hugging her tightly.

A cupboard banged closed. "Out you kids go," Esmerelda said. She twittered about her cottage like a spry young person. Her joints seemed to have loosened up, and she moved easily as she began pulling food out from hidden stores. "Get some fresh air while I make breakfast."

Dad leaned toward Kate. "Is that the old woman? She sounds different."

"Yes, she's had a good night's sleep, too. She's even looking younger."

Kate grabbed her camera, and she and her dad left the cottage, but Lidka took up her seat near the window and refused to move.

"My leg's a bit stiff after that hike down the mountain. Mind if I walk around a bit?" Dad asked.

"Let me show you the trees over here. You wouldn't believe how they are growing." As they walked, she described them, marveling at their new, strange growth pattern.

"Let me touch them," he said.

Kate directed his hands to the nearest tree. He felt the curve in the trunk and laughed. "You could sit on these. Wish I could see them."

"I'll take a picture, so maybe one day you can." She snapped the photo and wound the film. "Oh, there's Nessa." Kate waved. Nessa and Princess Kolodenko had emerged from their cabin. "Come meet them."

After introductions were made, Esmerelda called breakfast. They ate quickly as everyone was eager to go home.

Lidka ate silently, avoiding eye contact. Kate wondered if Lidka was proud of destroying the Kopciuszek treasures, or if she was feeling guilty.

When Nessa left to gather her bags from the cabin, she put her hand on Lidka's shoulder. "*Ciao*, cousin."

Lidka looked up from her vigil at the window, surprised. She gave Nessa a small smile and nodded.

"And thank you for helping me find my dad," Kate said.

Lidka nodded again. This new Lidka was quiet.

"I mean it. I couldn't have done it without you." Kate waved as she walked out the door to join Nessa. They met at the corner of the cottage.

"You don't think the boys will be too mad we left without them, do you?" Nessa asked, referring to Floyd and Johnny. She shifted the bag on her shoulder.

"Floyd might need some sweet-talkin' to get over it," Kate said, adjusting her own bag.

Nessa smiled. "Leave it to me."

"Are you sure you won't come with us?" Princess Kolodenko asked. She was talking to Esmerelda. "Your cottage is waiting for you in Italy."

An even younger-looking *babuszka* shook her head. "I haven't felt this good in years. I am happy to be alone again in a quiet place in the forest. If I need you, I will return. For now, I can make my way here with my garden." She glanced back at the cottage where Lidka hovered in the doorway. "And I have another orphan who needs a loving hand. Although this one might take longer to help than young Nadzia."

FORTY-FOUR

Quickly, they found the trail that would take them back to town. It went directly through the crooked forest. Kate made them stop for a minute so she could snap a quick photo.

"Babcia, what is that you have?" Nessa asked.

"This?" She held up a small package. "Lidka gave it to me. She said to open it when I got home."

"What are you waiting for? Open it now."

"I *am* curious. She didn't want me opening it in front of her." Princess Kolodenko pulled back the wrapping and stopped. "Oh."

"She found it at the castle," Kate said. "She said it used to be at your house in Krakow."

"When we had to leave, we packed what we could carry, and I didn't remember the maid figurine until I was on the train. I never thought I'd see it again. My mother gave it to me when I was a child, to remind me of our past, and to teach me that we are servants of one another. Oh, precious Lidka. Her heart is opening." Princess Kolodenko continued walking, holding the maid to her chest.

Lidka must have known how happy her gift would make Fyodora. She should have let the princess open it in person. For all Lidka's bravado, she didn't have the courage to show love.

"I'm sorry about the Kopciuszek treasures," Princess Kolodenko said. "If I had handled things differently, we would still have them. Now we must form a new identity as a family. I'm especially sorry for you, Nessa, that you never really got a chance to experience the magic."

"Oh, but I did, Babcia. I wore the ball gown on the *Queen Mary*. And again at the castle at Avanti. Kate took pictures, and it did feel magical to wear it."

Princess Kolodenko smiled sadly. "Then you will feel the loss as well."

Kate stared straight ahead, afraid if she looked at Nessa the princess would guess their secret. Nessa would have a hard enough time not telling.

Dad leaned over. "You want to explain all that to me later?"

"Just girl talk, Dad. You know how we feel about fashion."

Once they'd cleared the crooked trees, they came across two hikers.

Kate recognized them first. A familiar white-T-shirt-and-jeans-clad boy took her breath away. "Johnny!"

She broke away from the others to run into his arms. He scooped her up and spun her around on the spot.

"I'm so sorry I left you," she whispered, burying her face in his neck. "I've felt terrible ever since." Their separation hit her full force now that she was back in his arms. She could hardly breathe, the emotion was so strong.

"Sparky, it's okay. I'm not mad." he whispered back, relief evident in his tone. "Well, I was, but how crazy is it for me to be jealous of a dress? I love you too much." He set her back down and let her go. His eyes bored deep into hers. "Besides, remember at the beginning of the summer when I asked you if you trusted me?"

She nodded, searching his eyes. *He loves me?*

"Trust goes both ways. I need to trust you, too."

No blushing this time as she said, "I love you, too."

"See? I don't need magic shoes to find you. All I had to do was follow my heart." He grinned and put his hand on his chest.

Her stomach tingled as he slipped his hand into hers.

"Do we need to storm a castle or anything?" he asked.

"No, it's over. We can go home."

Meanwhile, Floyd had seen Dad and run to his side. "Dad!" He reached out and grasped Dad's hand to pull him into a hug.

"You don't know how long I've waited to do this," Dad said, his sightless eyes tearing up.

"I'm sorry," Floyd said, his voice catching. "I shouldn't have given up hope. I should ha—"

"Don't. I'm here. Nothing else matters now."

They separated, but Dad kept his arm around Floyd's shoulder. "You'll have to help me out, son. My eyes. I can't see."

Floyd looked to Kate in shock and she nodded.

"No problem, Pops. I'm right here."

"Are you ladies ready to go home?" Johnny asked. He squeezed Kate's hand. "Because I know I am. I've had enough of Floyd's attempts to speak Polish for a lifetime. You wouldn't believe what we ended up eating last night."

The trip through Poland and into Soviet-controlled Germany, and finally to the city of Wiesbaden, was happily uneventful. Kate got to see her dad and her boyfriend meet and talk about art, and when Nessa wasn't busy batting her eyelashes at Floyd, Kate filled her in on what happened at the castle with Malwinka. One of the first things they did was get Dad to a phone so he could call long-distance to Mom. Kate could hear her crying from ten feet away.

Before they left Germany, Floyd gave them a tour of the Wiesbaden Central Collecting Point in the Landesmuseum. Floyd, followed by Nessa at his heels, led them to a large open room with row after row of shelves filled with paintings. "There are three hundred rooms in this building," he said. "And here's just one of them."

"Dad, I wish you could see this," Kate said. "The paintings are stacked up like books at the library."

"Many of these are masterpieces," Floyd said. "I could

walk down this row and find a sixteenth-century portrait, turn around, and pull out a Renoir."

Dad shook his head. "Amazing. Wish I could see it, too." Dad clapped Floyd on the shoulder. "Glad to see you finally taking an interest in art."

Floyd shrugged. "All those years of you talking about it finally sank in, I guess. You know, I'm keeping my eye out for the amber room. It was taken from the Catherine Palace and moved to Königsberg castle here in Germany. But then that was bombed, and no one has seen the pieces since. There are rumors that some have been taken by private citizens. Wouldn't that be something? To hold a treasure no one knows about, but everyone is looking for?"

Kate and Nessa glanced at each other before feigning interest in a table of silverware.

While everyone moved on to the next room, they lagged behind. "How long do we keep it a secret?" Nessa whispered. "I was going to wear the gown at Princess Elizabeth's wedding in November, remember?"

"I don't know. You might need to wait until the older generation passes. If Malwinka and Ludmilla believe everything was destroyed, the feud is over."

Nessa pouted. "Figures. I'm the one who doesn't get to enjoy Kopciuszek's dress."

"You still have the shoes."

Her eyes gleamed. "That I do."

FORTY-FIVE

ecause it was Ferragosto, the big Italian holiday, the train was packed with last-minute vacationers, and they had to split up. Kate and Johnny waited in Rome for the next train, while Princess Kolodenko and Nessa carried on ahead.

"We will wait for you at the station in Sora," Nessa said. "Make a list of all the places you want to see before we go back to New York. I want to make sure you leave with good memories of Italy. Oh, and we have a surprise for you." She grinned.

They did not have to wait long before the train pulled out. Johnny was in the mood to talk, but Kate's eyelids were heavy. When he put his arm around her, she rested her head on his shoulder and felt the rumble of his voice as he spoke.

It was the train slowing down that woke her. She pushed herself up.

"Hey, Sparky." Johnny shook out his arm and flexed his fingers.

"Oh, I'm so sorry. I tried to stay awake."

He laughed. "I didn't want to disturb you. What good is an arm for anyway?"

"Are we here?"

"Yes. Are you ready for your surprise?"

"You know what it is?"

He nodded.

The town of Sora was decked out for Ferragosto. Italian flags hung from every available flagpole, and bunting and ribbons in green, white, and red were strung across the road and from building to building.

When Johnny and Kate stepped off the train, Nessa called out, "They're here!" Several people stood from the benches and waved: Princess Kolodenko, Mr. De Luca, Maria, Mr. Day, and a girl who looked awfully familiar . . . but couldn't be.

"Josie?" Kate stepped up to the station and was practically tackled by her best friend.

"Your charmed life is rubbing off on me," she said. "Mr. Day needed some costume changes, and my boss, Bonnie, liked that I was a fast worker so she let me come over." Josie lowered her voice to a stage whisper. "Besides, she's scared to cross the Atlantic—gets seasick." Everyone laughed.

"It is so good to see you. How long have you been here?"

"Apparently longer than you. I had no idea you were taking a sightseeing trip to Poland. I guess that came up last-minute, huh?" She fanned her hands in front of her face. "And your dad— Holy Toledo!" She looked at the train. "Is he here?"

Kate shook her head. "He took a plane home. He should be with Mom by now and hopefully seeing a doctor about his eyesight. I hope we weren't too late."

"That'll be some reunion. It's probably best you're not there while they get reacquainted. Good thing she didn't start dating Neil. And can you believe they've got palm trees here? Mom never told me about the palm trees."

Kate shook her head at the dizzying change of topics. It was good to see Josie again. Once all the greetings were made, they continued on to the park, where other families were also gathering.

Maria had spent all day in the kitchen from the looks of things, but she was beaming as she served a picnic lunch to everyone. She whispered something in Italian to Kate when she reached around her to place a salad on the table.

Mr. De Luca overheard and translated. "She says 'I like the happy ending.'"

"Me, too." Kate smiled at Maria and took in the scene around her. Good food. Good friends. When she glanced at Johnny, she saw he was looking at her. He winked.

Josie saw and wagged her finger. "No, no. You two have been together for weeks. I get her first after we eat. We've got lots to talk about before we have to go home." Josie made her eyes go big, emphasizing her point.

Johnny held up his hands in defeat. "Fine. I've got something to take care of anyway. Mr. De Luca, can I talk to you?"

After the girls helped clean up the picnic, Kate and Josie went off to catch up.

"Are you going to spill the beans about Johnny?"

"What do you mean?" Kate stopped in the middle of the bridge and stared out into the slowly moving water.

"I mean all those looks you keep passing each other. Everyone is noticing."

Kate blushed. "I had no idea we were passing looks."

Josie guffawed. "I still know you better than you know yourself. Something's changed between you two. What was it?"

What exactly had changed? Josie was right. There wasn't a moment she could point to, but they were at a different place than they had been when the summer started. Their separation at the border had been painful, but without it, she didn't know if she'd truly understand how strong her feelings were for him. When he came back for her at the forest, all ready to rescue her, she knew how deeply he felt for her, and that he was ready to accept her legacy.

"You're in love. That's it," Josie said. "You just needed me here to tell you."

Kate smiled. She'd already told Johnny she loved him. There was a love like her parents' where they could be so caught up in the day-to-day they sometimes didn't seem like they were in love. And then there was a love like Uncle Adalbert and Aunt Elsie, which was a sacrificial love. A lifelong commitment for better or for worse lived out in a working kind of love.

And what were she and Johnny? Mr. De Luca would say young love, and he'd punctuate it with a wink and a push out the door to look at the stars.

"Life is changing, isn't it?" Josie asked. "We can't go back to being kids again."

Kate continued across the bridge. "No." She slid her hand along the railing. "But we wouldn't want to, would we?"

∞

Josie threw herself into helping Nessa pack for New York, leaving Kate time for one last walk through an Italian garden with Johnny. He and his dad were staying on a few more days until filming wrapped up, and then Johnny was getting his promised flight home.

"Is everything okay?" Kate asked. "You seem nervous."

"What, me? No. I'm fine," he answered, wiping his hands on the sides of his jeans. "I told Dad about my plans for school."

"And?"

"Surprisingly, we've found a compromise. He is fine with me going to the art school I've chosen as long as I put in some time for him in the advertising department."

"Hmm, sounds like someone gave you good advice a while back."

"When did you get to be so wise?" He took her hand in his and pulled her into the flower garden. "You know it about killed me to walk away from you at the border."

Kate groaned. "I know. You never quite trusted Lidka. I suppose I didn't either, but I wanted to because she was the only one who seemed able to help me. You can say, 'I told you so.'"

"No, it wasn't that. Well, it wasn't just that. I got a taste of what you girls had to go through when saying good-bye to your soldiers. I didn't like it. At all." He tilted her chin and kissed her. "I never want to watch you leave me again. Ever."

He pulled a box out of his jeans pocket. "My opinion of Lidka has improved. She didn't trade the blue diamond after all. She kept it and gave it to Princess Kolodenko with a note suggesting she give it to me. It took some doing, but I found a jeweler in town willing to do a rush job." He opened a small box to reveal the square blue diamond nestled in a white-gold setting. "I had it made into a ring for you. A promise ring."

Kate sucked in a breath. Was he for real?

"You are the one for me, Kate Allen. I don't need to look for any other. With your dad coming home and all, my timing might not be the best, but I want you to know where my heart is. I love you. If you accept this ring, I'll know that you feel the same and are willing to wait for me, for us."

She could only gape at the ring, so Johnny continued. "I spoke to your dad when we were in Germany, and he admitted he still sees you as the girl you were when he left, and the idea of you marrying is hard for him. I won't even ask you to make a decision to leave your family just yet. But I've been serious about you, Kate Allen, for a long time, and I want everyone to know it."

Her thoughts raced back to their first meeting at the movie audition, then to the moment at the department store when she realized who he was . . . after she had thrown her shoe at him. And then all those sweet letters they wrote each other during the war. Finally, this trip to Europe, and how their relationship had been tested. He was still her knight in shining armor, even if Princess Kolodenko and Nessa wouldn't let him rescue her.

Beaming, Kate held out her hand. Johnny slid the ring onto her finger, then kissed her fingertips. The tingle went all the way to her heart, and she sighed contentedly. After questioning so many things in her life, she didn't need to question this. Johnny was her future. No matter how unpredictable life might be as a Keeper of Cinderella's dress, Johnny would always be there.

"I love you, too. Thank you for being so understanding about my family," she said. "The wait won't be long."

They continued their walk holding hands, the unfamiliar

feel of the ring pressing into Kate's skin as a reminder of what had taken place. So many thoughts raced through her mind she couldn't stop one long enough to properly think about it.

"Why are you smiling, Sparky?"

She punched him in the arm. "You know."

He grinned, then pulled her into his arms. They were already back at the patio. "I'll be up to say good-bye in the morning, but everyone will be watching. See you in New York?"

"I'll be on deck waiting."

Kate found the girls upstairs in Nessa's room. She stood in the door and lifted her left hand up to her cheek so her new ring was in full view. "Ahem," she said.

Josie noticed first. "Whoa. What is *that* on your finger?"

"Just a little promise Johnny made me."

Josie leaped forward and grabbed Kate, dragging her to the light. "Let me see this closer." She touched it gently. "It's so pretty."

"Peachy keen," Nessa said, looking over Josie's shoulder.

Kate laughed. "You need to stop taking English lessons from Josie. She's trying to start a new saying."

"Face it, Kate. I'm a trend spotter." She pointed at her trousers. "For example, everyone is wearing their pants like this this summer. You just roll them up to your knees."

Kate shook her head. Nessa's pants were rolled up, too.

"I'm going to go brush my teeth," Josie said. "Gotta get up early." She tapped the doorframe on the way out.

Nessa smiled. "Your ring is beautiful."

"Thanks. It's the diamond we found in the fresco. I had given it to Lidka to use as a bribe, but she gave it back to Johnny. Now I can't figure out how she managed to get us onto that train."

"Oh," Nessa said. "I know that one. She took more than the servant statue from the castle near Zakopane. She sent a note to your brother to let him know where to look for the piece she traded for your safety."

"Of course she did."

Nessa closed the lid on her trunk. Speaking of treasures, "Have you told Johnny our secret?"

"Your *babcia* already told him what happened with the explosion."

"Yes, but did you tell him what happened after?"

"Not yet." She looked at her ring. "But I will. He's going to have to know. Do you mind?"

Nessa shook her head.

"I kind of want to tell Aunt Elsie first. I feel that she ought to be the first one to know."

"I heard the *babuszka* tell you to let the former Keeper know that all was well so she would have peace of mind."

"Yes. It'll be the first thing I do when I get home."

ꙮ FORTY-SIX ꙮ

When they got off the ship, Kate's parents were waiting to pick them up. Mom was firmly attached to Dad's side, helping him navigate the busy pier. His eyes were bandaged, so he must have had the surgery. She gave them both a hug at the same time. The only one missing from their happy reunion was Floyd, and he would be home soon enough. No one was worried for his safety any more. Peacetime was a time to celebrate.

"I don't know how you did it," Mom said, "though I suspect Adalbert and Elsie had something to do with it. The Kolodenkos must have important connections."

"Is Uncle Adalbert with Elsie?"

"Yes. She is not doing well, Kate. You need to prepare yourself before you go."

Kate took the bus to the hospital. The castle-like turrets didn't seem so fancy now that she'd seen real castles. There was so much Kate wanted to tell Elsie, even if the old woman didn't understand any of it. Esmerelda, knowing Elsie's condition, had thought it would be a nice thing to do. "You don't know what sinks in," she had said. "You would be surprised what I recognized even when my brain was a bit muddled."

"How is she?" Kate walked tentatively into the room.

Uncle Adalbert stood and embraced her. "I am so proud of you, Kate. You showed great courage and we have all been rewarded for it. I've met your father. He is a good man. Still trying to figure out what has happened, but he is happy to be home."

Uncle Adalbert looked tenderly at Aunt Elsie. "You can try to reach her. I visit every day but I have not seen *her* in weeks."

Aunt Elsie had never looked so frail. Not even staring at the curtains, her eyes were fixed on the plain white ceiling.

Kate took the chair Adalbert vacated. He stood watch at the foot of the bed. An ever-vigilant sentry.

"Aunt Elsie. I found them. The shoes." Kate reached for her aunt's hand. Elsie's fingers remained limp in Kate's grasp. "They are beautiful. No, more than beautiful. Made of clear white diamonds, with heart clasps made of smaller light blue diamonds. I've never seen such a thing. And they are safe; the Kolodenkos have them again." There was no response from Elsie.

Kate shifted and continued her story, pouring her tale into her aunt, willing her to hear. To understand. "I met

Esmerelda. You know her as the *babuszka*, the one who tended the Kolodenkos' gardens. She was still alive and waiting. She was so old, but gathering together all her magical items, particularly the amber necklace, renewed her strength and she became young again. She gave us the option of changing the Keeper role. She asked Nessa and me. She saw how the world had changed, and let us change if we wanted to."

Adalbert leaned forward. "And?"

"We agreed to continue the tradition. It may seem old-fashioned, but we decided we liked it. We liked being connected because of Cinderella's dresses."

"Interesting decision."

"Would you have chosen differently?" Kate asked him.

He shrugged, palms up. "I have lived with this secret for more years than you. I've seen how it affected my bride. I don't know what I would have chosen. Plus, I am an old man. I like to think a practical one. But you are a young woman, still idealistic."

Kate frowned. After what she had been through, she was no longer as naive as she used to be.

"It is a compliment," Adalbert interjected. "Idealism is what makes young people try for something better. Believe in something better."

Kate pulled out the black-and-white photos she had taken in Poland and had developed in Italy. There were certain pictures she didn't want to share with Mr. G. "I thought you might like to see a little of the home country."

She started with the castle. "Kopciuszek's castle. Did you ever see it?" she asked Adalbert.

"I think she went one time as a child. Maybe twice." He turned his attention to Elsie. "Look, *moja ksiezniczka*, the castle. Do you remember?"

Kate added another shot from inside the great hall. Her focus was off and the lighting poor, but it was good enough to remind herself what it looked like. Malwinka was in the corner of the shot, but she had turned her head, creating a sort of blur.

Something about the photo triggered a memory of the detective showing her a thief they were tracking. A jeweler. A finder. "Punia!" Kate exclaimed, putting all the niggling pieces together. She couldn't believe she'd missed it earlier. "Lidka is the thief Agent Gillespie is looking for."

"What are you talking about?" Uncle Adalbert asked.

Kate laughed. "They think she's a man. Gillespie called her a go-between, which, now that I've met her, is an apt description." Gillespie thought Punia was a jeweler. The amber necklace. That was probably how Lidka got involved. "Well, they'll never catch her now. Especially if she stays with the *babuszka*."

Kate continued to hold the pictures in front of Elsie's eyes, though her aunt made no indication of seeing them. Adalbert gave a slight shrug, as if to apologize for Elsie. Undaunted, Kate showed off the rest of the pictures. "Here is the train we took across Poland. The house in Krakow. Is this where you met Princess Kolodenko? Your friend, Fyodora?" She didn't say it was Malwinka's house now. The pictures showing the aftermath of war, she handed directly to Adalbert. "Did you want to see these?" she asked. "Or would you rather remember things the way they were?"

"I have already seen pictures such as these," he said. "I will always have the memories of before." He flipped through them quickly and handed them back.

Kate gave him the picture of the crooked forest. "And this is where it all ended." She told him how Lidka tried to destroy everything and the resulting explosion that damaged the trees. "They are still alive, but now they are bent like this."

Adalbert laughed. "I wonder what legend will arise from this forest once people stumble across it. People always need an explanation."

"I think Mr. G will like this one. It might inspire a new store window."

Kate put the pictures away, then squeezed Aunt Elsie's hand. "I'll come back another day." She let go, but her aunt's fingers tightened and held on.

"Aunt Elsie?"

Her aunt's gaze fell to the blue diamond on Kate's finger.

Kate sat back down. "Uncle Adalbert, quick, she's holding my hand."

"Because of love," Elsie said. "*Dziekuje.*" *Thank you.*

Adalbert rushed over and grabbed Elsie's other hand. "I'm here, Elsie. I'm here."

She did not speak, but her eyes locked onto his.

Kate gently removed her hand from Elsie's grasp and left the two alone. As their story was drawing to a close, hers was only beginning.

She had much to do before Johnny flew home. She and Nessa were going to meet up with the carpenter who installed the false bottom into Kate's hope chest. They wanted him to build her a wardrobe that included a hidden place for a special pair of shoes.

⌬ ACKNOWLEDGMENTS ⌬

Ever since *Cinderella's Dress* was published, I'm often asked when I knew I wanted to be a writer. Back in school, several wonderful teachers put books into my hands, planting seeds, but fifth grade was a standout. Halfway through the school year, Miss Swetlikoe swept into our classroom like Mary Poppins and her umbrella, except our beloved teacher arrived with a guitar and books and changed everything. She read to us *The Hobbit* and *Watership Down*, and I thought I would burst if I didn't try writing my own novel. So I did. Turns out I wrote fan fiction of *Watership Down*, but it was my first attempt at a novel. That teacher is now a high school librarian, continuing to inspire students to greatness. Thank you, Mrs. Lunde, for all you do.

For this second novel I picked up two talented new critique partners who helped hold my feet to the fire and fix plot holes. A big thank-you and hugs go out to Kristi Doyle from the back of the room at Phoenix Comicon, and Sarah Chanis, who likes to hang out in book-signing lines. I also want to give a shout-out to Ms. Bieszczady who shared countless Polish historical and cultural pins for my Pinterest board. Thanks also to ever-faithful Andrea Huelsenbeck who, as a first reader, supplies equal parts enthusiastic support and critical eye. And to my final first reader, Rebekah Slayton, thank you for gasping in all the right places and giving me good ideas.

I wish we could publish an edition that includes all the editor notes, because my editors Stacy Cantor Abrams and Lydia Sharp can be a hoot. So many times their notes had me laughing, sometimes because they were tactfully pointing out my errors, and sometimes because they were being encouraging cheerleaders. Erin Crum, I especially appreciate you holding my commas accountable. Ladies, you are a joy to work with. I cannot properly express how much I appreciate the careful time you put into editing my story.

Alexandra Shostak, you created another beautiful cover. One day we will hold a joint book signing so people can get your autograph on all that prettiness.

Thanks also to all the behind-the-scenes folks at Entangled: Heather Riccio, Debbie Suzuki, Melanie Smith, Anita Orr, Jeremy Howland, Liz Pelletier, and any others who have touched this project.

I especially can't forget my patient and supportive family. You didn't know what was involved when the first book came out, but now that you do, you still signed up for another go! Thank you for encouraging me to live my dream. It's better with you there to share it with me.

And to my readers, it's been so much fun to connect with you. I love getting mail, so please visit me at my website ShonnaSlayton.com and send me a note. While you're there, you can also sign up for my Reader's Group. (In the newsletter I spill a lot of the behind-the-scenes happenings in an author's life.)

CINDERELLA'S DRESS

By Shonna Slayton

Kate simply wants to create window displays at the department store where she's working, trying to help out with the war effort. But when long-lost relatives from Poland arrive with a steamer trunk they claim holds *the* Cinderella's dresses, life gets complicated. Now, with a father missing in action, her new sweetheart, Johnny, stuck in the middle of battle, and her great aunt losing her wits, Kate has to unravel the mystery before it's too late. After all, the descendants of the wicked stepsisters will stop at nothing to get what they think they deserve.

MY NOT SO SUPER SWEET LIFE

By Rachel Harris

The daughter of Hollywood royalty, Cat Crawford just wants to be normal. But when her prodigal mother reveals that she has something important to tell her daughter . . . causing a media frenzy, normal goes out the window. Lucas Capelli knows his fate is to be with Cat. Unfortunately, a scandal could take him away from the first place he's truly belonged. As secrets are revealed, rumors explode, and the world watches, Cat and Lucas discover it's not fate they have to fight if they want to stay together, it's their own insecurities.

Well, and the stalkerazzi.

OLIVIA TWISTED

By Vivi Barnes

Tossed from foster home to foster home, Olivia's seen a lot in her sixteen years. She's hardened, sure, though mostly just wants to fly under the radar until graduation. But her natural ability with computers catches the eye of Z, a mysterious guy at her new school. Soon, Z has brought Liv into his team of hacker elite—break into a few bank accounts, and voila, he drives a motorcycle. Follow his lead, and Olivia might even be able to escape from her oppressive foster parents. As Olivia and Z grow closer, though, so does the watchful eye of Bill Sykes, Z's boss. And he's got bigger plans for Liv . . .

TIL DEATH

By Kate Evangelista

Sixteen-year-old Selena Fallon is a dreamer. Not a day-dreamer, but an I-see-the-future kind of dreamer. Normally, this is not a problem, as she has gotten pretty good at keeping her weird card hidden from everyone in her small town. But when Selena dreams of her own rather bloody death, things get a little too freaky—even for her. Enter Dillan Sloan. Selena has seen the new guy in a different dream, and he is even more drool-worthy in person. Beyond the piercing blue eyes and tousled dark hair, there is something else that draws her to him. Something . . . electric. Too bad he acts like he hates her.